SPEAKING OF HORROR II

Interviews with:

Joe R. Lansdale
Carrie Vaughn
Lisa Tuttle
Kim Newman
Fred Chappell
Elizabeth Massie
Brian A. Hopkins
Harry O. Morris
Sephera Giron
S.P. Somtow
Hugh B. Cave
Robert Weinberg
Gahan Wilson
Ramsey Campbell
David J. Schow
Graham Joyce
Brian Lumley
Peter Straub

SPEAKING OF HORROR II

INTERVIEWS CONDUCTED BY
DARRELL SCHWEITZER

Darrell Schweitzer
Capclave 2018

WILDSIDE PRESS

To the memory of Robert Reginald, to whom I owe a great deal. He always favored this sort of book.

*

Joe R. Lansdale first appeared in *Worlds of Fantasy & Horror* #3 Summer 1996. Copyright © 1996 by Terminus Publishing Co., Inc. *Carrie Vaughn* first appeared in *Orson Scott Card's Intergalactic Medicine Show* #26, January 2012. Copyright © 2012 by Darrell Schweitzer. *Lisa Tuttle* first appeared in *The New York Review of Science Fiction* July 2008. Copyright © 2008 by Dragon Press. *Kim Newman* first appeared in *Science Fiction Chronicle* December 1995/January 1996. Copyright © 1995 by Darrell Schweitzer. *Fred Chappell* first appeared in *Worlds of Fantasy & Horror* #1, Summer 1994. Copyright © 1994 by Terminus Publishing Co., Inc. *Elizabeth Massie* first appeared in *Cemetery Dance* #50, October 2004. Copyright © 2004 by Cemetery Dance Publications. *Brian A. Hopkins* first appeared in *Cemetery Dance* #41, December 2002. Copyright © 2002 by Cemetery Dance Publications. *Harry O. Morris* first appeared in *The Silver Web* #9. Copyright © 1999 by Buzzcity Press. *Sephera Giron* first appeared in *Weird Tales* Sept-Oct 2007. Copyright © 2007 by Wildside Press. *S.P. Somtow* first appeared in #314, Fall 1988. Copyright © 1998 by Terminus Publishing Co., Inc. *Hugh B. Cave* first appeared in *Cemetery Dance* #29, October 1998. Copyright © 1998 by Cemetery Dance Publications. Robert Weinberg first appeared in *Cemetery Dance* #40, October 2002. Copyright © 2002 by Cemetery Dance Publications. *Gahan Wilson* first appeared in *Cemetery Dance* #39, July 2002. Copyright © 2002 by Cemetery Dance Publications. *Ramsey Campbell* first appeared in *H.P. Lovecraft's Magazine of Horror* #1, Spring 2004. Copyright © 2004 by Wildside Press. *David J. Schow* first appeared in *Cemetery Dance* #26, Summer 1996. Copyright © 1996 by Cemetery Dance Publications. *Graham Joyce* first appeared in *Cemetery Dance* #43, May 2003. Copyright © 2003 by Cemetery Dance Publications. *Brian Lumley* first appeared in *H.P. Lovecraft's Magazine of Horror* #3, Fall 2006. Copyright © 2004 by Wildside Press. *Peter Straub* first appeared in *Worlds of Fantasy & Horror* #4, Winter 1996/97. Copyright © 1996 by Terminus Publishing Co., Inc.Copyright © 2014 by Darrell Schweitzer. *All rights reserved.*

Published by Wildside Press LLC.
www.wildsidebooks.com

INTRODUCTION

More archival conversations. These interviews were done between 1995 and 2012. What I usually say in the introductions to interview books is that interviews of this sort are not *news,* but, in retrospect, efforts to capture how a creative artist felt and thought at a specific point in his or her career. You can go to an author's website to find out what he's doing now and what his latest books are, but this is more about what he said ten years ago, or five, or whenever. Here we have one of the last reminiscences by the great pulp writer Hugh B. Cave, about six and a half years before his death. The point is not news, but he tells a great zombie chicken story.

In the period covered by these interviews, the horror market boomed and busted. My coverage of the field was itself was affected by this, as, at times, the market for interviews with horror writers became erratic. But among our interviewees, other than Cave, who died in 2004, we have a mixture of old-time masters like Ramsey Campbell, Peter Straub, and Brian Lumley, who have ridden out the crash, and new voices like Carrie Vaughn and Sephera Giron, who emerged during it or after. There is still a wide variety of perspectives, and a clear sense that for all there is less horror on the bestseller lists now than there was in, say 1995, this is a field that either is not dead, or comes back from the grave again and again and again, like some of the more persistent characters in many of the stories.

That being so, I hope to do a third volume in this series in a few years.

—Darrell Schweitzer
Philadelphia PA
December 26, 2013

JOE R. LANSDALE

We start with a writer who probably needs no introduction. Joe R. Lansdale lives in Nacogdoches, Texas. He writes horror, westerns, crime-suspense, and comics. A lot of his work shows a profound sense of the absurd, so that the reader might shudder and laugh (nervously) at the same time. His novella "Bubba-Ho-tep," which was memorably filmed, embodies these qualities. His other works include the *The Drive-In* and sequels, *Savage Season, The Magic Wagon, Dead in the West,* and the Hap and Leonard series. He was won the Bram Stoker Award nine times and been nominated another nine. He has thirteen World Fantasy Award nominations. He was won the British Fantasy Award and been named a Grandmaster by the World Horror Convention.

Q: In the introduction to By *Bizarre Hands*, Lewis Shiner goes to some length to define your place in the horror field. I have my own theory that you're the Warren Zevon of horror. I'm thinking of the song "Excitable Boy," which, if it had a Texas accent, would be a Joe Lansdale story. Where do you see yourself in the context of the field?

Lansdale: I don't give any thought to where I see myself. I just do what I do. Whatever interests me at the time, that's what I pursue. But I don't have much conscious attitude about it, other than I try to write about the people I know, the characters I know—which is not to say that everybody I know is bad people, but those are the ones that interest me.

Q: Is it because there aren't enough plot conflicts in the lives of good people? What's the fascination with the bad ones?

Lansdale: I think we all know bad ones from afar. I think it's that they're so different. I think too that anytime you see something that's bad, you recognize something of yourself in it, whether you admit it or not. I think that the worst things that people do are in all of us—not that all of us do those things—and also the best things people do are in all of us. So I think it—the evil side—is an interesting side to explore, because it's a side that you don't think about too much. Publically you have to pursue something else. So it's kind of nice, in fiction, to be a human monster for a while, or at least try and understand what makes 'em tick. It's just one of the mysteries of life that this kind of stuff exists. It doesn't mean that I want to be these people or that I'm impressed with them. But I'm amazed by them.

Q: How much of your material is based on fact? Have you ever found yourself confronted by such people? A lot of your stories seem to be about secret murder-rituals in back-country towns.

Lansdale: Yeah. A lot of them are based on the truth. One story, "The Night They Missed the Horror Show," most of the things in that story either happened, or they were apocryphal stories that I'd heard when I was growing up, and I put them all together. They didn't all happen to those people in one night, but a friend of mine is actually the guy that dragged the dead dog around. He wasn't a bad guy like in the story. He was just drunk and a little stupid that night. But the events that happen to these characters supposedly did happen to some people and I just took them and consolidated them. The two guys who were the villains, Vinnie and Pork, I knew those guys. They weren't called that. But they were real and they did things very similar to that. So, that's realistic, yeah.

In "The Pit," it's not so much that that happened, but a lot of those attitudes I have personally encountered. And I've known people who fought dogs, which I always thought was pretty despicable.

I write about things which I generally think are despicable, but I often write about them straight-on to the point where people sometimes think I have sympathy for them, which always surprises me.

Q: You always write about rural degenerates, which seems to give rural people a bad name.

Lansdale: I think about that sometimes, but I think what it is, is that I'm so drawn to the horrific, and crime in general that I'm not going to be writing about the good people. I'm not trying to say this is the way all the people I know are, or this is the way all the people are in East Texas, but these are the sort of people I'm writing about. If I lived in Maine or California or New York, I'd still write about those people. They may not drive the pickup trucks, but they're there. Stephen King has certainly written about rednecks in Maine. They're everywhere. I don't think ignorance is a Southern thing by any means. I think we Texans know ignorance when we see it though, and I am not sure that some others do.

Q: For the longest time everyone seemed to assume that that sort of behavior was a Southern thing, but then I come from Philadelphia where we had Gary Heidnick's infamous body shop.

Lansdale: I think it's just that the Southerners are fascinated by that. We have the term Southern Gothic because for some reason it has always been part of the culture to observe weirdness. We look at it straight on. I think Flannery O'Connor said, "We still know weird when we see it."

Q: Some of your stories strike me as being like more straightforward Faulkner. I'm thinking of Faulkner stories like "The Hound," for example.

Q: I like Faulkner. I tend to lean more toward the humorous grotesque he did, stuff like "Mule in the Yard." I thought that was good. Or one that was very creepy, was "Barn Burning." To me, that's the way I tend to think of horror. I don't think so much of ghosts and rattlings in the attic. Stuff like that doesn't do much for me. I'm not saying that I haven't read stories like that that don't work for me, but as a writer, if I'm going to spend any time on something, it's hard for me to believe in something like that. I'm more interested in what people do to one another, because that scares me more. Therefore I'm able to make that more real, because those things happen. I don't mean that I feel obligated to write about that, or that I only write about that, but the older I get and the more I write, the less interested I am in things that go "Boo!" in the night, unless it's somebody doing it.

Q: You'd say, then, that you're not all that much interested in supernaturalism?

Lansdale: I am as a reader, but not so much as a writer, because I don't have the patience for it. As I reader, I have to be in the mood. I grew up on supernatural fiction, and I loved it, and I still love it in a certain compartment of my mind, but I don't read as much of it and I certainly don't to be drawn to write it as much. Once in a while a story will occur to me. I have written some supernatural things, but it doesn't seem to be what I'm designed to do as a writer. I often like a lot of things as a reader that I'm not interested in writing.

Q: How about using supernatural lore from Texas? Robert E. Howard made a couple of attempts, but otherwise I don't know that very much of it has ever been done. It's probably a very rich subject.

Lansdale: Most of the stuff that's been done has been non-fiction books, Texas ghost books, and such, most of them not too good. But, as a writer, that doesn't interest me too much. I won't box myself in and say I won't do that. If something interests me enough and excites me enough, I just might; but it seems that my mood is more toward the more realistic horrors. It's what really scares me. It seems to be what I am able to put down in a convincing manner, and that's why I pursue it.

Q: At what point does this sort of "horror" become what we at least used to call crime fiction? Is there a meaningful difference between horror fiction and crime fiction?

Lansdale: I don't know that there always is a difference. I thought a lot of the stories I wrote were crime and that's where I tried to publish them, but the horror editors bought them. I thought "The Night They Missed the Horror Show" was a crime story. I had written part of it and had it lying around for a long time, and then David Schow was doing the anthology, *The Silver Scream*, and asked me to write a story for him. I said, "Well, I've got one, but it's not spooks. It's the stuff that really scares me. It's the attitudes that really scare me. "And he said, "Hey, write it." So I did. And when I wrote *The Nightrunners*, I thought it was a suspense novel, and that's the way I tried to market it for five years. Nobody would buy it. A lot of the stuff that I wrote that was later published as horror, I wrote as crime or mainstream. I didn't have any it was horror. I have nothing against horror. It just never occurred to me. When people started buying it and wanting to call it horror, they didn't hurt my feelings any.

Q: Since you're so much of a regional writer, your background must be important to what you write. So, could you describe where you grew up, traumatic childhood encounters with hatchet murderers, that sort of thing?

Lansdale: I had a real happy childhood. I did grow up very rural, small towns, in the country much of the time. My father couldn't read or write, but he was an extremely good man, a powerful man. I had sort of a Huck Finn existence growing up because of where I grew up, in East Texas. Most people when they think of Texas think of sand and cactus and stuff like that. Texas is very varied. Where I come from is more like Arkansas or Louisiana, a lot of woods and a lot of rivers and creeks.

I did grow up with a lot of old ghost stories, though. But as far as things that happened in my life, it mostly happened to others that I observed. And there were stories I heard my father tell. My father was in his forties when I was born, so it was sort of like being raised by grandparents, to some extent. My people date back through the Civil War. My grandmother, who died in her nineties, remembered travelling in a covered wagon and saw one of the last Buffalo Bill Wild West Shows.

So I grew up with a storyteller tradition, too, which a lot of East Texans have. I think that, in the past, a lot of it may have come out of the fact that they couldn't read or write. So they passed on what they wanted to tell through stories, which of course were embellished as they went. I heard stories from my father which were obviously stories handed down from the middle 1800s and still going. I've used variations of them. I don't think I've ever told any of them literally. I probably should, to preserve them. I'll probably tell my children those stories. But my background was rural, country. Among the people I grew up with, there was no college education at all. They were mostly blue collar, a lot of farm stock. My generation was the first where anyone went to college. I had a couple of years. My brother had a couple of years. I think his son, my nephew, is the first one to have a college education among the Lansdales that I know of, at least on my side of the group.

Q: Coming as you did from such a background, what made you become a writer?

Lansdale: My mother was a reader, of non-fiction especially. But she always encouraged me to read, and by the time I was nine years old, I never wanted to be anything else. I really don't know how to explain it to you. I think a lot of writers find that. I don't know about you, but as a writer I seem to have a knack for remembering things from my childhood real well. I distort them a lot, for stories, which I'm sure every writer does, but I can't remember anything coming to me and saying, "You ought to be a writer, "or striking me. I do remember wanting to be one since I was nine. I do remember, when I was about twelve or thirteen discovering Edgar Rice Burroughs, and then I knew that was what I wanted to do. I read the *Iliad* and the *Odyssey* as a kid. I used to keep Iliad under my pillow because I read that Alexander the Great did that. I've just always been fascinated with stories.

Q: Did your family encourage you?

Lansdale: Yeah, they did. My father, he always said, "Whatever you want to do, you'll do it." I never lacked for confidence. I don't want this to sound like plain ego. I certainly know how to fail. But I think learning how to fail is important too. But if you have confidence in yourself, failure doesn't scare you any. That's one thing that my parents instilled in me, confidence. They were very straight-ahead people, who always felt, "Eyes forward, ears back, go get it done."

Q: A lot of writers from blue-color backgrounds encounter parental pressure to "get a real job."

Lansdale: My mother always used to have something to fall back on. I think a lot of parents did that. I never really had anything to fall back on. I did all the blue collar jobs. That's always what I had. I went to college for a little while, and I was going to be an archeologist, but at some point I said, "Hey, I want to write." So I dropped out, I didn't drop out because of a lack of interest in archeology but because I had a greater interest in writing and I felt like what I was being taught in school wasn't helping me any. Even in the English courses I don't think they knew much of what they were talking about, and for the most part still don't. I don't think a course in writing will do you any good unless it's taught by a writer who's published; somebody who's writing now, not someone who wrote thirty years ago.

Q: So you wouldn't want to take a course from a brain surgeon who had never taken a brain out . . .

Lansdale: Exactly.

Q: What sort of things did you do while you were learning to write?

Lansdale: Actually, I dug ditches. I was a bodyguard very briefly. I was a bouncer. I tried farm work. I was a janitor. I worked in public relations for Goodwill Industries, and as a transportation manager for Goodwill Industries as well. And, I worked in a rose field as a farm laborer for other people. Just every damn, dirty job you can think of, just about. When I was in high school I worked on garbage trucks in the summer. Whatever there was to make a buck, to survive, I've done it, just about, that's legal.

Q: Presumably all this really paid off by adding to the background of your fiction.

Lansdale: Oh, yeah. That's where I get a lot of the assholes I write about, and all of the good people I write about too. Some of the best people I ever met, I met them on those jobs. And still, while a lot of the people I hang out with are writers, a lot of my friends are carpenters and people who do blue collar work. I was the guy they'd say to, "You hold the hammer and nails," because I couldn't build anything. I always tore things up. But those are the kind of people I hang around with. I generally prefer their company, most of the time.

Q: Because they're more straightforward and less pretentious?

Lansdale: Yeah. Less bullshit. Also, too, I think it's because their backgrounds are similar to mine, so I know where they're coming from and what they're talking about, and I have a lot of respect for people who make their living with their hands. I certainly couldn't do it, other than I was the guy who could lift the big rock. That's as good as I got. I didn't have any real skills. I wasn't a carpenter or a painter or anything. Everything I did like that, I screwed it up. [Laughs]

Q: How long were you trying to write before you started to sell?

Lansdale: It depends on how you look at it. I had been writing, as I said, since I was nine. It took me about two years from the time I decided

I was going to start writing to when I started to sell. Actually, the first thing I ever wrote, though, was an article I did when I was twenty-one. It sold, and I did four more articles, and they all sold. Then I decided to switch to fiction, and I didn't sell anything for two years, I think. Then I started selling, and gradually it picked up, more and more. *Mike Shayne's Mystery Magazine* bought my first fiction, a thing called "A Full Count." It was a novella. I went on from there.

Q: The earliest thing of yours I can remember is *Dead in the West* as a serial in *Eldritch Tales*.

Lansdale: Which is very different from the book. The serialization is pretty sloppy. That's my fault. But, actually I had a novel before *Dead in the West*, which was *Act of Love*. And then I wrote one under a pen-name which I revealed—Ray Slayter—because everybody knows it, called *Texas Night Riders*. I wrote it in eleven days, and it shows it. That was actually my first novel sale, but it came out three years after *Act of Love*. I was writing short stories well before that. In the middle to late '70s I was writing short stories for different magazines, and non-fiction for *True West* and *Frontier Times*.

Q: Have you thought to write more on the order of horrific westerns? You might be uniquely suited to do this.

Lansdale: It's occurred to me. I don't know that I will. I really would like to write westerns. I don't know that I'd want to do that and nothing else. I'm happy with what I'm doing now. I'm writing two crime novels for Mysterious Press right now. But I feel that the western aspect of my work is far from finished. At least I like to think so. As for there will be any more horrific westerns, I don't know. You see, horror tends to creep into everything I do. It seems to be there in one form or another.

Q: Does the western today have very specific, generic expectations which restrict the writer?

Lansdale: About like horror. About like science fiction. The same ones. It's there for every genre if you let it take you over. I don't think it's any more restrictive than any of the others. I think if you want to do interesting work, you can. When I wrote *The Magic Wagon*, I thought it was a western. It just had some potential fantasy elements in it. It depends on how you look at it. If you read it one way, there are no fantasy elements at all. But the characters perceive them as fantasy elements. So, I don't know. I don't think the restrictions in westerns are any worse than anything else. I think it's what you do with it. It's what you bring to it. If you can't find your own voice, if you can't find something about the subject that interests you, you're going to write the same dull, old stuff.

Q: How does the creation of a story occur for you? Do you write it out in a burst, or take notes, or what?

Lansdale: Very seldom do I ever take notes. Once in a while something will come to mind and I'll write it down on a sheet of paper and promptly lose it. But usually if I write it there, it'll stick with me. But more likely, a couple of ideas will hit, and I'll think about them and I'll sit down—I work a regular schedule. I try to work in the mornings until noon, then take off for lunch and go back and work in the early afternoon. I used to to do that seven days a week. I don't work seven days a week now. It's about five and a half.

But the stories vary. Usually it's some particular scene or a character will come to mind and a story will grow out of it, or an incident. But there's no set pattern to the way I work. I don't outline, if that's what you mean. I don't take a lot of notes. If I feel like a story needs research to make it believable, I'll research.

Q: Have you had much feedback from the sort of people you write about? I don't particularly mean the crazed murderers, but the farmers and blue-collar people. Do they read your stuff? How do they feel about it?

Lansdale: No, I haven't heard much from them. I've had a couple of people who wrote and said, "I hate niggers too," and I had to write back and say, "I think you missed the whole point of the story." They didn't catch the satire. A lot of my stories certainly have that interest or edge in them. I got that from Mark Twain. He's one of my favorite writers. But, other than that, no, not really.

Q: A friend of mine once described the typical Joe Lansdale story as, "You don't know whether to laugh or throw up. "

Lansdale: [Laughs]

Q: In order to prove the point, she then proceeded to read to those assembled, "My Dead Dog Bobby," from your Pulphouse collection.

Lansdale: I don't know what to say to that. Yeah, that's true. That story is certainly a sick puppy, if you'll pardon the expression.

Q: You can read that story as horror or as humor. You've got both sides of the coin there.

Lansdale: I learned that from Robert Bloch. I doubt Robert Bloch would claim any connection to my stories. [Laughs] I love his work. I grew up on it. I think he showed me that horror and humor are very similar. You can walk an edge there. You can also fall off and the story can be destroyed. It can be too horrific, just plain, ugly, nasty, or it can be just too damn funny to get your point across. So it's a hard line to walk, but that's what has always interested me, walking that line between the outrageous and the horrific. Actually I find that the outrageous stuff is what has actually happened. And that's what you'll think I made up. The stuff that seems no so outrageous, I made up.

Q: You must indeed get some interesting fan mail.

Lansdale: Yeah, like I said, I get a note every now and then that says, "Yeah, I hate niggers too," and that upsets me, but I can't be the Cliff Notes for everybody. Most of the stuff I get is pretty intelligent. I was talking to a lot of other writers who have some real weird fans, and I've had a couple of odd things, but for the most part it's been real intelligent and interesting because they seem to run the gamut from your blue-collar to your academics who read it. A lot of the stuff that I've written has appeared in literary magazines, so it's an odd audience.

Q: I'm surprised they'll let you be that violent in literary magazines.

Lansdale: Well, I don't know that they would publish "The Night They Missed the Horror Show." Some of the things that were done were things like "Trains Not Taken," which is just strange. It's an alternate universe western sort of thing. There's that western influence again. And there was another one I did for the literary magazines, called "A Car Drives By," which was redone—"Not From Detroit"—but I've also done some other oddball things of that nature that I wouldn't have expected to appear in those kind of magazines, but did.

Q: No writer can remain creatively healthy and do the same thing over and over. Presumably there must be a limit to the number of stories of strange, secret rituals in back-country towns and crime-suspense novels you can write. What next? Where would you like to evolve as a writer?

Lansdale: I think you've got to change. If you look at the collection, *Stories by Mama Lansdale's Youngest Boy*, which contains primarily my earliest work, you'll see that most of it isn't about that at all. It's about weird false teeth and creatures out of the dump—more traditional horror subjects—and then you have the stuff in *By Bizarre Hands*, and then the stories I'm doing now are a bit different. They're much more crime-oriented. They're a little more traditional in structure, but I don't think of them as traditional stories. I think you have to change or else you die. I don't want to be known as the guy who writes the same type of story over and over. You can write one redneck story after another, but after a while, what's the point? I'm doing something new now, and I hope ten years from now to be doing something new again. I hope it doesn't take that long.

Q: You also have to watch out for repetition of details or devices. I noticed recently when I put together a collection of my own stories that I had three stories in a row in which people came back from the dead and manifested themselves by rustling around in the kitchen. You had two stories in a row in *By Bizarre Hands* which cars break down.

Lansdale: No matter what you do you're going to repeat some themes, but if you're careful you can try and not repeat them as often. But you have certain themes and certain obsessions and you can't get away from them, but if you find new approaches and new ways to express yourself, you can do better work. I find that I'll think, "God damn, I used that element in some other story." So you're going to repeat yourself to some extent. But the ideal is to tell a different story in a different way, and that's the best you can do. What makes your stories work if they work at all is the fact that you do have certain obsessions.

Q: Most writers have a limited cast of characters. There are usually about five, and they're based on yourself, a few people you've known, and so on. But sometimes you deliberately try to vary this—

Lansdale: I think you can try so hard that you develop artificial material. Some people just have a very limited approach and there's not anything they can do about it, no matter how hard they try. I think to some extent, I have forced myself to relax and say, "Okay, just back off and let's just see what else is inside your head, and what new themes you can put into your work." The best thing to do there is to be observant, to read in a wider spectrum, to observe people, to run in different circles. That's what's happened to me in the last couple of years: my work is usually changing before I'm able to change it. By the time I'm writing certain stories, I already have a new attitude, new emotions, new stories in mind, and it'll take me two years to get to them. Recently Ellen Datlow picked one of my stories for *The Year's Best Fantasy and Horror* and she said that this sort of thing is getting tired, redneck horror. And if you really look, only seven or eight of my stories are like that. The rest of them are totally different. Those are the ones that people remember, see. I didn't think of it as a criticism. I thought she was right. I don't want people to remember just those. Technically she was wrong, because there's only a handful of stories of that nature.

Q: But if you wrote New England yuppie horror no one would believe you.

Lansdale: Well I have to write what interests me. I don't write for other people so much as I write for myself. I think that's the best thing I can do, because I'm the one who's going to get bored quicker than anybody else over a certain type of story. I'm the guy who has to labor over a story that somebody might read in an hour or less. That may take me a week or a month to write. Or a novel might take six months or a year to write.

Q: The public perception of your work is obviously based on what has been published. What about the material that hasn't yet appeared, which will surprise them?

Lansdale: I hope it'll surprise them. You never can tell. I don't want to say that the fiction I'm writing now is more upbeat—that implies something I don't mean to say—but it has a totally different attitude, even though the voice remains the same. I have no way to describe it until people see it and they can tell me. I seem to be working more directly into the crime field than horror. I am still using some of the off-the-wall things that interest me, as for what kind of stew I put together, I guess the readers will have to tell me.

Q: Do you think you'll ever face a publisher-typecasting problem? I've always wondered what would happen if Stephen King wrote a romantic comedy. Would they bring it out with a black cover and something menacing on it?

Lansdale: Probably. Obviously I don't have the great popularity that Mr. King has, which makes him more of a brand name in the eyes of the publishers, but if you look at my books, for *Act of Love* I think it said "Novel" on the same. *Dead in the West* was obviously published as horror. *The Nightrunners* was published as horror. The two *Drive-In* books were published as science fiction. *The Magic Wagon*, I think I mentioned, was published as a western. *Cold in July* was published as a novel. *Savage Season* was suspense, although they're both akin to each other. *By Bizarre Hands*, horror. *Stories from Mama Lansdale's Youngest Boy*, horror. Now I'm doing two novels that are being published as crime-suspense from Mysterious Press. But I think everybody wants me to buy a label and say, "This is what I do." Probably the closest I've come to doing that is what I'm doing for Mysterious press, because they're giving me an opportunity to reach out for a bigger audience. As for whether I will continue to say, "Yes, I'm a crime-suspense writer," that remains to be seen. As long as I am interested in those types of stories, I will write them. When I get interested in something else, I won't write them. Even though I'm doing these two for Mysterious Press, I'm also doing one small *Drive-In* book, the last one, and I am also doing a novel that takes place in East Texas in the 1930s and has some possible supernatural elements. So I am keeping the subjects mixed.

Q: If you get popular enough in a certain way, some publisher may say, "Here's five million dollars. I want another book just like the last one."

Lansdale: I'm not that popular and I've already had that. I've had publishers tell me "You're never going to make a career until you settle down to do one thing or another." And to some extent, Mysterious Press is saying, "Okay, we'll call these suspense novels, but what we want is Joe Lansdale." Obviously I'm not going to write a romance for them. It has to have a crime element. So much of my work has that anyway and I seem to naturally lean in that direction. I find suspense such an open and varying field. I think you could write a horror novel and be suspense, of a sort. I think it's true of science fiction, whatever. It excites me right now. It's a wide-open field. It's a different approach. Hey, they're paying me money too, so what I say? I'm not in this just for the art. But I'm going to do what I think is both artistically-correct and Lansdale-correct. That's really all I can do.

Q: Has there been any movie interest in your work?

Lansdale: I've sold a lot of it to the movies. *Cold in July* to John Irving, who did *Ghost Story, Hamburger Hill, Tinker, Tailor, Soldier, Spy*. He has a real varied career. He did the *Robin Hood* made for Fox. He's had *Cold in July* for about four years now. I did a screenplay for it. *Savage Season*, John Badham has that one. *The Drive-In* has been optioned. *Dead in the West* has been optioned four years in a row. There's interest in it again right now. "The Far Side of the Cadillac Desert" was optioned a couple years in a row. I don't know if it's going to be renewed or not. "The Pit" is supposed to be filmed soon. Whether it'll actually happen, or not, I don't know. I read the screenplay. It didn't owe a lot to my story that I could sell. They used the lines out of it, but they didn't understand the essence of it at all. And there's been some interest in a couple of others that I think will be nailed down before long.

And a lot of comic-book interest. There will be a lot of things adapted into comics, and I will be doing some original comics inspired from some of my stories. There may even be a *By Bizarre Hands* comic book. That's being kicked around right now.

Q: Well, to wrap this up, any thoughts on where you'll be twenty years from now?

Lansdale: I hope I'll still be writing novels and short stories. I hope I'll still be writing films and comics. Primarily it's the prose that I'm interested in. Short stories are what I love, but right now I feel that I'm temporarily burned out in short stories. That's one reason why I've put a lot more effort into the novels. But, who knows? I go where the wind blows, at least where the Lansdale wind blows.

Q: Thanks, Joe.

CARRIE VAUGHN

Carrie Vaughn is most famous for the bestselling Kitty Norville series of novels, which began with *Kitty and The Midnight Hour* (2005), about a female werewolf who runs a late night radio talk show for supernatural creatures. She is also the author of five published non-Kitty novels and about fifty short stories. This interview was October 16, 2011 as the Capclave convention in the Washington DC area, at which she was guest of honor, was winding down.

Q: I am sure that a lot of people now think of you as "the werewolf lady." There must be more to you than that. So why don't you start by telling something about your background?

Vaughn: I have been writing since high school, sending stuff out since high school, but I didn't sell my first story until I was about twenty-seven, to Marion Zimmer Bradley's *Sword and Sorceress* anthology. I am not sure how many people know that. I probably sold a couple dozen short stories before my first novel finally came out. As you said, I am best known for my werewolf novels, but I do have this other short-story career that I am quite proud of. I still try to do as much as I can in the short format, because I do like it.

In other news, I have a master's degree in English Lit. I am a military brat. My father was in the Air Force for twenty years. So I have lived all over the country. I've settled in Colorado. I have been there about fifteen years now and I have a dog. What else would you like to know?

Q: Did you set out to write in this field and the kind of books you are writing, or did it just happen? I know I once thought I was going to be a science fiction writer. That's not how it worked out.

Vaughn: It just kind of happened. I grew up reading the science fiction and fantasy that was on my parents' bookshelves. So, all of the classics, Clarke, Niven, anybody you can think of. The old anthologies. So I did read a lot of short fiction, even when growing up, and that was the kind of thing I wanted to write. I was one of those daydreaming kids who wasn't any good at sports. Writing was one way I could daydream productively, I guess. So I tried to write the kinds of things that I read, and the short story was part of that. I really did think I was going to be a hard-science fiction writer. I was very much into the science classes, watching National Geographic, and reading the magazines, that sort of thing, and then I kind of realized that most of what I was reading later on was Ray Bradbury and Ursula Le Guin's Earthsea series and Robin McKinley and I took a lot of mythology classes in college and started writing more and more fantasy. My first three novels that didn't sell at all were traditional fantasy, medieval world, quest-type fantasy novels, which I think would surprise some people.

Then I got the idea for the Kitty novels. It started as a short story. You know this. I wrote a short story about this werewolf with a talk radio show. It seemed like such a crazy idea that I could get maybe a short story out of this and nothing else. I wrote the short story, and it appeared in *Weird Tales* in 2001. Thank you, Darrell. [I humbly explain that the late George Scithers and I were editing *Weird Tales* at this point.—DS.] I had a great time writing it, and I had a lot more ideas in that world. The big push on this was when you sent me the letter that Gene Wolfe had sent to the magazine, saying that "Dr. Kitty Solves All Your Love Problems" was his favorite story in that issue. I was so incredibly happy that I immediately went and wrote the next Kitty story. I've gotten to speak with him about that just a little bit. When the novel was coming out, my editor asked me for people who might be willing to give blurbs, I immediately mentioned Gene Wolfe. I didn't know if he would blurb the book, but he did. That also made me very happy.

Yes, it started as a short story, and it turns out that the idea was a lot bigger than I thought it was. I am working in the 11th novel right now. But I do have three traditional fantasy novels tucked away, and I still write lots of other things in short fiction. I am slowly branching out in the novel realm as well.

Q: So if you were to take these three traditional fantasy novels and put werewolves in them …

Vaughn: I don't know. Maybe I should try it.

Q: But seriously I think that the appeal of the Kitty Norville series is that this is about a werewolf who is a part of modern life.

Vaughn: Absolutely.

Q: So just putting a werewolf into a generic fantasy setting wouldn't be nearly as interesting.

Vaughn: That's exactly right. I think that's the appeal of urban fantasy, the reason for its surge in popularity over the last few years. It's not just the supernatural creatures. It's supernatural creatures that are recognizably like us, in a culture that's recognizable, in the modern world. That is my favorite thing about writing the Kitty books. I can have her go to Senate hearings. I can have a reality TV show. I can deal with werewolf veterans of the Afghanistan War. I can look out at the real world and ask myself what this would look like with vampires and werewolves or magic or fairies, and the stories keep coming. There is just so much out there. Not even dealing with it on the level of metaphor, it's fun, and the thing that makes it fun is the real part of the equation.

Q: And as long as the real world exists, I suppose it will continue to supply you with material.

Vaughn: Yeah. The thing that is going to limit the series is that, dealing with Kitty, there is a character arc, and I do want to give that arc an ending someday. I don't know when, but I do know how that story ends. I would like to do that. But, in the meantime I am up to eleven books because I keep getting ideas that don't fit into the book that I am currently writing. Then I put them in the next book. You just have to look and see how many people are writing urban fantasy with how many ideas. It has touched some kind of chord, and yeah, it's relevant.

Q: Considering that you live in Colorado, why not contemporary western rural fantasy?
Not all the world is in cities.

Vaughn: That is a big debate right now. Why do we keep calling it urban fantasy when a lot of it takes place in the boonies, or in small towns, or suburbia? Suburban fantasy is the next big trend, I predict. That is one of the ways I am a little ambivalent about the term "urban fantasy," because it does have so many different definitions for so many people. The great thing about having Kitty be from Denver is that Denver is a great urban city. I can tell an urban city if I want to, but it's also thirty minutes away from a national forest and the Rocky Mountains. I can go to those places if I need to as well.

Q: Taking a scholarly turn, I wonder if you've read much of the fantasy that was published in *Unknown Worlds*? Presumably in reprints. Do you know what Unknown Worlds was?

Vaughn: No.

Q: There was a whole school of fantasy developed in it, of which Fritz Leiber's *Conjure Wife* is probably the best remembered example. *Unknown*, which was later titled *Unknown Worlds*, was a companion magazine to *Astounding Science Fiction*. It was edited by John W. Campbell between 1939 and 1943, and it specialized in what we now call urban fantasy. It was about Old World supernatural creatures living in contemporary Chicago. There were stories about elves learning to adapt to the 1940s. This is where Leiber's "Smoke Ghost" was published. I wondered if there was any link between what you're doing and this older school of urban fantasy.

Vaughn: That's the other thing that I wish people talked about with urban fantasy, that it is not new. It has been going on for decades. People have been writing this kind of story for a long time. It's the modern fairy tale in some ways. It really is the modern take on magic in the world and dealing with the world in terms of magic. Yes….I recently picked up Jack Williamson's *Darker Than You Think*, which would be completely at home in today's market. It's just the same kind of thing.

Q: And it was first published in *Unknown* in 1940.

Vaughn: The story I probably talk about most when people have me on werewolf panels to talk about where werewolves come from is Marie de France's "Bisclavret."[1] For that audience it was a contemporary story. It was set in a contemporary world that they would have all recognized. It just happened to have a werewolf in it. So we've been telling these kinds of stories for a really long time. It's only recently that people had paid attention and compartmentalized it into this particular brand with the action-adventure mystery component.

Q: We've been telling werewolf stories since, at least, Petronius's *The Satyricon*. You must know that one, too. But I have a theory that a good deal of what we are seeing in present-day publishing consists of the immediate descendants of *Buffy the Vampire Slayer*.

Vaughn: It's the descendants of Buffy and a couple other veins. Through the '80s we had Chelsea Quinn Yarbro and P.N. Elrod, as well as Anne Rice. What is interesting to me is that in the '80s it was just vampire fiction. Now it's become this big, huge sub-genre. I have also heard the idea that it is also an inheritor of Gothic fiction, 19th century Gothic. I think there is a component of that just in the dynamic of how some of the romances work. It really is Jane and Rochester and Cathy and Heathcliff. It's that kind of romance played out in a different setting with different creatures.

Q: I think it also has a substantial component of the hardboiled detective story. Raymond Chandler got into the mix.

Vaughn: Yeah, very noir. Which is one of the things that is so fascinating, that it does draw all of these different components from all

---

1   12th century French poet. The title means "The Werewolf."—DS

of these different areas. It's mystery, thriller, romance, erotica in some cases, all rolled up into one strange brew.

Q: At what point does it become a formula, in which someone can take standard elements off the shelf and just put them together? I am sure that sooner or later someone will write a totally generic urban fantasy.

Vaughn: [Laughs.] It's already there. If you talk to some people, it was like that from the beginning. As we said, these aren't necessarily new stories. Yeah, it is a formula. I have talked to people who think that for it to be urban fantasy you have to have a kick-ass woman who's in a love triangle doing X, Y, and Z. I keep telling them, no, please, you can do other things. You don't need to have it just like this. It's a bigger umbrella than that. But a certain kind of story appeals to a lot of people, and a lot of people deal with the familiar, rather than trying to branch out, I think.

Q: Do the readers want the familiar? Are we getting into the condition of prose television?

Vaughn: I don't know. I am not sure I can answer that, being one of the producers in this genre. I don't always know what readers want and what they are looking for. For my own series, I do try to tell a different story with every book. I try to bring in issues that I am interested in. I try to challenge myself as a writer. So, just for myself, I am trying to do as much as I can within the constraints of the genre that I've agreed to.

Q: Do you know yet if your readers are Kitty readers or Carrie Vaughn readers? I am sure they are discussing this at your publishers' a lot.

Vaughn: I think there's a Venn diagram. I have Kitty readers who will only read Kitty books. At the same time there are readers who would never read the Kitty books, because of the covers. The covers mark them as a certain kind of book. There's a group of readers that will never, ever touch that kind of urban fantasy. But they'll read my standalone books. They'll read *Discord's Apple* and *After the Golden Age*. Then there's a chunk in the middle, who will read anything. I do have Carrie Vaughn fans. Just at this convention I have signed stacks of books for people who have both the Kitty books and the Young Adult and the standalones. I think it's too much to ask for everybody to read everything, because it is not all going to appeal to everybody. But I do have a really solid split in the middle of that Venn diagram.

Q: So, has there been any Hollywood interest in Kitty yet?

Vaughn: Not serious, let's say. I've gotten some nibbles, but when you hear words like "I can't pay you anything up front but can give you a percentage of the back end," it's best to walk away from those. But nothing serious. Nothing I'd be willing to sell the rights for.

Q: Obviously someone is going to do a series like this as a TV show. It might as well be yours. But on another subject, I wonder if the appeal of the werewolf as continuing character is in some ways opposite that of the vampire. The problem with vampire, if you really get down to it, is that he's dead. He may be superficially charming, but he's still a corpse. The werewolf is not only alive, but possibly excessively so. It has self-control issues. So do you think the appeal of the werewolf might be that if people are tired of vampires, here they can turn to the exact opposite?

Vaughn: I occasionally get asked, "What's sexier, vampires or werewolves?" and I say, "So you're asking me between necrophilia and bestiality?" [Laughs.] It's a facetious way to put it. Just personally, I didn't feel I had anything to add to the vampire mythos. As you said, traditionally, yes, they're dead. But it's so interesting to me how that has become less and less of the vampire mythos as we've gone on. The vampires in the Twilight novels don't really follow that mythos, and a lot of people don't even think about that part of it. What appeals to people is the longevity, the immortality. With werewolves it's the self-control issue. There is something about werewolves that doesn't appeal to people the way the genteel, long-lived vampire does. I am not quite sure what it is. Once again, personally, I find werewolves much more interesting. They are much more vibrant and have a lot more diversity. For me there are many more stories to tell. They're not all the Lestat character that seems to attract readers.

Q: Your werewolves act like a combination between a wolf pack and a biker gang. But they'd be less appealing if they acted more like wolves, because wolf hygiene is not the same as human hygiene. It's all that sniffing in the wrong place.

Vaughn: I am sure that appeals to some people. [Laughs.] I don't know that people give wolves enough credit for being civilized in some cases. I've done a bit of research into wolf behavior and pack dynamics to write the books, just because it's a great source of ideas and material. They are actually pretty civilized. There is some research that's been done that suggests that the leaders of the pack aren't necessarily the strongest, meanest wolves. They might be the wolves that are the best at organizing. They may be the best peacemakers. They're the wolves that can keep the most members of the pack alive the longest, which sort of speaks to a human bureaucracy. The thing I really enjoy doing is picking and choosing the traits I want to deal with. Every werewolf is going to fall somewhere on the scale, either more wolf or more human. They're not going to be either/or. They're going to be more one or more the other. Their place on that scale might change, depending on the story. That to me is the interesting bit, is getting to pick and choose.

Q: Was it the first story, in which somebody called in to Kitty's radio show because they were in trouble with a fundamentalist preacher who claimed he could "cure" werewolves? What I notice is that the larger, religious/spiritual dimension is neglected in most werewolf stories. The traditional medieval werewolf usually had serious damnation issues. It used to be that the basic method of becoming a werewolf, other than selling your soul to the Devil, was being an unwanted child born between Christmas and Epiphany. Lycanthropy was seen a curse. This is not to suggest that someone write a fundamentalist Christian werewolf series for the Left Behind market—though I suspect that someone could—but it does seem that the larger supernatural aspect—supernatural context, we might call it—is being neglected.

Vaughn: I believe werewolves got their own chapter in *Malleus Malificarum*, which is the witch-hunter's handbook in the Middle Ages, because it was seen as a form of witchcraft as much as anything else. That's another aspect, like the undead part of vampirism, the whole damnation thing has just vanished. We have very secular supernatural creatures. It's something I'd like to deal more with. The faith-healer who was going to cure vampires and werewolves showed up in the first two Kitty books. Once again, that was more of a reflection of our modern American culture. That is a growing concern for a lot of people, this idea that your faith is a big part of you. The way that works out in the political arena is, I think, just fascinating and a little frightening. Yeah, I hope to deal with it more. I've got a vampire character in the book I am writing now. He was born in 15th century Spain. He was Catholic. He was pretty devoutly Catholic. He was turned into a vampire against his will. So is he still Catholic? How would you be a vampire and a Catholic at the same time, and is it even possible? That's something that I hope to deal with.

Q: This opens a whole new can of worms, but what your faith healer reminded me of, very much, was certain religious fundamentalists who claim they can "cure" gays.

Vaughn: That was exactly where that came from. I remember being in college, and you could turn to the back classifieds in the alternative weekly, and there would be an ad that said, "We can cure you. Call this number." That was exactly the thread I was following for that storyline.

Q: It would be an interesting statistical datum if you could get it: what percentage of the readers of this sort of supernatural novel series are gay? Is it above average for fantasy readers generally? Both the vampire stories and the werewolf ones are about alternate, secretive societies which are not mainstream and not respectable. They exist on their own terms. I am sure that parallelism must be working in both the writing and in the marketing.

Vaughn: Purely anecdotal data says yes. I don't have numbers because I don't ask. It's not something I ask everybody who comes to a signing, but I think you're right. There probably is a readership that responds to that.

Q: There is also probably a readership that just responds to the feeling of being different. These are probably great books for teenagers.

Vaughn: Teenagers love it. It's one of the reasons that *Twilight* has become so popular. Ironically enough, everybody can relate to alienation. Everybody has had that moment, no matter what it looks like from the outside, that they fell like an outsider. Sometimes being in the middle of everything can make you feel even more of an outsider, if you feel like you're putting on an act or trying to pass. So I think that definitely people are responding to that.

Q: Adolescents surely feel their hormones getting out of control in scary ways. What is a male werewolf anyway except a terminal testosterone explosion?

Vaughn: Not just that. I don't know if you've seen the movie *Ginger Snaps* . . . ?

Q: No.

Vaughn: You need to see *Ginger Snaps*. It's about two teenaged girls. One of them gets infected and slowly transforms into a werewolf. It's the best treatment of that metaphor I have ever seen. Highly, highly recommended.

Q: But werewolfery is no longer purely a curse. It used to be the tragic story of how the werewolf had to be destroyed. Now they're coming to terms with it.

Vaughn: If you're going to have stories, that's where it has to go. You have to come to terms with it and move in if you're going to tell different kinds of stories. I feel like for a long time the main werewolf story has been "Dr. Jekyll and Mr. Hyde." The werewolf always dies in the end. That is one reason that werewolves have never been as popular as vampires, I think, because they've stuck in this story-loop in which they always have to be destroyed. The wild urges have to be controlled. If vampires do represent death, that's why they keep winning. That kind of where the Kitty series started, saying let's have werewolves who can control themselves. Then where do we go from there?

Q: Then there is the idea, rarely presented convincingly, I think, that vampirism is a treatable condition. Just get them their ration of blood, etc. I confess to being something of a fundamentalist on this. I think it's more dramatic to have vampires as evil. You do have a bit of a narrative problem, I suppose. You are writing about a person who terms into a ravening beast…but not a bad one.

Vaughn: This is why you get Oz, on Buffy, being locked in a cage once a month. What are your rules? What boundaries are you willing to put up with? If you set up rules in your world, and if you've decided that in your world werewolves can go off to the mountains by themselves and run around and kill deer and rabbits and then come back and be fine, then that's your world. Or you can write about the lone wolf who can't control it and is always killing his neighbors, and that doesn't last very long.

Q: Let's talk about your other books for a bit. After the failed generic fantasy novels, you wrote several werewolf novels. Then what was next?

Vaughn: *Discord's Apple* and *After the Golden Age* are my two stand-alone fantasy novels. I actually wrote those right around the times of the first and second Kitty novels. I didn't know whether the series was going to take off or not, so I started working on other things. Those are the two that came out of that. Oddly enough, they're both contemporary fantasy as well. I got into that vein and found it a very rich vein and kept going with it. *Discord's Apple* is my near-future, pre-apocalypse, Greek mythology and magic novel. I have been calling it my "kitchen sink" book because everything I love went into it. *After the Golden Age* is my superhero novel. My main character is the daughter of the most famous superheroes in the city and she has no powers of her own, and she has to save the city with accounting; because not only does she have no powers, she became an accountant, and has never lived it down.

Q: What is immediately forthcoming? What are you working on now?

Vaughn: Those are both out. I also have two Young Adult novels out, *Steel* and *Voices of Dragons*. Right now I am working on another science fiction YA. I'm not finished with it yet, so I don't want to talk much about it. I've got more Kitty books in the pipeline. I am considering doing a spinoff novel and branching out and doing more in that world. And short stories. I'm always working on short stories. One of my problems right now is that I've got lots of stuff I want to do and not enough time to do it. So I am having to pick and choose what I work on.

Q: Thanks, Carrie.

[2011]

LISA TUTTLE

Lisa Tuttle was born in Texas 1952 but has lived in Great Britain since 1980. She has been selling stories since 1971 and won the John W. Campbell Award for best new writer in 1974. Her first book, *Windhaven*, written in collaboration with George R.R. Martin, was science fiction, with parts of it published in *Analog*. Her later novels have been mostly fantasy and horror, including *Familiar Spirit, Gabriel, The Pillow Friend, The Mysteries*, and *The Silver Bough*. Among her collections are *A Nest of Nightmares, A Spaceship Built of Stone*, and *Ghosts and Other Lovers*. PS Publishing published her novella *My Death* as a short book in 2004. She has written for children (*Catwitch*, etc.) and edited *The Encyclopedia of Feminism* and a celebrated horror anthology, *Skin of the Soul*. She was a Guest of Honor at the 2007 World Fantasy Convention.

Q: You're a Texan transplanted to Britain for some time now. Your last two novels have been set in Scotland. Do you have any sense of being a "regional" writer? Has being a non-native but long-time resident given you a special angle or insight?

Tuttle: I've never thought of myself as a "regional" writer, but I do prefer to write about places I've actually been, and the better I know them, the more comfortable I feel about setting a whole novel there. Which is why I may set short stories in China or Seville (both places I've visited), but my novels tend to be set in places where I've lived, with Texas, London, and Scotland predominating. This is the problem I always had with writing science fiction—making up a whole new world has always seemed far, far more difficult than inventing characters or plot.

Another reason for using familiar (to me) settings is the autobiographical impulse. It's not always obvious, but I'm as autobiographical a writer as a lot of more "realist" writers. I may be telling stories about the dead returning to life, weird relationships with ghosts, impossible pregnancies, and other intrusions from beyond reality, but I've always drawn heavily on my own life.

And ever since I first visited this country in 1976, I've found the landscape and history of Britain incredibly evocative and inspiring. Sometimes I get ideas from the scenery around me. That didn't happen to me with Texas; but because Houston and the Gulf plains and eastern woodlands of Texas were the earliest landscapes I knew, they're a deep part of me and naturally affect my writing. I love Austin and the hill country, but I was an adult before I got to know that part of Texas, and only lived in Austin for about five years...so I'm really more an outsider there than I am on the west coast of Scotland where I've lived for the past 17 years.

I don't know if it gives me any special insight, but I think the position of being an outsider, never entirely part of the place I call home, has been fertile for me as a writer.

Q: So, do you find yourself deliberately collecting bits of interesting lore about places you've visited?

Tuttle: Actually, yes. I can never resist a locally-published pamphlet about ghosts or folklore or mysteries of the area. I also own a lot of books on those subjects, from all over.

Q: I note that *The Mysteries* touches on disappearances everywhere, but of course it centers on Scotland. Do they still have an on-going abduction mythos in Scotland?

Tuttle: Not that I'm aware of, if you mean specifically abductions by the Gentry...if you're talking the modern version of alien abductions, that mythos is alive and well, although possibly not as wide-spread as in America.

Q: And, how do you adapt autobiography into fiction? Is this a matter of fantasizing about how your life might have gone differently, or using things that did happen?

Tuttle: Both, I guess, although there's more to it than that. My life goes into my work—I don't really see how it could not. It's hard to explain exactly how it works; I don't just write about something that really happened to me and then give it a little supernatural twist; the autobiographical element is something I play about with and change quite dramatically, but the beginning of a story is often something that's really happened to me...or that I've been afraid might happen...or that I've fantasized about happening.

Some examples: I wrote a short story called "In Jealousy" which I deliberately wanted to make sound like a true ghost story—even though it absolutely isn't. I began with something factual—I did go on a tour of China in 1985, when my first marriage was breaking up, and I did spend a certain amount of time (far too much!!) brooding over my unhappy marital situation while I was there. But it was a special women's tour (organized by the Society for Anglo-Chinese Understanding)—which it isn't in the story; in the fiction, the narrator begins an affair with a man who's in much the same situation as herself: lonely and unhappily separated. I based the relationship on a very brief one I'd had with a man several years later—and although I changed every physical fact about him, the psychological details of what drew us together and quickly split us apart were true.

Familiar Spirit, my first horror novel, is full of the real, physical details of my life at the time that I was writing it. I think I included the lamp shaped like a cowboy boot that I found in the first apartment I rented—or maybe I put that in a later book. It's set in Austin in the 1970s, and Sarah, the heroine, probably has some of my characteristics and personality traits (I'm not sure—it's been a long time since I read it)—and, like me at the time I was writing, she'd just split up with her boyfriend. Although unlike me, and for reasons to do with the plot, she wasn't at all happy to be on her own and wanted her boyfriend back. But probably the major autobiographical element there was the setting: at the beginning of the book, she moves into a rather decrepit old house on West 35th Street, the very real place where I'd lived for several years. Obviously that house was important to me, because I also used it (even though I had to move it out of Austin and deep into the piney woods of East Texas) as the setting for a section of *The Pillow Friend*. The real house is long gone, knocked down and replaced by a condo, so I'm glad to feel I preserved it in fiction.

Quite a bit of my real life fed into *The Pillow Friend*—incidents, such as my having my appendix out when I was seven; the emotional turmoil of adolescence and unrequited love; my marriage to an English writer; my feelings about Texas, London and Scotland—and the whole geographical arc of the book reflects the course of my life—Houston, Austin, Harrow, Scotland. All the rest—especially all the weird stuff—is just totally and completely made up.

Q: There are a lot of unhappy people in your stories. There are a lot of unhappy people in most stories, because that's the obvious way to generate conflict. Would it be possible to write a story about a completely happy and contented character, or is the whole point of fiction, particularly ghostly fiction, to probe the things that make us unhappy and uncomfortable?

Tuttle: For a moment there I thought you were going to ask if this was autobiographical! (I am quite a cheerful person, in general, I think.)

Actually, this is something I've thought about—I think it is possible to write about someone who is happy and contented, but if they remain that way from the beginning to the end of the story, well, I doubt it would be much of a story. So, they might be happy at the beginning—and then something terrible happens!—and/or they can win through to happiness or contentment at the end, but in the middle, that is to say for most of the story, there has to be something that at the very least tests them or unsettles them. Fiction, not just supernatural fiction, does usually involve change and conflict to some degree, which kind of rules out "completely happy".

Having said that, I must admit that quite often in my fiction I write about people who are troubled and maybe even psychologically disturbed or borderline if not outright mad. There's lots of genre fiction about people who are put into stressful situations, but the reader never thinks they're going to crack up; the suspense is how this strong or normal person is going to manage to win through—this is the traditional hero, whose sanity one does not doubt. Then there are the characters you might find in stories by Poe, or Ramsay Campbell or me, where—possibly from the very beginning—the reader is thinking, this person's hold on reality is precarious. Is she really being haunted, or does she just think she is?

Q: Do you believe in ghosts?

Tuttle: Basically, no, I don't. Or at least, I don't believe ghosts are the spirits of the dead, and I'm very very skeptical about the existence of any psychic or paranormal powers that a lot of people believe in. Yet although I think of myself as basically a rationalist, I'm not a hard-liner, or a total materialist. If I were, I'd probably have no interest in ghosts, whereas in fact I am fascinated by the whole subject: by ghosts and hauntings and people who believe…and by inexplicable experiences. I do not doubt that people do see ghosts and have other strange experiences which can't be satisfactorily explained away in scientific terms. (Although I think also that many of them could be explained, but sometimes people will resist that explanation, refuse to accept it because they know it was supernatural—and that's interesting, too.) My own fascination probably suggests a chink in my rational armour. Maybe I really, deep down, long to be convinced.

Q: How do you think this affects your ability write about ghosts, then? Lovecraft suggested that the non-believer had a certain advantage, since a true believer would take the supernatural for granted and not give it sufficient buildup.

Tuttle: The fact that I'm not a believer maybe suggests why, to write a supernatural story that convinces me, it has to be ambiguous; on some level there's usually at least a hint that maybe none of this is "really" happening—or at least nowhere outside the brain of the main character. (For example, in short stories like "The Nest," "Riding the Nightmare," and "Bits and Pieces"; and the protagonists of both *Lost Futures* and *The Pillow Friend* are quite likely clinically insane....but then again maybe not.)

As for how belief or non-belief in the supernatural affects a person's ability to write about it...well, I can only speak from my own experience, which suggests to me that no one *un*interested in the supernatural would bother to write about it. (And if forced into it would probably do a poor job.) But obviously I don't think that being interested in the so-called supernatural necessarily implies belief.

I think this question could be asked about religion without any stretch—people's beliefs obviously must influence how they write...but it also affects how they read. Do devout Catholics take a different message from Graham Greene's *The End of the Affair* than totally non-religious me does? Presumably their understanding of/appreciation for that book would be closer to what the author actually intended. I recall having this feeling about Gene Wolfe's writing—particularly after talking to someone (a Catholic) who obviously had a much more powerful response to one of his books than I did; perceived it in a different way.

So—I don't know how to answer this question. It must have an impact, I suppose, but I don't know exactly what it is, or how you'd begin to disentangle it from everything else that affects a written text.

Q: Okay, if you WERE convinced, if evidence of ghosts were presented to you in a compelling manner, would you find this frightening or reassuring? On one hand, it tells us that we don't cease to exist at death. On the other, it suggests that some people could suffer an eternity of torment because of some tragedy.

Tuttle: I would love to see some compelling evidence— but it kind of depends on what ghosts were proved to BE. A non-material yet conscious survival of dead human beings? Or (what's always seemed more likely) "recordings" of events that took place in the past; or some perhaps telepathically-triggered perception which exists in the mind of the person(s) experiencing the ghost rather than 'out there.' Maybe it's some other form of "being" that has nothing to do with death. (After all, there have been apparitions of the living...and what about bi-location?)

Whether I found it frightening or reassuring (or, more likely, a bit of both) would depend on what this evidence convinced me of.

Q: I notice that real, true religious believers (maybe more in the US than in Britain—you tell me) actually AVOID ghostly and supernatural fiction, because they are afraid of it. On the crudest level, this is because they believe that if you talk about the Devil you may summon him. So I wonder if our fascination with the supernatural stems out of some delicate combination of skepticism and desire for the magical. We don't believe the supernatural is true, but we find artistic reasons for pretending it is. Any thoughts?

Tuttle: Is this actually the case? I don't know enough about most writers' religious beliefs to be sure. Of course you don't have to "believe" in ghosts and spirits and evil curses and all that to write convincing stories about them. Also, it seems to me that it's possible to be a devout Christian, with a belief in the after-life, without believing that the dead return as ghosts on this earth. (What kind of a way is that to spend your eternal life?) However, as for writing about supernatural matters—I think a strong belief in the reality and power of evil (as something which exists in and of itself, possibly as personified by the devil) could have two possible results: either you avoid writing about it because you don't want to somehow encourage it by leading your readers to dwell on it and maybe even having them attracted to witchcraft, spell-casting, vampirism, etc (readers being the perverse creatures we all are, you can't be sure they'll decide to emulate the hero rather than the villain!) OR you might want to depict how awful it is and how necessary it is for good to triumph by writing about the supernatural out of a deep belief that it not only exists, but permeates the world. And maybe that is more British than American, because the two examples that I can think of are both English: G.P. Taylor (I haven't actually read his books, but I've read an interview with him which set it out pretty clearly what he believes—I think he is or was a vicar, and he writes supernatural fantasies about the battle between good and evil) and James Herbert (a practising Catholic).

Your idea about a fascination with the supernatural among unbelievers being a balancing act of those two very different attitudes reminds me of Todorov's definition of the fantastic, which he said required three conditions: first, the text must be sufficiently, convincingly realistic to make readers "hesitate" between a natural and a supernatural explanation of the events described; second, this same hesitation may be experienced by a character in the story; third, the reader must adopt a particular attitude towards the text, so that he rejects a purely allegorical interpretation. Critics who follow Todorov emphasize this "hesitation" or ambiguity as a basic part of the fantastic, and I think it defines the appeal supernatural fantasy holds for me. Of course, and especially these days, there is a lot of genre fantasy to which that definition emphatically does not apply: there's no ambiguity about it; it's pure fantasy, whether set in an imaginary realm, or in "our world" but with the existence of ghosts, vampires, werewolves, magical powers, etc. added on.

But for me, what's most appealing about fantasy is exactly when it's on that borderline between real and unreal; when the rational gives way; when I as reader (and even as writer) sense the presence of something "other" which can't be explained…a mystery. That's what I love about it. And as soon as a ghost is explained it becomes less interesting—to me, anyway—even if the "explanation" is a bit of fantasy itself (e.g. spirits of the dead are forced to walk the earth until they get revenge or are exorcised by some ritual). This is also why I don't care for most genre fantasy; I'm not a big fan of "other world" fantasies (no, not even Tolkien), or the type of supernatural/paranormal fictions that establish loads of "rules" about how vampires came to be and how they exist and co-exist with ordinary mortals, not to mention werewolves and witches—I know a lot of people enjoy them, but it strikes me as being similar to role-playing games, and that doesn't interest me, either.

Q: Who are some of your favorite writers of ghostly fiction, particularly ones you think have influenced you?

Tuttle: Writers I think have influenced me—and long-term favorites in the field—include M.R. James, Ray Bradbury, Shirley Jackson, Henry James, Theodore Sturgeon, Kate Wilhelm (although she always comes immediately to mind when I'm asked about influences, I guess she's mostly SF and thrillers…not sure if she's written any ghost stories, but a lot of her work, and in particular her novel *Margret and I* had a huge influence on me), Edith Wharton, E. Nesbit, Robert Aickman, Joyce Carol Oates, Walter de la Mare, Arthur Machen, Charlotte Perkins Gilman (just one story—"The Yellow Wallpaper"—but, wow, did that have an impact!), and more recently (that is, I didn't read them until after my own career was established) Peter Straub, Angela Carter, W.G. Sebald, Jonathan Carroll.

Q: You don't write much science fiction these days. You started out in science fiction. Why the shift?

Tuttle: I think the shift was more in the market (or genre definition) than in me. In other words, I think I'm writing in the same genre or general area I've always written in.

If you look back at the very first stories I sold, they were mostly horror stories or ghost stories. But there wasn't much of a market for that in the '70s (mainly it was *The Magazine of Fantasy and Science*

Fiction) and because I wanted to sell, and because I was a fan of science fiction as well as supernatural fiction, I did keep trying to write SF. My SF usually tended to be on the "soft" side—I'm interested in people involved in strange situations, and also in speculating about "if this goes on..." or "what if?" but I have no hard science background, am not especially interested in technology (except as it impacts on people—for whom it might as well be magic), don't really go for space opera, and just generally tend to feel more comfortable writing about locations and backgrounds I've actually experienced rather than trying to create an entire new world or far-future scenario from my rather limited imagination (this goes back to our earlier discussion about the role of autobiography in my writing).

When it came to publishing my first short story collections, the first one, *A Nest of Nightmares* in 1986, was all horror stories (and includes the first two stories I ever sold: "Stranger in the House" and "Dollburger"); the second one followed the next year, *A Spaceship Built of Stone* in 1987, was supposedly my SF collection, and yet at least three of the stories in that ("No Regrets", "Birds of the Moon", "The Hollow Man") are the sort of cross-over, borderline genre stories I like best and are hard to really define: are they psychological horror? Contemporary fantasy? They have elements that appear in science fiction (alternate realities; astronauts; medical technology to revive the dead) but they are really about ordinary people trying to live in the face of some extraordinary circumstance.

My first novel was a collaboration with George R.R. Martin—it began with the novella "The Storms of Windhaven" and grew into the novel *Windhaven* (first published in 1981). We thought of it as science fiction; I guess it still is, although when I look at it in the light of SO many fantasy novels which have been published since I think that if the publishing scene had been then as it is now it would probably have been labelled as fantasy— possibly George and I wouldn't have felt it necessary to provide the SF rationale as the "deep background" to the story (i.e. having it set on a distant planet with a "lost colony" cut off from other worlds and cannibalizing the wrecked spaceship and remnants of their former technology). "The Storms of Windhaven" was originally published in *Analog,* and one of the reasons for the collaboration, on my part, was the desire to sell to a "hard SF" market that I was sure I'd never break into on my own.

My second novel—the first one I wrote solo—was *Familiar Spirit*— and that was a horror novel. Before writing it I was working on an SF novel, but finding it really hard going—I got bogged down in the hard work of building a futuristic setting and providing a rationale for it and imagining new technology. I think in general I would rather read SF than write it. Although I do have a half-baked idea for an SF novel which I hope to be able to develop and write one of these days... I haven't given up on that genre. I find it very difficult, but also rewarding. There are some ideas which can only be explored through SF.

Lost Futures—my fourth novel—was science fiction—but it was very "domestic" and contemporary and low-key; most of the book doesn't read like what most people would consider SF. Which probably explains why it was not very successful! A lot of what I write seems to fall into the cracks between genres. It's certainly been a problem for me in the past... but I just write what I write and hope for the best when it comes to finding my audience. Over here in the UK, *Lost Futures* was published as SF— but with a very "girly" cover that wouldn't appeal to many fans although it may have reflected the contents well enough— but in America it came out packaged as horror, with a kind of horrific, mummified-looking head on a dark cover, and raised red lettering dripping blood. I think it was one of the last books published in Dell's "Abyss" line (as the horror market was just about to collapse), and I can only imagine that a lot of hard-core horror fans would have found it hugely disappointing, as there are no mummies or dripping blood and gore within at all.

The novel I'm writing now has both magic and time travel in it; I suppose I would have to classify it as fantasy, like my last two novels— *The Mysteries* and *The Silver Bough*.

Q: Thanks, Lisa.

KIM NEWMAN

Kim Newman is the has published several acclaimed novels, including *The Night Mayor*, *Anno Dracula*, *Jago*, *Back in the USSA* (with Eugene Byrne), and *Johnny Alucard*, plus numerous short stories, often sarcastic and outrageous, frequently appear in *Interzone* and other publications on both sides of the Atlantic. His "The Man Who Collected Barker" is particularly recommended. He is also the author of *Nightmare Movies: A Critical Guide to Contemporary Horror Films*. He has won the Stoker Award, the International Horror Guild Award, and the British Fantasy Award. He had also written a good deal of work as "Jack Yeovil."

Q: So, how did you get to be the striking figure in the horror field you are today?

Newman: [Laughs.] I was born. As a pre-teenager, I certainly read comics and watched *Dr. Who* on television. I think probably my passionate interest in the horror genre, and also in film, was started as an eleven-year-old by staying up late to watch the Bela Lugosi version of *Dracula*. I think I can date from that my complicated interest in these things. Before, I'd just consumed comics. But after *Dracula* it became not just something I was interested in, but something I wanted to do. I remember writing my earliest and doubtless least literary effort, a play version of *Dracula*, which I put on in my drama class with eleven-year-olds. Also, through my teenage years, as I saw more and more horror movies and read more and more widely in the field, I wrote stuff. It was unpublishable, of course. I wrote my first novel as a fifteen-year-old. I haven't yet burned it. Oh, I must do that. [Laughs.] All the way through university, I was fiddling around with bits of writing. I was one of those awful kids who was a writer, who was working on a novel. It was drivel, of course. I think it's useful that I wrote all the real drivel that I had in me at a point wherein there was no chance of it getting published. I actually submitted my first novel to New English Library around 1974 and got a form rejection.

So, I did it all. I expanded from all the old Hammer movies. I saw in the credits, based on the novel by Bram Stoker, or Robert Louis Stevenson. So I actually started with the classics. I read *Dracula*, *Frankenstein*, *Jekyll and Hyde*, when I was eleven or twelve. At the same time, because I had this interest, my parents, who were always buying books, bought me a few anthologies. They went into W.H. Smith and there wasn't a horror section. There wasn't a category like there is now. I remember that one of the first horror book I saw, a work by a living writer, was an anthology of Robert Bloch stories. It was called *The House of the Hatchet* in Britain. I think it is probably called *Yours Truly, Jack the Ripper* over here. It contained his post-Lovecraft stories, the ones in which he had cast off the big Lovecraft influence and was starting to write in a more vernacular tone and to deal with more modern subjects. From then I must have read Lovecraft quickly and spread out in my interests.

This was before Stephen King had come along. James Herbert had just started publishing. But when *The Rats* came out, Herbert's breakthrough book, I remember that was the first novel I had ever read about which I'd thought, *this is terrible*. I had read books before that I had not enjoyed, but previously I'd not had any critical opinion. I remember reading this and thinking, this is a *bad* book. There are things in this book which just do not work. It's a hundred-and-twenty-page novel and the hero takes a thirty-page holiday in the middle of it to have sex.

That's slightly off the point. What I mean to say is that back then horror was basically Dennis Wheatley. I read one or two of his things and didn't really get on with them. Now I might find them somewhat more interesting as artifacts from the '30s and '40s, with all the prejudices of the time. But then I found them just stuffy and tedious. Wheatley spends a lot of time describing the meals his characters eat. It was a mannerism of his.

I never read *Famous Monsters*, but because I was interested in film, I did read books about horror films. Carlos Clarens wrote a very good one, and there were a few others out. As I had discovered Stoker and Stevenson, etc., I discovered that these guys Robert Bloch and Richard Matheson had also written books. I'd seen films they were involved with.

I probably read a lot of books that were made into films, even though they were not particularly major books, because it was something that interested me. To this day I will pick up copies of *Executive Suite* or whatever because I have reviewed the film based on it. I remember looking out for things like *Conjure Wife* because I had seen the movie.

So that's how I got interested in the horror field. As for how I got into it as a professional was just that I couldn't get a real job. I graduated in 1980 as an English graduate at time when there wasn't a use for my talents, whatever they were, in any of the fields I applied to. So I spent two years, three years, something like that basically on welfare doing bits of theatrical work, writing for fanzines (mostly music fanzines), doing bits of cabaret, and stand-up comedy. The kazoo-playing which always comes up in my biography is from that period. After a couple years, I had a conversion-on-the-road-to-Damascus experience with an amplifier falling on me in the back of a van after a particularly poor engagement at a biker pub in Bath, where we had been thrown off by the management in the middle of our set. That ended up with a screaming row in the street. I'd like to say we went on to become rich and successful. We didn't. We really just got depressed and broke up. I committed myself to moving to London, away from where I grew up, and I just followed what interested me. I started sending out stuff I had written. I sold journalism first, but quite quickly thereafter I sold my first short story to *Interzone*. I went on to *Fantasy Tales*. I sold my first book, which was non-fiction, about film, within four months of selling my first article. That fixed me on maybe I should stop applying for these jobs I'm not even getting interviews for, and maybe I should dig ditches, or be a writer.

Q: I note that some of the writers you mentioned, James Herbert, and especially Dennis Wheatley, are not really known in the United States. Do you think you had a different perspective by becoming acquainted with them early?

Newman: I didn't actually read those people religiously. I didn't actually like their work. They were horror. If you went to the horror section in a British bookshop, it was Dennis Wheatley for a long time. I think Herbert came along slightly before Stephen King. By the time King was publishing his first book, I had given up reading modern horror, because I had the false impression it was all rubbish. I spent my time reading Arthur Machen or H. Rider Haggard. I didn't actually catch up with King or Peter Straub until the early '80s.

Q: Most of your books have an outrageous or iconoclastic sense to them. Were they perhaps written out of protest, a sense of "this stuff is really stupid; I can do better"?

Newman: I'm not particularly arrogant that way. I think what I came to do when working on a novel in particularly, or a story as well, is that I have whatever I want to write about and I start messing around with the theme and the characters. But often I think, what would be the conventional way of doing this? And I'll do something else. What would normally happen in a book like this?

Only time did I ever do what you're talking about, saying, "Hey I can write this better," which is an appalling attitude, and if someone talked like that at a convention you'd punch them in the mouth.

But I did it under a pseudonym, in the Jack Yeovil books. The first of those is the one that is only just being published. It was written in 1987, and it is coming out in Britain under the title *Orgy of the Blood-Parasites*. I had written something like a novel and a half, and those were going the rounds of the publishers and getting rejections. Both of those books, in the end, sold, but they didn't sell quickly. I realized that I needed to have another work out there going the rounds, because I couldn't just keep devoting six months of my life to something that wasn't selling. So I thought I'd write the book in a week, because if it doesn't sell, I'd only lost a week. If it does sell, even if it sells for three hundred pounds, at that time that would have been more than I could have earned in a week doing anything else. So I sat down and wrote this thing. Its original title was *Bloody Students*. It's a splatter novel set on a university campus. I thought that even in a week I could write a better book than—I will mention the names—Shaun Hutson or James Herbert or Guy Smith. And I wanted to write that type of book, something with lots of action, lots of gore, a bit of sex. Being my work, there was a kind of seam of humor running through the book which I don't think those other guys would be comfortable with. And, being me, I couldn't quite bring myself to the heights of frothing misogynist frenzy that I think runs through all their books and, to my mind, makes them unreadable, even on a camp level.

But I was trying to do a trashy paperback, very much in the way that John Brosnan has written the Harry Adam Knight books, which I admire greatly. Later on, when I was Jack Yeovil, I was asked to write fantasy novels. Again, I looked at the field and said, "I really can't write this stuff in which a bunch of people go on a quest and save the kingdom from the forces of darkness." Again, I looked at the other stories and wondered why you can't have fun and do something interesting and play around with different sets of conventions and clichés. So one of my fantasy novels is a kind of Dirty Harry, hardboiled detective novel about tracking down a serial killer in a grimy city. It's sort of a medieval version of one of those really complicated Italian murder mysteries. Another is essentially a backstage musical-cum-murder-mystery. I got fed up with the fact that all these books seemed to have aristocrats as heroes. They all depend on the idea of the divine right of kings. Some prince would come along, and even if he's disguised as a peasant for most of the book, in the end he gets his throne. Personally I think such people are probably scum. So I wanted to write from a slightly more street-level perspective.

Again, I'm not sure if that was through dissatisfaction with what was going on, because I didn't read particularly widely in the field. It was just my perception that there was a lot of fluffy, lazy thinking going on in the production of formula work. I think that doing that would bore me stiff first, and then bore the editor stiff who had commissioned it, and finally it would bore the reader stiff. My books didn't sell at all better than those by someone who took the path of least resistance and wrote the barbarian-on-a-quest stories in the same series. (That was David Garnett, by the way.)

Q: Your *The Night Mayor* has a sense of "Can you top this?" as if you're out to out-do all that has gone before in this genre.

Newman: I write first to amuse myself. I do sit there at the typewriter and sometimes think, "Nah, that's stupid," but sometimes I think it's stupid but I'll try it anyway. I think my books do often tend to topple into the ridiculous. I like to feel there is a kind of grounding in seriousness. For instance, none of my books are just funny in the way that Terry Pratchett books are, because I do think there is still a rooting in nastiness. I think my characters are seriously jeopardized. People are seriously hurt. There's not this kind of funny stuff. And the most overblown things I've done have a kind of savagery. I think I write more out of anger than anything else. Again, I'm just analyzing my own work. It's not something I set out to do. It's something I find I have done.

Q: Your *Anno Dracula* may be one of the few Dracula spinoffs that anyone is going to remember. You're doing something very familiar, but taking it to an ultimate extreme.

Newman: That project grew from the original novella, which Stephen Jones published in *The Mammoth Books of Vampires*, to repay his earlier plugging of my work. I was asked to do a story for the anthology. I thought, well, I ought to do a Dracula story, since Dracula is the big vampire character. So I had an idea which hadn't, I thought, been done. There were similar things. One of the reviewers pointed out all the others that were kind of like mine, but no one did it exactly as I did. I wanted to do something that was inclusive, that included all different types of approaches to vampires. I didn't want to do the ultimate, though some people have said that. It's still literally a vampire book. It's a parasitic book in that it feeds off of other vampire novels or even other types of novels. I looked at our culture—I don't mean European/American, but our culture of horror, people who grew up on Hammer films and Bram Stoker, and now all the way down to Anne Rice or whatever—and I wanted to write from within that culture. But also I wanted to write about things that horror doesn't usually deal with. I don't think that all that much horror is interested in the things you find in science fiction, in how societies work. I'm not entirely sure if *Anno Dracula* is even a horror novel, because it's not scary. It doesn't set out to be scary. It's about horrible things. The characters are in terrible jeopardy, but I don't think it's go that kind of Lovecraftian sense of supernatural awe or fear. In fact, what I think I was trying to do was to present a world in which the vampires and the monstrous were just a part of everything else, in a way that I think that monstrousness is a part of the real world.

I wouldn't say that it's the only *Dracula* spin-off which anyone will remember. I think, for instance, that Brian Stableford's *The Empire of Fear* is a pretty strong novel, and there are a few others. But I'm starting to feel really embarrassed about having done this book. As much as I like it and as nice as people have been, it's hard not to say there are lots of these around now. I was just browsing through the convention book room downstairs and I came across two new *Dracula* spin-off books. I thought well, I've got one of these as well. And what's more, I'm going to do it again, because I have finished a follow-up book, *The Bloody Red Baron*. I'm beginning to feel like I've gotten into a lift and it's getting very, very crowded with fat people with halitosis....[Laughs. Stephen Jones cackles in the background.] I may want to rephrase that.

Q: No, it's a striking image. Very trenchant...But, well, what happens now if the publisher wants more and more Dracula books and starts waving large sums of money at you for a third one?

Newman: I've got ideas for three more. I'm not going to do—and I'm going to name names again—the Brian Lumley thing of having one series that's a big hit and writing more and more of them until the quality declines. The thing is, this is a big subject and because of the basic idea allows me to go back and do other books set in completely different places, times, and with a completely different feel, I will not go back and do a second book set in 1888, or in London anyway. The next book is set in World War I, in France in 1918. I may well come back and do a 1920's gangster-flavored one. I've also always wanted to do a western. The other idea I have is one that has something of the feel of an early '60s blue movie, set in Rome, in a La Dolce Vita type setting. That would be called *Dracula, Cha-Cha-Cha*, which was a big hit song of the time.

But I'm not going to do these one after another. I may well abandon these ideas for stupidity or whatever. I've made some money out of these books. It certainly has been my most successful book. In fact, I immediately went away and did something far less commercial. I would hope not to be remembered as a one-subject author, and I've never been in the position of this Faustian bargain. I don't really believe it works that way anyway. But I would hope that I am incapable of writing a book as bad as *The Tale of the Body Thief*. That's a terrible thing to say. [Laughs.]

Q: Well, if you want to malign the dead for a bit, the one author who really seems to have made the Faustian bargain was Frank Herbert, with his endless multi-million-dollar Dune books. The running joke is that he does the soap-opera version, which is called *As the Worm Turns*, and the horror version, *Charnel House Dune*, and so on. But, more seriously, if you extend your Dracula series into a western, how do you propose to handle the American setting? I know that if I were to set a story in contemporary London, I'd try to restrict the scope as much as possible. I'd try to keep it in one hotel room, or something. I'd hope to get a couple street names right and leave it at that. So, how do you feel about big, sprawling foreign settings?

Newman: I've done it quite a lot. I think I probably know as much about the Wild West as I know about London in the 1880's. I've seen a hell of a lot of movies and read a lot of books. I was for a while nervous about doing it. I was particularly nervous every time I read an American book which was set in London. I will allow the incredibly honorable exception to be Peter Straub's *Julia*, which is one of the best books about London written by an American I've ever come across. But, that said, there was a case recently of a major, big-name American horror writer who wrote a book with a scene set in contemporary London where someone is paying for their drink with pound notes. You Americans should know that we haven't had them for ten years.[2] Things like that, I would hope to get right. I am sure people could go through my books and find such things. I have done it myself. I have gone back through stories set in America and found, not terrible mistakes, but things that were wrong that I've like to change.

One of the other things I've been doing, another strand of my work, is a series of alternate-world stories in collaboration with a historian-journalist named Eugene Byrne. They have been predominantly set in an alternate America from the 'Teens through to the Fifties. So far, no one has come up to me and pointed out some really stupid error. I am sure they're there.

I feel that I can probably write American reasonably well, though I wouldn't want to give up all the British things about the way I write. I think that those stories which are about America are not like the stories that Americans write about the same things. Obviously I am slightly more critical of America than some American writers tend to be. For

2   The last convention I was at in London, David Hartwell did try to buy a drink with a pound note. Big laughs.—K.N

instance, it is a well-known fact that Dennis Etchison's first great success was his highschool essay, "What America Means to Me." I think you would be rather interested to find out what America means to *me*, and I think it would be very different from what it means to Dennis.

Q: There is an absolutely unique form of TV and film dialogue, which probably your ear can't quite pick up, namely a British actor impersonating an American. The best example I can think of is the actor playing the cowboy in the Louis Jourdan version of *Dracula* for the BBC. He has a totally unique accent, which made me understand what a Hollywood English butler sounds like to you.

Newman: I would have to say you're quite right. I think Americans do British much, much worse. Again, I'll mention names. Stephen King, "The Langoliers." There's a character in that who is supposed to be a British secret agent, and every single line of dialogue that comes out of him is like the toad that pops out of the princess's mouth in the fairy tale. It is as bad as introducing a Scotsman who goes, "Och aye, 'tis a broa bricht moonlicht nicht the nicht." It is just awful. And Stephen King has been to London. "Crouch End," a story of his, also has this completely phony, completely false vision of Britain and the way British people talk. There always used to be a thing in the '60s where every adventure show or cop show would have one episode set in Britain. Most of it would be set in Los Angeles or New York—*Macmillan and Wife* or *Columbo* or whatever. The American episodes would be on the street, people going into restaurants, and the like. You'd go to London and you'd get fog, gaslights. Here's another fact: since the Clean Air Acts of the early 1950's, London doesn't have fog anymore. Cobblestones. Cockney knife-grinders, that sort of stuff. It's not like that, although I've written about London like that. I've seen what the appeal of that is.

I am sure if I wrote a whole book with an American setting, I am sure I would have Americans read it. In my second novel, *Bad Dreams*, the heroine is an American, and I gave the whole manuscript to Lisa Tuttle to have her go through it and find what an American would not say, and so forth. In fact, she only picked out one thing, and that was that I had her arranging to meet someone at tea-time. [Laughs.]

Q: So, how do you avoid being merely mid-Atlantic and appealing to neither British nor American readers?

Newman: You try to be honest. I write the best book I can, *Anno Dracula*, I had a really good deal on in America. The thing had just come out in hardback in America. I don't usually think of wide commercial appeal. The book I wrote after *Anno Dracula*, I didn't think would even get published in America, because it was a deeply British sort of thing.

Also, in Britain, we read things like *Carrie*, for instance, which is about a school system which is completely alien to British experience. We can understand it. It only takes a while to fit in and see what is going on. So I don't see why American readers should fail to make that same adjustment for books about Britain. Clive Barker has said about his novel *The Thief of Always* that he has de-nationalized his work. He avoids British settings. His work could be set anywhere. But I think that hurts the book. I think that it had a specific setting, be it British or American, it would have been a stronger book. As it was, it was a story about someone who lived in a real world and went to a fantasy world. In order for that sort of story to work, the real world has to be Kansas or Oxford or Manchester. It needs to have something real. And, by going with this nebulous, non-specific setting, he hurt the book. I think that what I'm saying that I don't want to hurt the book, even if doing so would make it, in the short term, more instantly commercial. I'm not, I think, a particularly difficult writer. I'm not doing particularly off-putting work. So I think I will always will have a certain audience. I have reached a point where I am making a living. That means I have reached a point where I can afford not to compromise.

FRED CHAPPELL

From a genre standpoint, Fred Chappell is "one of us" who is also "one of them." He is a major poet, and was poet laureate of North Carolina between 1997 and 2002. He has published numerous well-regarded mainstream, often regional novels. There is *Fred Chappell Reader* which you will find in the Literature section of the bookstore also contains the complete text of his Lovecraftian, albeit non-supernatural novel *Dagon* (1968). At the same time he has been published in *The Magazine of Fantasy & Science Fiction* and *Weird Tales*, written Cthulhu Mythos stories (including a novella for my own *Cthulhu's Reign* in 2010), and is the author of the very distinguished fantasy/horror collection *More Shapes Than One* (1991). He has won the World Fantasy Award twice.

Q: When you accepted your World Fantasy Award you described the experience as being like a homecoming. So, could you start out by explaining that? What were the beginnings of your interest in the fantasy field?

Chappell: In fact it's very much like a homecoming indeed as we sit in a deserted bar at the Calloway Inn and look through the glass window there and see L. Sprague de Camp and his lovely wife pacing up and down as they wait for a taxi to the airport, I expect. I recall that the first time I saw Mr. de Camp was in 1951, at the New Orleans World Science Fiction Convention. So it's a full circle for me.

I was quite an active fan from 1950 until up about 1954 when I went off to college and had to become interested in other things, other kinds of books, in the struggle to stay in school. It's the struggle that most people have. And so I developed other literary interests, and when I began publishing I published very different work from science fiction or fantasy. So, now that my last volume of short stories, *More Shapes Than One* has been so well received by fantasy readers, I feel that I've kind of come back to the people I grew up with, so to speak.

Q: But you started out trying to write fantasy and science fiction.

Chappell: That's correct.

Q: You've mentioned submitting things to fanzines in the early '50s. How much did you actually publish back then?

Chappell: Actually, I published a great deal in fanzines at the time. I published in one called *Sirius*. I'm sorry but I can't remember the editor's name. I also published a lot with an editor named Sheldon Deretchen, until he became an ardent Marxist, which bored me. But I also published quite extensively in Bob Silverberg's *Spaceship*, in fanzines—Boy, it's hard to pull names out at this point—edited by Joel…somebody. But in most of the well-known fanzines of the time. I think I published in Charles Riddle's famous *Peon*. I was quoted in Lee Hoffman's *Quandry*.

Q: Was this fiction, non-fiction, or what?

Chappell: I did a little bit of non-fiction. I tried to write science articles and I still have no aptitude for that. I published a fair amount of poetry in fanzines, but mostly fiction. Short stories.

Q: Are any of them ones you'd want to see the light of day again?

Chappell: [Laughs.] I'm not ashamed of having written them. I'm a little ashamed that they're so patently terrible. But I don't have to apologize for that. I wrote then the best that I could write. That's my practice now. I did publish a couple of stories under a pen name in professional magazines, not because I was trying to hide my identity, but because I thought that was a romantic thing to do. Now, because I don't like those stories, I don't give that pen name away. Somebody'll dig it up, I am sure, but I hope not.

Q: So you went away and served an apprenticeship in other types of literature. So, could you tell us about your subsequent career? What happened next?

Chappell: I published six novels. I've published about twenty books of poetry and fiction—that includes novels and short stories—over a period of thirty years. I published my first novel in 1963 with Athenaeum. I moved to Harcourt Brace following an editor. Hiram Haydn. I've always stayed with editors rather than publishers. I've been in and out of mainstream literature, mostly as a poet. I have a reputation for poetry, I expect, if I have a reputation, but also for fiction. I've won the requisite number of awards and prizes. Of course my real career is teaching college.

Q: Before your very recent work, what the fantasy reader knew you best for was a book called *Dagon*, which seemed to come out of nowhere around 1968 at a time when only the immediate minions of

August Derleth were writing anything having anything at all to do with Lovecraft or the Cthulhu Mythos—and suddenly Dagon happened. How did it come about?

Chappell: It came in my mind to write it, and so I wrote it. My publisher had no notion of what I was doing or what it was about. I didn't enlighten him. He had never heard of H.P. Lovecraft, and I didn't tell him, because I knew it would do no good as far as marketing went and nobody needed to know it. I figured it would have a very obscure, short-lived career in the United States, which, as a matter of fact, at first, it did. Then it won the most prestigious of French literary prizes. It won the Prix de Meilleur des Livres Etrangers, the Best Foreign Book prize from the French Academy, and has had a Continental reputation since then. It's now still in print in a wonderfully gaudy mass-paperback edition from St. Martin's Press with a cover that is the kind of cover that you dream of when you are fourteen or fifteen years old, but then when you get to be thirty-four or thirty-five years old you hide from your mother.

Q: How was this book received by your regular mainstream readership?

Chappell: Insofar as I had one, they were just puzzled, but not that puzzled because my other books were also rather strange to them. I've never published any work but one that didn't have some touch of fantasy or irrealism in it—and that one had a science fiction fan club stuck in the middle of it. So most of my readers expected oddness. But my first novels were very difficult, hard metaphysical exercises. They weren't very attractive to readers. This was because that was the kind I wanted to write. Then after a certain period I figured I'd had enough of that and I wanted to write a more popular book, one that would sell pretty well and would pay my poetry publisher back. He was obviously going to lose money publishing my poetry. So I thought I'd write him a novel that would sell some copies. So I wrote a more humane novel, and, sure enough, it worked out about as we'd predicted.

Q: Did your mainstream or academic colleagues regard your involvement in fantasy as a bad habit to be apologized for?

Chappell: They didn't understand it in the least, to tell the truth. They didn't understand it so much that I had received comment on it at all. Writers in the academy rarely receive any direct comment on their work. You have to be Brett Easton Ellis to get any comment from your colleagues. Nobody reads it because they all have their own concerns. They all have their own careers to pursue. When I book comes out, they say "Congratulations," if they remember to, and that's the end of it. But after I got some reputation, my fiction was looked at a little bit, and critical articles began to appear, so they figured it must be all right, because people are writing about it. The one credential a writer can establish in academia is that the scholars are writing about your work. That's about the size of it. [Laughs.]

Q: How do you feel about that? Is it rather like being stuck in a museum while you're still alive?

Chappell: It's kind of like receiving a lifetime achievement award when you're thirty-five. You figure it's all over but the tombstone.

Q: I am thinking of one instance I know of: a teacher was actually fired from a university job when they found out he was writing science fiction, back about 1950.

Chappell: I'm not surprised but I'm sorry to hear it. The prejudices of academe are so well known that they don't need to be remarked on by me today. We have to admit that the prejudices of the science fiction and fantasy community are pretty well known too. They don't read much outside their field. They don't care for what we would call mainstream poetry. But I don't mind this. As far as I'm concerned, a story is a story is a story, and if a story is good enough, it will reach readers of any persuasion.

Q: What is the attraction of the fantastic for you? It seems you've stuck with it even when you weren't immediately rewarded for doing so.

Chappell: It was the most attractive thing to me when I was that age when we read everything, when childhood is one long series of books interspersed with boring other things you have to do. My chosen reading was science fiction and fantasy. The reason for this was, growing up in a small mill town in northwestern North Carolina, that I had very little access to mainstream literature that was of any interest to me at all. Of the other genre literature around, detective stories, westerns, love pulps, that sort of thing, only science fiction seemed exciting or interesting. I learned a great deal from it and owe a great deal to it. I learned how to write by reading science fiction pulp magazines. Also, at the same time, I learned how not to write.

Q: Are you still a reader and collector of this sort of thing? The reason I ask is that it's clear in "The Somewhere Doors," which is a story about a science fiction writer, that you had a copy of the August 1936 *Astounding* on your desk as you wrote it.

Chappell: I'm not a dedicated collector. In fact I shouldn't admit this, but I have a whole attic full of terrific pulp magazines from the

1930s. I have an especially large collection of *Astounding* and *Famous Fantastic Mysteries*, which I have not taken care of. They're falling into sawdust. Every time I think about them, a red blush of shame creeps up the back of my neck and over my ears. But life is full of things one should take care of and don't find time.

Q: At what point did you discover H.P. Lovecraft?

Chappell: I discovered him through the letter columns of the pulp magazines, in *Famous Fantastic Mysteries*. One of the great things about the pulp magazines of the era was the letter columns. There was a real give-and-take between the readers and the editors, and the writers to some extent, in those days, which was not only interesting to read, but rather comforting for a reader to come in and find that other people read these things too, that it must be all right, that the people who can actually write letters also read these magazines.

Famous Fantastic Mysteries had a letter column in which people kept requesting again and again that they reprint some stories by an H.P. Lovecraft. They rarely did, almost never, and so this was very intriguing. Well, Victor Hugo's comment that nothing is so interesting as a wall on the other side of which something is happening springs to mind. It just intrigued me so much that when I finally did read my first Lovecraft story, I was rather disappointed, because of course nothing could live up to the expectations that these accolades had aroused. But then when I read some other, better stuff, I found that he held up for me. He still holds up for me. The best stories still hold up in my mind. I esteem them almost as highly as any other literature I know of.

Q: In your collection *More Shapes Than One*, there is a definite impression of H.P. Lovecraft in story after story. Can you define that special something about him?

Chappell: The thing he worked hardest on, which seems to be his forté, was atmosphere. He claimed that the supreme achievement available to horror fiction was the creation of atmosphere. The landscapes that he created in fiction remain as vivid in my mind as many real landscapes I've seen, and certainly many of the paintings I've seen. Outside of that, the use of recondite or forbidden knowledge seemed particularly wonderful. A great many writers use that, but Lovecraft uses it with wonderful force and appeal. Where he was not good are exactly in the places he knew he was not good, in the creation of character and in the construction of plots. Sometimes these are not the things we most value in a writer.

Q: In your story entitled "Weird Tales" you did something I've always wanted to see someone do in a Cthulhu Mythos story. The last two lines are written from the point of view of someone living in a time after the Old Ones have won and repossessed the Earth. The rest of us are wondering why, if they're so powerful, they haven't won long ago.

Chappell: It seemed to me that if I could end the story correctly, it would treat all the Mythos stories of Long and Derleth as well as Lovecraft as being reportage rather than fiction—disguised reportage in order to save their lives. That's what I wanted to pull off with it. As far as I know, you are the only reader to point out in print that the story takes place in the future. But that's not revealed until the last words of the story.

Q: I was getting entirely tired of the sort of Mythos story that goes: Scholar discovers moldering book, then is eaten by Things. I once wrote a parody in which the Old Ones win, just to get it all over with.

Chappell: Yes, I've seen the parody. It was inevitable that someone would write it, and I thought you did a good job. I must say that there are some interesting details that scholars might like to know. One of my dearest friends in the early '70s was the great Southern poet Allen Tate, who, as it happened, was a close friend of Lovecraft's associate, Samuel Loveman in those years. Well, not a close friend, I shouldn't say, because he did not like Samuel Loveman, but he gave me all sorts of personal information about Loveman—who is really an obscure figure in American literature—and so I was able to use that as background. I felt I had access to a kind of information not many people would have. All the quotations that are in documents in the story are real. Those came from Hart Crane's letters or from H.P. Lovecraft's letters.

Q: If you ever got to meet H.P. Lovecraft, what would you say to him?

Chappell: Thanks a bunch, kid. I owe you one. [Laughs.]

Q: What brought you back to writing more fantasy, all of the sudden in the past few years?

Chappell: That's not exactly true, the "sudden" part. If anybody had a world enough and time and wanted to paw through my earlier fiction, they would see that even the realistic novels shade into fantasy, then shade back out again. I try to make this seamless, but I don't draw a distinction between what is real and what is imagined. It seems to me that what is real is what is imagined, that we can only know the world as we imagine it. Out problem is not that we imagine too much, and therefore become unreal, but that we don't imagine fully enough, and don't understand the reality that's out there.

Q: In the sense that we don't create the world by imagining it. We recognize the world by imagining it.

Chappell: We discover the world by imagining it.

Q: But there are those who try to shape the world by imagining it. It seems to me that they tend to get hit by something hard and sharp fairly soon.

Chappell: That's absolutely true. It's one of the first signs of maturity, when we first realize that what we thought and hoped ain't gonna be it. But that's not a fundamental or serious mistake. That's just a mistake of youth and of incomprehension. Sooner or later the real mistake is always going to be not daring to imagine fully or surprisingly enough.

Q: So this would make fantasy a kind of training for coping with reality.

Chappell: Yes, I think it is a method of coping with reality or trying to comprehend reality. Actually, in order to cope with reality, it takes willpower, which is not something that fantasy is very good at developing.

Q: There'd also a type of realism whose virtue is being completely realistic, and any intrusion of fantasy renders it false or dishonest. That too is a method of coping with reality.

Chappell: I agree with that. I would not want to be reading one of Hemingway's stories in which magical transformations suddenly began to take place. That would just ruin the story and ruin the vision of reality that Hemingway's stories set up. On the other hand, I would not like to read a Marquez story or a Borges story in which there was just plodding detail after plodding detail. There are some writers who are very good at that, and there are some writers who are not good at it.

There is a great deal of talk, and there has been for some while, about Magic Realism, but that's always really been with us. I would recommend to any fantasy reader that he might have a look at a novel by Emile Zola, the naturalist, called *The Sin of Father Mouret*, because there's where the mythic and the fantastic are developed straight out of the most raw, naturalistic basis for fiction that you can imagine. And yet, it's still realistic and still fantastic at the same time. It's very powerful.

Q: A most intriguing contrast is the recent film *The Fisher King*, which hints at fantasy all the way through, but the whole honesty and validity of it is precisely that there is nothing fantastic at the end. It's a story about coping with delusions.

Chappell: Some psychological studies are like that, like de Maupassant's stories. "The Horla," for example. Or Fitz-James O'Brien's "What Was It?" These are stories which start out seeming to be fantastic, but are actually portraits of a sensibility or of a diseased mind. Behind the fantasy is a terrible reality. Poe invented this mode. He was probably the best at it.

Q: You've at least touched on that. But one of the things that's so impressive about *More Shapes Than One* is the range. A couple of the stories are science fiction. Some are purely whimsical, the one about the highway blocked by a symbolist poem waiting to be written—

Chappell: I enjoy writing humor when I can. It's very difficult. I know it is the hardest thing for me to write. Perhaps it is for other folks too. But I enjoy it because readers enjoy it. I give a lot of readings, and people are so happy to have a humorous story read to them rather than a grim story that leaves them depressed. You sign more books when you have a humorous story, I think. [Laughs.]

Q: But a lot of humor dates in a way that grim things don't.

Chappell: That's because humor depends on topical elements.

Q: However, I suspect that those who deliberately write for immortality do not achieve it.

Chappell: [Laughs.] I think that's probably true. If we do, how the hell would we know?

Q: Or be able to enjoy it? But to change the subject, what are you writing now?

Chappell: I have a book of poems out, if anyone's interested in that, called *C*, that is, the Roman letter One Hundred. After that comes a book with a very hot title. *Plow Naked*, it's called, but it's a book of essays on modern poetry. And after that, I hope to do another book of fantastic short stories. I have about half of them written, and a satiric novel about philosophy.

Q: What are your writing methods like?

Chappell: I write everything out longhand. Even the novels I write in longhand. When I am writing fiction, I try to write two pages a day, which will amount to about twelve hundred words. The next day, I go over it and I rewrite those pages, sometimes extensively, sometimes not so extensively, and then launch in after that to the next pages, which goes on until I'm halfway through a novel. After that I can't do it, because the bulk would be too much. I'd spend the whole day rewriting and rereading. So when I've got half the book, I just go writing straight on. Then I do an enormous amount of revision, constantly. If a young writer wants to make his living writing, I'm the worst model he could follow. I will rewrite stories time and time and time again. Even after they're published I sometimes revise them.

I determined early on that I did not want to make my living writing. I wanted the freedom of what I wrote. I wanted to be able to write poetry in freedom. So I decided to acquire another profession, besides the writing, so I can keep on writing, but also have fun.

Q: This is a very important point. A writer shouldn't quit his day job until holding it literally costs him money. Otherwise you may be forced into over-production and end up imitating yourself. Suppose somebody said, "Here's five million dollars. I want you to write five sequels to *Dagon*. Don't give me this stuff about not having anything to say. Just do it." What would you do then?

Chappell: I would have to say, "No." I would love to write more Mythos stories, but none having to do with *Dagon*. By the way, I've got to tell you, *Dagon* was not a fantasy book I put out, a horror book I wrote just for the fun of it. It was a different book for me. It was very personal. It caused me a great deal of personal anguish. I had to live through that book. My first two novels I had written in fairly short order, but that one caused me a lot of troubles. I think it's a real failure. My ambitions were much too large for such a short book. I wanted to make it very powerful and very concrete, hard. That was probably the wrong approach. I could not write that book again. It's all I can do to reread it.

Q: But other people seem to like it, or it wouldn't still be in print.

Chappell: I one of the reasons that they like it is because it cost me so much. I suppose you can tell that this is a genuine book. The writer cares about this book, whatever kind of botch he made of it.

Q: Surely there are some books which are more admirable for their ambition than for what they actually achieve. A very, very competently-rendered nothing is still nothing.

Chappell: Yes, but sometimes I just love competent nothings. One of my favorite writers is P.G. Wodehouse, for example. There is nothing terrible about works which are competent nothings. On the other hand, I do admire more works by writers like Faulkner and Lovecraft and Poe because they tried to go—to boldly go—where no man has gone before.

Q: Surely this is what writing is all about: following your obsessions.

Chappell: Yes. I think it has to be more than obsessions. It has to be a kind of vision of what we think or hope or dread is out there, rather than what one person has to get off his chest, but I'm not sure that I'm equipped to distinguish between the two.

Q: Maybe we only find that out after we read what we've written.

Chappell: Yes, and after it's published and some decades have gone by.

Q: That's a pretty good ending line. Thanks, Fred.

Recorded at the World Fantasy Convention,
Calloway Gardens, Georgia,
Halloween weekend, 1992.

ELIZABETH MASSIE

Elisabeth Massie is probably best known for *Sineater* (1992). Her other books include *Shadow Dreams* (1996), *Wire Mesh Mothers* (2001), plus novelizations, Buffy the Vampire novels, and a quite extensive body of distinguished short fiction. She has won the Bram Stoker Award twice.

Q: I am sure your relatives frequently ask you, "Why do you write all this weird stuff?"

Massie: Oh yes, they do.

Q: So what do you tell them?

Massie: I just tell them that I write "this weird stuff" because it's really not all that weird. Life is full of all sorts of frightening things. I was an overly sensitive child and have become a very inquisitive adult. I like to explore all sorts of darker shadows, to turn over stones to see what's under there.

Q: Remember the line in Lovecraft about the painter who paints all the horrible things and says, "I paint what I see."

Massie: Yes.

Q: Would you say then that your techniques are those of a realist?

Massie: I think so. Even though I haven't witnessed a great deal of horror in my life—I've lived a relatively peaceful life in caring family within a small community—I have made a point of exploring human horrors throughout the world. As a long-time member of Amnesty International, I've read quite a bit and have interviewed people who have experienced harsh realities first-hand. Not just for research sake, but so I can do something as an activist. In addition, closer to home, I was a public school teacher for nineteen years, and teachers learn a lot about what goes on behind closed doors in "other families." Kids will tell you anything.

I tend to be a realist in that I like to create stories that ring true.

Q: Most of the fiction of yours that I've read has no supernatural content—

Massie: That's true, and that goes back to the fact that, honestly, there's very little supernatural that scares me. I've had folks say, "You must believe in ghosts and vampires and other monsters." Ghosts, vampires, and monsters can be good fun and—when written well enough that I can suspend disbelief—they can be incredibly frightening. But I usually write about things that frighten me personally, scary things I believe in. I tend to write psychological horror as opposed to supernatural.

Q: Supernatural horror would be frightening if it were actually real.

Massie: Yes. Amen. [Laughs.] It would be. And I'm not saying there aren't some unknown aspects of the world that don't creep me out and worry me just a bit! As an aside, the word "supernatural," I think is interesting. It's a moot term to me, because if something is real, it is real. What exists is natural, whether we like it or not, whether we understand it or not. It is not "unnatural" or "beyond natural." To call something "supernatural" is like saying it's real but it's not really real.

Q: The novel that put you on the map, *Sineater*, has nothing supernatural in it, but for the people in the story, I am sure there is something (as they see it) supernatural going on.

Massie: The characters in *Sineater* are in a very isolated community in western Virginia. They do have connections to the outside world, but they've been isolated to the point that there's a lot of, not exactly inbreeding, but people don't move away. Families stay close, and they've created their own mythos and believe it very much. It's an old mythos that the sineater can absolve you of your sin by eating the food off your chest after you've died and sending you to heaven. When their traditions and their beliefs get mucked with by an outsider, everything starts to fall apart.

I don't believe a sineater is going to absolve anybody, but these folks certainly do.

Q: It seemed that the actual horror of the story was the narrowness of the community's mindset, and how few possibilities anyone could see. If the protagonist had merely headed for civilization [Massie is chuckling]—all he'd have to do is get on a bus and go to, where? Wheeling, maybe.

Massie: Hey, this is Virginia, not West Virginia! They'd head for Richmond.

Q: Or Richmond, and he'd be fine. Suddenly all those rules would no longer apply.

Massie: It's those invisible bonds that you are taught as a child, and unless you're really given an opportunity to see something outside yourself, you tend to believe them. You've got your little invisible chains. Really, though, I can't imagine there are many people in the world who aren't bound by mental or emotional bonds in some way or another—a religious teaching, a moral code, a prejudice, certain aspects of a culture or community. People are bound by things they don't entirely realize. Even if we're aware of it, there are usually some things that will control us that appear to be beyond ourselves.

Q: This is certainly a potent theme for horror, the idea of mental boundaries and controls. You could turn it around. If somebody actually did break through all of this conditioning, would he be a complete psycho?

Massie [Laughs]: Maybe a psycho, maybe the next new prophet.

Q: Surely real-life serial-killers and psychopaths merely think themselves free of social restriction.

Massie: True, and yet there are others who say that feel compelled or driven to kill. In that is their own binding. Something is telling them they need to do that.

Q: We don't want to get too far into the area of serial-killers, a very trite subject by now. We are already past the stage of funny serial-killer stories, so I am not sure how far you go yet go.

Massie: That's true . . .

Q: You didn't have another idea for a funny serial-killer novel?

Massie: No…[Laughs.]

Q: There remains the long-running argument of what precisely constitutes a horror story, then, and where does a non-supernatural horror story merely become a crime story. Something like Robert Bloch's *The Scarf* was published as a mystery novel in the '40s. Today we'd call it horror. Do these distinctions mean anything?

Massie: A crime story can be horror, it can be suspense, it can be a thriller, it can be a mystery. But it's all fiction. Distinctions mean a lot to publishers. They also do to bookstores. These folks are afraid someone might pick up a novel in a genre they aren't expecting, and go haywire. I figure, books have synopses inside the jackets. A reader can check it out before he/she lays down their cash. I like the idea of a "contemporary fiction" section. I've quit trying to figure out how to classify horror. I think authors should classify their own work, if indeed it must be classified. I like the category "horror." To me, horror fiction is scary fiction.

My first short story was a creepy psychological tale called "Whittler." It was published in *The Horror Show* in their winter 1983/84 issue. It was a spooky tale, so that seemed to be the best place to send it. My second sale was "Dust Cover," also with *The Horror Show*, less than a year later. It hinted at supernatural but could have been the character's imagination. But, it was scary, so it was horror.

Q: Well, if we look into the ancestry of the modern horror story, to Poe, for example, we find that although "A Cask of Amontillado" is actually very funny, it's also a very effective horror story with no fantastic content. Or "The Pit and the Pendulum." So non-fantastic horror has always been there, and the ghostly does not define the genre.

Massie: The "scary" element defines horror, not the realistic or surreal element. Let me say that I do on occasion write supernatural horror. Sometimes a dream or a fleeting thought will inspire me to write something surreal and scary. My newest collection of short fiction, *The Fear Report*, contains a novella called "Dooka Dee." It's about shrunken heads and their power. I thought, what if someone with ADD got involved with shrunken heads and the power they wielded? It creeped me out, so I wrote it.

Q: So, why did you start writing horror when you did? Sometime in the '80s, was it?

Massie: I started publishing in the 1980's, but have always written darker-edged fiction. Even as a kid, I explored things that scared me through my writing. In high school and college I continued to write but never tried to have anything published. Then I started a family (Hi Erin and Brian!) and began a career as a seventh grade life science teacher. I didn't stop writing. I just didn't have the time to even consider what marketing was or how you went about it. In the summer of 1983 I attended a convention in Boston, where Stephen King was attending. That wasn't the highlight. The highlight was meeting Brian Hodge, who is another writer. He had just sold his first short story to *The Horror Show* and he recommended that I go ahead and send something out and see what happened. I was really lucky because I sent my first story out, and within two weeks I had a letter of acceptance, my check for two dollars. I received all this great news on my thirtieth birthday.

Q: Had you been writing for a long time before that?

Massie: Since I was five and could put word to paper. I always wanted to be a "writer" but had no idea of how to get started, which was one reason I went to the convention in Boston in the first place. It was perfect. It was the best launching-off experience I've ever had.

Q: So fame and fortune follows…

Massie: [Laughs.]: We wish.

Q: For a while your *Sineater* was something of a cause celebre among horror writers, because it was only published in England and New York publishers wouldn't take it, which made a lot of people critical of New York publishers. What is the story behind that?

Massie: Stephen King had set the standard for conventional horror and *Sineater* wasn't a conventional horror story. That seemed to confuse American publishers just a tad. The British publisher—it was Pan—seemed to understand it, and once it came out in print, it was taken a little more seriously over here, so it got a hardcover deal. But I really think because it didn't fit the Stephen King type of supernatural, *Cujo*, *Christine* kind of mold, that they were disinterested at the time.

Q: The book is also narrated in the present tense.

Massie: Yes.

Q: I think that's your problem right there. For really low-brow readers—if you're going to publish a book for morons buying it in a supermarket—anything "literary" is too much. There have been present-tense narrations since the beginning of time, but the technique is still avant-garde in some circles.

Massie: I had forgotten that. I am glad you brought that up, because I do think that had something to do with it.

Q: Basically, the New York publishers don't like to take risks. They wanted you to write a book just like Stephen King only a little bit different.

Massie: [Laughs]: With a different villain.

Q: Close enough to get his sales but not close enough to get sued. So, do you have any sense now that publishers want you to write *Sineater* again?

Massie: Not really. *Welcome Back to the Night* had a surreal or supernatural aspect to it, *Wire Mesh Mothers* did not. *Publishers' Weekly* said "Massie's sharp observations and eye for detail bring her characters to life." I sense that is what they want from me, and it is what I want to continue to provide—intense stories in which realistic characters struggle with the terrifying, the bizarre. The last year or so, I have been wanting to explore another "subgenre"—horror historical fiction. I've done quite a bit of historical fiction for young adults along with writing horror fiction for adults. I want to meld the two together. I did that once in a middle-grade book, and I thought that worked great. In 2003, my first horror historical short story, "Flip Flap", was published. I'm now working on a new novel set in 1909 on Coney Island. I am still working on the proposal, so I've not marketed it yet. But I think it's going to be my best novel yet. Old amusement parks, now those are frightening!

Q: I hope it's a successful new direction for you. I know Robert McCammon had a great deal of trouble getting his historical horror novel published.

Massie: Yes, he did. In fact, I read *Sings the Night Bird* last summer. It is my understanding that he wanted to write historical novels, and he ended up doing a horror-historical combination.

Q: You make use of Southern folkloric material, certainly, if not always history. You could he the heir to the mantle of Manly Wade Wellman—

Massie: Well, again, I'm probably a very rare creature these days, because I live only four miles from where I was born. My family is still around. The only time I lived elsewhere was when I was in college. I travel quite a bit, so I've seen many other places. But I love where I am.

Q: Where are you?

Massie: The Shenandoah of Virginia, which, if you head due west you can hit West Virginia in about 45 minutes. In the shadow of the Blue Ridge Mountains. I am very much influenced by the people and their ways. They speak slowly and politely for the most part. They're relatively conservative, which drives me crazy, but in a way I understand. I know the traditions, the slang, the customs, and the stories. More often than not, I write out of what I know. Well, not counting Coney Island, but that is place just fascinates the hell out of me. Much of what I write is based on the area where I am. Stephen King does the same thing. Not that I have to do what Stephen King does, but, you write what you know, and then you expand outward. I definitely am a Southern person, so that's where I'm coming from.

Q: Didn't you once get the sinking feeling that all of the Stephen King imitators would also set their novels in Maine, and this would become demanded of them, a genre like a western . . .? [Massie is laughing.]

Massie: Yes, and I've never been to Maine, so if that was the case I would be in deep shit.

Q: I would guess what you get with Southern material is a conflict between modernity and tradition. And probably some people think you've sold your soul to the Devil to be writing this stuff.

Massie: I think they might but they're too polite to say it, because we're Southern. [Laughs.] I live in a very polite community. I've had relatives say, "Why don't you write yourself a nice little story for *Redbook*?" And they were thrilled to death when I started doing historical fiction. "Oh good. She's got it out of her system. She'll be all right now." But then they find out I'm doing historicals and horror.

My immediate family and my circle of friends are not so hideously conservative that they think I've sold my soul to the Devil, but if you extend that circle out a little—to some cousins and aunts and neighbors, they would probably say, politely of course, "Yes, the poor dear's going to Hell."

Q: Ray Garton has some really colorful stories, about getting shot at and his tires slashed, and that sort of thing.

Massie: I don't know where Ray lives, but folks here are too nice to do that. They'll just go, "Beth, bless her heart, she doesn't know where she's heading."

Q: You could write a novel about where you're heading.

Massie: Oh yes. Oh yes. [Laughs.] In fact my novel, *Welcome Back to the Night*, is not exclusively about that, but I do have an opening scene at the family reunion. It's set in a town very much like mine. The family all gathers and they're all talking about each other behind their backs. To their faces they're very sweet and very polite, but behind their backs, oh, everybody's just worried about this one character. She's just gone down the wrong path. What are they going to do? It's not an aggressive group, but they definitely have their views about what's going to go wrong with that person. No tire-slashing. Just a lot of prayin' for the lost soul.

Q: Did you come from a family where people told stories, or are you just the weird one?

Massie: I was lucky. In my little community, my family was considered free spirits, though not rude or impolite ones! My mother is a professional water-colorist. My Dad was a newspaperman, a poet of sorts, who owned a motorcycle with a side-car, and he would take us riding around town, and that just startled the town folks. It was like, "God, what does he...uhhh! Does he think he's a Hell's Angel?"

On long-distance trips in the car as a family, we would entertain each other by making up round-robin stories. So it was definitely a family that was in love with the idea of creating, whether art or stories or just being wacky.

Q: At some point you had to think about how to make a story come alive and work on the page. Everybody has an idea for a story, but there's a big difference between that and actually writing one. So, how do you make it work?

Massie: Being a person who grew up in the age of television, I am very visual. I know a lot of other people have said this, but it's true for me as well. I visualize a great deal before I even start writing. If you dropped in on my home at any time, more than likely you wouldn't find me at the computer. You'd find me wandering. I wander in the house and I wander outside, and I stare out the window—and I'm working. I'm visualizing a scene. I'm imagining it and I'm feeling it and I'm smelling it. If it doesn't work, then I rewind my brain and I take it off in another direction. So, when I sit down, I can see it pretty well in my head.

I am not the kind of person that composes entirely at the computer. A lot of it comes from just letting my imagination fill me up. I think that is what helps with being able to get in characters' skins, get into other locations and come up with a good description and hopefully a good plot and a good story.

Q: I take it you're not an outliner.

Massie: I only outline when I am required to outline. It is agony for me, if an editor wants a good outline or a good synopsis. I can give you a paragraph or a page about a novel I have in my head, but if I have to do a four or five page outline or a ten page synopsis, it is agony. I might as well write the damn book. It takes that long. With *Sineater* and with my earlier novels, I knew where it was going to end, but, good God, there's so much in the middle that changes as I'm writing, and to have an outline just kind of pisses me off. Not that I can't change an outline. Nowadays it seems like editors are already getting blurbs and cover copy written before you finish the book, and so if something changes, you're in trouble. It may say something on the back of the book—and I've had that happen—that didn't happen in the novel, because it changed. And so, outlining is really excruciating. Unfortunately, it's more and more required.

Q: Maybe the solution—a little risky, but sneakily effective—would be to write the book first, then write an outline, and tell the editor you have this idea. You describe what you've already done. That has to be a lot easier.

Massie [Laughs]: Not a bad idea, except as a writer trying to make a living, time is precious. Writing anything completely on spec is very scary. Most of my books for younger readers have taken five or months, and my shortest novel for adults has taken a year. So during that time there would be no paychecks. Yikes!

Q: Probably the *Cemetery Dance* readers don't know about these books you've done for younger readers. What are they?

Massie: I have a series for young adults called *The Young Founders*, a trilogy for middle grade readers called *Daughters of Liberty* and some single, stand-alone titles. It wasn't such a stretch, moving into historicals from horror. Much of history is quite frightening. One of the Young Founders novels is set in Jamestown, 1607-1609. These guys faced hardships from which I would shrink mightily. My main character was on the list with the first settlers, though no one knows what actually happened to him. His experiences are based quite carefully in what really happened Jamestown. Speaking of terrifying events, one in the book involves Gabriel Archer. He was captured by the Powhatans, tied to a tree, and skinned alive with mussel shells. He died in extreme agony. This is from an actual diary. Horror? I would think so.

Q: I'm surprised you don't run up against barriers of political correctness. I gather than in much of juvenile publishing today, it is not correct to suggest that the American Indians were ever a menace to white settlers.

Massie: That's true, but what got me through, I believe, is that I balanced it out by showing how brutal the British were, telling what happened to people who committed treason, or even if they were caught stealing. So everybody's bad. [Laughs.]

Q: Well, if life is so horrible, why are we so cheerful?

Massie: [laughing]: Because we're morons…because we have imaginations and can imagine how wonderful it can be.

Q: But that's not what we write about. So are we writing to depress ourselves?

Massie: I'm purging my soul when I write [laughs] and I say that with a wink.

Q: Thanks, Beth.

Recorded at NECon,
July 2003.

BRIAN A. HOPKINS

Brian Hopkins won the Bram Stoker Award for "Five Days in April" in 1999. His novels and collections include *These I Know By Heart, Lipstick Lies and Lady Luck, Cold at Heart, Salt Water Tears, El Dia de las Muertos*, etc. He has won the Stoker Award four times, and been nominated for the Nebula, Sturgeon, and International Horror Guild Awards.

Q: I guess we can start by discussing how you got to be your famous self. So, how did it all begin?

Hopkins: I originally started writing as a child and mostly thought of it as self-entertainment. I read voraciously, and enjoyed that, and I thought, well, I can create my own stories. So I did, and exchanged them with friends and everybody loved them. I wrote up through high school, but stopped for a bit in college. After college, I eventually started writing again. Then friends suggested that I should try and sell some of my fiction, which seemed preposterous to me, that people would actually pay me for this. But they pushed, and finally I did send out a story. It became my first published story, which was in *Dragon* magazine in 1990.

Q: Despite that story in *Dragon*, am I wrong in saying that in the horror field, at least, you've come up mostly out of the small press and electronic publications?

Hopkins: I've written across quite a few different genres. Lately it seems I am becoming best known for my horror. A lot of that came from having won the Stoker for "Five Days in April," and again for *The Licking Valley Coon Hunter's Club*, which are aren't pure horror—in fact I wouldn't call "Five Days in April" horror at all. *Coon Hunters* is more cross-genre. It's more mystery and adventure with some vampires thrown in, and they're not even real vampires. So I've actually written across all genres, and in the early '90s I was in the small press with 75 to 80 or 90 stories, in early magazines like *After Hours, Deathrealm*, Dave Wilson's *The Tome*, and all the magazines that were done by John Herron: *Midnight Zoo* and all those small-press magazines. I had a lot of stories in those small-press magazines, and then a lot of stories in the early sci-fi small press too.

Q: It seems that there are only a very small number of writers who have emerged this way into real visibility, and you're one of the few. Thomas Ligotti is the case that everybody wants to be. So—were you submitting stories to the bigger magazines at the same time and getting rejected?

Hopkins: I don't respond well to rejections, so rather than taking the road that a lot of writers take, where they keep beating on the big magazines, taking the rejections, and sending in more stories, I would try the big magazines, and as soon as I got a rejection, I would sell it somewhere in the small press. Eventually, after a number of years of that, I would write something, and someone in the small press would ask me for a story, or I would see a place where I knew it was a perfect fit and sell it immediately to the small press, even if it was for peanuts. Sometimes I just got to where I would bypass the big magazines completely. If I had to do it again, I think I would definitely be a little bit pickier about where my stories went. The reason I say that is that I am an author sitting here with basically no inventory, and now that I'm known and getting read a little by professional editors, and not getting lost in the slushpile, I could probably sell a lot of those earlier stories to better markets. If I was to give advice to newer writers, I would definitely say be a little bit pickier about where your stories go.

Q: You also have to give the advice of don't write for the drawer. Surely if you're going to continue as a writer, you want to publish what you write now on the assumption that when they ask you to be in the prestigious anthology next year, you are capable of writing another story then.

Hopkins: I agree. I have no drawer stories. I am not one of those writers who, when asked, can pull out an older story and say, "Do you want it?" Everything I'm being asked for now, with the invitations that are finally starting to come in, it's always a matter of having to come up with a new story, which is generally not a problem. I have far more stories in me than I have time to write them.

Q: Without pressing you to the point of vanity...do you have the perception that the big magazines are too narrow in their focus, and you need the small press so you can write and sell the kind of things the big magazines do not publish?

Hopkins: Yes, definitely. In my case what I perceived was happening was a matter of the slush pile. When you talk about a magazine that publishes a dozen stories a month and receives a thousand stories a month, I think the editors are going to have stories that they may never even get to read. It's a matter of building up a rapport with them, where they actually get to reading your stories and eventually they take something from you. I am not a prolific enough writer—I've never cranked out more than eight or ten stories in an entire year—to sit there and bang on their door repeatedly with story after story to the point where my name was popping up in their head and I was getting out of that slush pile....You're looking quizzical.

Q: I'm looking quizzical for a couple of reasons. First of all, I have been on the other end of this process enough to know that everything gets read by someone eventually, but for the illiterate scrawls on orange paper or the single-spaced printouts in microscopic type. Further, it doesn't necessarily help to be remembered as the person who sends the editor eighty-five stories he can't publish. Then he tends to dismiss the next one. But, I can also tell you, the submission process is not a lottery. It's only a lottery from the point of view of the editor, who is hoping to find a publishable story. Maybe only one envelope in a thousand will contain one. But if you submit a publishable story, you're way ahead of the pack. Only in the top five percent of all submissions to such considerations as taste and editorial policy come into play. Most stories simply aren't good enough, and it is obvious. So I should think that if you were to submit a story now, whether the editor knows your name or not, you will get sufficient attention. The function of the first reader is to tell if something is decently enough written so that someone else should look at it. Surely anything of yours would pass that test every time.

Hopkins: Okay....[Laughs.]

Q: So that means you will get read.

Hopkins: In time I did, but I had moved on to the small press, and my own quirks and my own desire to see my stuff out there, if only in the small-press arena, kind of overrode any rapport I might have built up with any of the larger press magazines.

Q: What larger magazines are we talking about here? *Fantasy and Science Fiction*, *Alfred Hitchcock's*, *Playboy*, or what?

Hopkins: Primarily it was *Fantasy and Science Fiction*. I had personal rejection after personal rejection from Kris Rusch, "Great story but I just can't find a place for it," or "I can't use it," and eventually I got tired of reading those notes from Kris Rusch.

Q: You know she didn't write those to everybody.

Hopkins: That's what people would tell me, but the rejections I used to get were rarely the form rejections. They were, "This is a great story, but ___." Those actually got to be more of a deterrent to me than form rejections.

Q: When you write a story, do you give serious consideration to what genre it will be, or where it will fit in? Like, for instance, your story "Crocodile Gods." The reason it is not a *Weird Tales* story is that it has no fantastic content. It doesn't even suggest a fantastic content. This is one of those stories that's good enough that questions of taste and editorial policy come into play, which is very late in the process. But, do you think in those terms when you're writing?

Hopkins: No, I don't think in those terms. When I wrote "Crocodile Gods," I didn't set out to target *Weird Tales* with that story. I rarely ever target a story anywhere. I will typically write what interests me at the time. "Crocodile Gods" is based on an actual event. I read about the actual event in a sailing magazine, and thought this the absolute worst, most horrific thing I can think of: You're on an island in the South Pacific, and your husband dives in to check the bottom of this lagoon to see if the anchor is going to hold, and these crocodiles just rip him to shreds right there in front of you, and this woman is left on this boat alone, sitting there, with her husband just having been ripped to shreds. I read of this actual event and wanted to write about it in more depth and detail than was in the article. So it was something I wanted to write. I wrote it, and then I worried about where the story was going to go after it was written.

That's basically how I work. Only with a few rare exceptions have I ever said, "I want to be in this publication," and then sit down and write something specifically for that. I tend to write whatever is interesting to me at the time. My research also drives what I write.

Q: So you're not going to try for *Alternate Historical Zombie Cats* this week?

Hopkins: [Laughs.] Not unless I suddenly took an interest in cats and just had to write about them.

Q: What are your ideas about what a horror story should be?

Hopkins: Well, there are a lot of different types of horror. The type that I write, or what I like to deal with in the way of themes and so forth usually addresses human loss, tragedy, and then how that tragedy or loss is dealt with or overcome. I'll rarely write a true fantastical, monster story. I've written a few, but mostly they don't interest me. I would much rather stick to a reality-based horror story, such as "Crocodile Gods," where the monster is a crocodile, a real, horrific thing that you could encounter, and then have to come to terms with and either overcome, or, as is the case in this story, she doesn't overcome.... It's kind of a downbeat story.

Most of my stories seem to be rather downbeat. In fact, I have a science fiction collection out, that I had originally asked Jack McDevitt, a friend of mine, to write the introduction for. He read all the stories that would be in the collection and said, "I'm sorry, but I just can't write the introduction to this." This is my collection *Wrinkles at Twilight,* which is a CD ROM collection through Lone Wolf Publications. Jack called me up at home and said, "Brian, I really wanted to write this introduction for you, but I just can't do it, because it is so different or far removed from the type of science fiction that I write"—Jack writes the typical 1950ish science fiction stories, with the standard plot where there is a problem they overcome through some technological means, and it has a happy ending. Jack said, "Brian, have you *ever* written a happy ending?" and I had to sit down and actually think in terms of, "Have I ever written a happy ending?" and couldn't come up with one. He declined writing the introduction for that reason, and then Gary Braunbeck wrote the introduction for that collection.

But those are the type of stories that I like to write. They are more reality-based, than they are pure fantasy with werewolves or vampires or Cthulhu-like monsters or elder gods or what have you.

Q: What do you find to be the uses of the fantastic in horror fiction?

Hopkins: If a horror story is done well, you take the fantastic element and you create a metaphor for reality, and you have something to say about the human condition or real-world events. For instance... thinking, thinking, thinking ...

Q: "Five Days in April"?

Hopkins: Yes, for instance, the angel that's in "Five Days in April," a fantastic being. People will argue, but I don't personally think that angels exist. But I can still write about them. The angel is used as a metaphor for lost hope. In using that metaphor, I am able to show that humans can overcome anything, in that case the horrific bombing in Oklahoma City, and still have hope for mankind. When horror is done correctly, I believe that is what those fantastic elements do. They create a mirror in which we can see reality and come to terms and understanding with events that happen in real life, either to us personally or to us as a society.

Q: Let me guess, you didn't grow up reading H.P. Lovecraft.

Hopkins: No, actually, I didn't. I actually came to horror fiction, reading-wise, rather late. Let me clarify that I did, as a youngster, read

Poe and some Lovecraft and Shirley Jackson and a lot of the other early horror writers. To me that was Literature. That was the stuff where you sat down in English class and they said, "We're going to read Edgar Allan Poe." I never identified that as being horror. For me, growing up, with my early reading period in the '70s, horror was either the older films with the giant spiders that had been mutated by radiation—which I kind of enjoyed but really felt were silly—or horror was slasher films. I actually identified that as horror when I was growing up. My early reading was all either fantasy or science fiction. I read all of Robert E. Howard and Edgar Rice Burroughs, and I read all the Asimov and Clarke that I could get ahold of. My father, who is still a big reader and goes through a couple paperbacks a week, would read these horror novels, and I would see him with them and think, "Why's my Dad reading that crap when he could be reading this excellent science-fiction novel?" He also read those too. But I couldn't understand why he read the horror. And at some point in time I picked up a horror novel, it just happened to be Stephen King's It, and read it, and my eyes were just opened. Then, probably for the last fifteen years, I read almost exclusively horror. I probably read some science fiction, and I still buy tons of science fiction, but never have the time to read it. I haven't read any fantasy other than some of the standards like the Donaldson books, and now I am reading George Martin's excellent fantasy series; but other than that I have ignored all the current fantasy that seems to be in endless series type volumes.

So I didn't set out as a reader to really focus on horror, and I didn't set out as a writer to say I'm going to be a horror writer. I just found things that really interested me and I wanted to write about, and it seemed like, more and more, those stories were falling into what other people wanted to classified as horror.

Q: You seem then to be diametrically opposed to Lovecraft—or Ligotti, to cite another more recent practitioner—whose great interest was "the weird," the intrusion of unreality into reality. That doesn't seem to be your thing.

Hopkins: I am certainly not opposed to them. They just weren't part of my early reading. I have read a lot of their stuff in later years and enjoyed it, but, again, it's different from what I write. I don't think I write anything like either one of those two gentlemen.

Q: It would seem you're going through your intense horror-reading period now, after you have become a writer, which is unusual. Most people who become writers read exclusively in the genre when they're 15, and by the time they're writing it, they're reading all sorts of things. Do you read, mainstream fiction, non-fiction, all sorts of odds and ends?

Hopkins: Yes, I do. I read a lot of stuff. I read an awful lot of non-fiction, and if you've read my work, it's all very detail-oriented. So I do an awful lot of reading in the non-fiction area for research for what I write. And, like I said, I pick up a book that's interesting, a non-fiction book, and that will drive my fiction too. I will say, "This is really fascinating. I will write a story around these details, around these facts." A prime example is Richard Preston's *The Hot Zone*, which is a book about emerging filoviruses in Africa: Ebola, Marburg, and other types of hemorrhagic fevers. I read that book, an absolutely terrifying book, and knew I had to write a story about it. I wrote a story in January 1995 called "All Colors Bleed to Red," which is about an Ebola virus that mutates and reaches the next step, airborne transmission, which could very well wipe out everybody. I tried to sell that story, which I think is one of the best stories I've ever written, throughout the summer of 1995, which just happens to be when the Dustin Hoffman movie *Outbreak* came out. All the rejections I got said, "This is a great story, but we just saw that movie. It's old hat now." Of course I had written it before I ever heard of the movie.

Q: Have you sold the story since?

Hopkins: I wound up selling it in the small press. I can't remember which magazine it appeared in. I think it appeared on the Web. It's included in my collection, *These I Know by Heart*.

But that story is another prime example of, yes, it's a horror story, but it is very detail-driven through the research I did on Ebola and so forth. It's also a hard science fiction story. In fact some of the rejections I got from the horror market said, "Well this is too much like science fiction," and some of the science fiction rejections I got said, "Well, this is great, but it's too much like horror."

Q: This doubtless shows the ultimate futility of genre. If you try to follow trends and categories, you will wind up producing a second-hand version of something someone else already did.

Hopkins: I pretty much ignore trends in most fiction. I am going to write whatever interests me at the time, and then when I'm done writing, whenever I'm ready to check it in, I would rather have a body of work that my readers will read, not because they say, "Brian Hopkins was a good horror writer and we like horror stories," or they're science fiction fans and they say, "Brian Hopkins wrote good science fiction and I read his science fiction books, but ignored his horror." I would rather my fans learn of me as a good writer, and if tomorrow I turn around and write a romance story, they're going to be confident enough in my ability as a storyteller to want to read that romance, even if they're more or less fans of horror. Again, a lot of that, when I blend genre, I think, helps build that appeal.

When we talked about H.P. Lovecraft and elder gods and stuff...my new novella that is coming out in time for the World Fantasy Convention is called *El Dia de los Muertos*, and it deals with fantastic creatures, old Aztec gods: Coatlicue, Huitzilopochtli. These gods are resurrected by a man who has lost his daughter in a Mexican earthquake. So, I do write, occasionally, about fantastical creatures and in a style that might be construed as Lovecraft-like. Readers who like that sort of thing should watch for *El Dia de los Muertos*, but my point is that just because I haven't written in a certain voice or certain themes doesn't mean I won't next week or next year, because I am constantly changing what I do and evolving as a writer. In fact, I've got a mainstream novel that I've been working on for five or six years. When I've finished that, I'll make a push for getting a mainstream novel out there. After that, if I feel like writing a western, I might write a western. You just never know.

Q: Have you had a talk with an agent about career strategies at this point? An agent will tell you that if you publish this mainstream novel, that will make you a mainstream writer, so publishers won't want a romance from you. You know how all convention panels are ultimately about marketing? I was on a panel the other day, which got onto that subject rather heavily. We were talking about the early marketing of Stephen King. Publishers had to establish what the Stephen King brand name means. Therefore they didn't want to publish his quasi-science fiction novels as by Stephen King, because if *The Running Man* had been put out right after *'Salem's Lot*, it would have greatly diluted what the Stephen King name meant. So, I guess if you're a careerist, at some point you're going to have to think about what the Brian Hopkins name means.

Hopkins: [Laughs.] I guess I'm not a careerist. I am going to be writing as long as I am around, but am I going to focus on and target a career? Had anyone encouraged me when I got out of high school—I mean, here I was, a young kid; through my four years of highschool, I must have written twenty novels. I'd punch holes in them and bind them up with shoestrings. I still have them stored away in my attic. I won't show them to a soul. They're very amateurish. But if someone had at that time encouraged me and said, "Brian, you've got to be a writer. That just makes sense for your life." This would have been 1979 when I got out of highschool. It would have been a perfect time, if I wanted to write horror, to have launched a horror career. But I really wasn't encouraged to go that route. My parents said, "Are you going to college?" I said, "Well, I guess so." "How are you going to pay for it?" "I don't know." "Well you need to get a scholarship." My Dad was in the Navy, so he said, "Why don't you try to get a Navy scholarship?" and "Why don't you apply for an Air Force scholarship on the ROTC program?" And I applied to both, and the Navy offered me a two-year scholarship and the Air Force offered me a four-year scholarship. However, to take the scholarship, I had to focus on a career that, naturally, the Air Force needed. So I chose engineering, because I had an interest in electronics and all sorts of gadgets. So then I focused on building an engineering career. As I said, for a few years in college and afterwards, building that career, I didn't write, but I returned to it because it was something I loved. Later I started publishing my work. But, had I set out as an 18- or 19-year-old to become a writer, I think I would probably be more career-oriented, because it would have been more a matter of making enough money from my fiction to get out of my parents' house, to feed myself and later my wife and my children. So I think I probably would have been more focused on what I needed to write to make money.

Instead, I am comfortable. I make plenty of money in my day job. I don't want to say that writing is a hobby. I certainly don't approach it as a hobby, something I do purely for fun. But it's something I do, and I'm going to write what I want to write, rather than worrying about the market or building a career. I am more worried about building that body of work that I talked about.

Q: Maybe you can use pseudonyms and publish the western as "Bart Hopkins" and the thrillers as "B.A. Hopkins" and the romances as "Bernadette Hopkins."…Not quite kidding. They probably are going to ask for something like that if you start selling a lot of novels in different genres.

Hopkins: I'll probably balk at it and go on and do what I want anyway. [Laughs.] You asked about agents. I actually don't have an agent. I am waiting for somebody to discover me.

The mainstream novel that I am working on, which is called *Wading Inland,* deals with a man dying of AIDS—he is a musical composer and he is determined in the last six months or so of his life to decipher the music of whales, which he thinks contains some cryptic message about God and the universe and our fate and how it's all intertwined. I have about half of it written, which is about 70,000 words, and probably 50,000 words in notes to write the rest of it. At one point, a friend of mine, Janet Berliner, had read it and thought it was fantastic, and I had hoped at that time that it was good enough to secure an agent on what was written. So, through Janet making some connections for me, we approached a couple different agencies, but they weren't interested. So that is the only attempt that I've made to get an agent at all, is with my mainstream novel. I had hoped that on the half that was written it was strong enough to get an agent and possibly even get a book deal out of it. You hear all the Cinderella stories. An example is Nicholas Sparks's totally awful book, *Message in a Bottle,* which was made into a very good movie. But you hear all the stories about how he was paid a four million dollar advance for the book, because somebody found him and wanted to make him a household name. Now maybe he is, in mainstream, or he's almost a romance writer now, I think, but he's marketed as mainstream. I had hoped that maybe something could be done for *Wading Inland* like that, that it was certainly stronger than most of what I was seeing being pushed as mainstream.

Q: Here I think you do have to think with some deliberation. When you type "The End" on the final draft of *Wading Inland*, what do you do next?

Hopkins: That's a good question. [Laughs.] I assume that I will take the route that so many other authors have taken, and send it out to half a dozen different agencies, and hope that one of them will take the time to read it and see in it what I see in it and what those who have been reading it as I write it have seen in it. Everyone who has looked at it thinks it is probably the most powerful thing I have ever written. So hopefully that will be true, so it may launch a mainstream career that could very well overshadow everything else. If I want to make a career decision on what I write, then perhaps that will focus the remainder of my career.

I seriously doubt, though, that I could ever be a pure mainstream writer without there being fantastic elements in my work.

Q: But you could be marketed as one.

Hopkins: But I could certainly be marketed as one. I'm quite certain that from a money perspective, that would be a smart move.

Q: My guess is that after you become a famous mainstream writer and sell millions of copies, you can still, for old times' sake, put short stories in the small press.

Hopkins: [Laughs.] I've always been a sucker for invitations, so any time a small press asked me for a story, I almost felt obligated to write something for them.

Q: Do you have a sense of community in the horror field, that, in essence, you're a member of an exclusive club and you want to stay part of the club and therefore you write for these anthologies or whatever?

Hopkins: Yes, I would say there's a feeling of community. I have hundreds of friends who are horror writers or horror fans. I certainly can't see myself walking away from it. Like I said before, I hope that people who read my work, even if they're just horror fans, when they see my mainstream book out there, they're going to want to read it because it's Brian Hopkins.

An example is Robert McCammon. After years of retirement, he's coming out with this new book that's totally different from anything that he's written before—or so they say, I haven't read it. I'm a big McCammon fan. I have everything that he has ever done, and I will certainly buy this book and read it. I fully expect to enjoy it as much as I have enjoyed all his other work, because McCammon is an incredible writer. I hope that one day people will equate me in that same light.

Q: You can't really get away from the horror because it's in the blood . . .

Hopkins: [Laughs.] It definitely is.

— Recorded at the World Horror Convention, April 14, 2002.

HARRY O. MORRIS

Can there be anyone in the horror/fantasy field who doesn't know the marvelous artwork of Harry 0. Morris, Jr.? His Lovecraftian/Surrealist magazine *Nyctalops* was an important influence in the 1970's, both for its written content (Morris discovered Thomas Ligotti) and, perhaps even more importantly, for its visual style, which introduced its audience to the grotesque collages and distorted and artfully doctored photos—the work of the then unknown J.K. Potter and Harry 0. Morris himself. Today, Morris is designing and illustrating some of the Dell/Abyss horror line, and changing the whole look of horror publishing as profoundly as, say, Richard Powers changed science fiction in the 1950's.

Q: I am sure fans of your art have sometimes wondered "Where did this weird stuff come from..." Well, more precisely, could you give us some idea of haw you got started as an artist and what sparked your interest in the macabre?

Harry O. Morris: I seem to have always had an interest in horror. The biggest influence probably came in 1964 when I found a copy of H.P. Lovecraft's *The Dunwich Horror* in the Lancer paperback edition. It exerted a big influence on my life, which led to starting my own Lovecraft-oriented magazine in 1970 called *Nyctalops*. As far as artwork goes, I'm not someone like Jeff Jones, who was constantly drawing since he was a kid, but I did draw off and on all through junior high.

My parents bought me a Famous Artists Correspondence Course, which has influenced my artwork, maybe for the best, maybe for the worst, and I guess around age twenty-one I discovered the collages of Max Ernst and combined that with Lovecraft and surrealism, and after that it was just a lot of experiments to achieve a dream-like effect by various means.

Q: It does indeed seem that there's as much surrealism as Lovecraft in your work, which is very much in the tradition of a lot of late 19th or early 20th century collage artists. But collage is very different from other sorts of art, and ideally suited for surrealism because of its use of incongruities. Is this how it works for you? How do you choose the images you want to use?

Morris: It's a matter of juxtaposing two distant realities on an unfamiliar plane, as from Lautreamont, his example being an umbrella and a sewing machine meeting on a dissecting table. That's the theory behind the collage.

I leave a lot of my stuff up to chance. A number of people—and I do it occasionally—will find a background and elements to put on top of that background. I often do that. Otherwise I just get a bunch of stuff on the table and try something until I think it works. The next morning, either I'll go "Yuck, it doesn't work" or "Yes, it does." It's just playing around with different images.

One thing I like to do is cut and put staff in a more 3-D effect, something behind a building, partially exposed, rather than sticking one image on top of another—which I often do if it looks good, but I prefer to cut into the thing.

Q: Did you make any sort of formal study of the Surrealist movement and its ideology?

Morris: Yes, especially in my earlier years. I've eased up on it. I'll still go back and read the Surrealists occasionally. I am still impressed. I haven't outgrown that, as old as I am now, but especially in my twenties I was in awe of the Surrealists. I did read a lot of Andre Breton, Louis Aragon—not so much Salvador Dali—a lot of intellectual stuff that was kind of over my head. But it made a weird sense to me and I believed in it a lot.

Q: Which brings us back to Lovecraft perhaps? The Surrealists and Lovecraft have something in common, and not merely that both are popular in France.

Morris: Yes, they do. *View Magazine* published an article sometime in the 1940's, which related Lovecraft to the Surrealists. I think I read one of Lovecraft's letters in which he said he didn't care that much for the Surrealists. But they admired him. They admired Clark Ashton Smith and other pulp writers. You can make connections. If anything, I think Lovecraft was darker than the Surrealists. He was more of a pessimist. The Surrealists, despite their going into the subconscious and finding all these evil devil-images sometimes, were basically willing to improve the state of mankind and provide some kind of hope to change the world and transform Man; whereas Lovecraft was a cosmic materialist. You know:

Mankind doesn't mean anything. Man is a speck of dust So Lovecraft was a lot more negative than the Surrealists.

Q: The Surrealists have a more playful element. Duchamp, for example, is certainly playful.

Morris: Duchamp's was an intellectual playfulness, as you say, where Lovecraft was more Victorian, classical, structured. He did have a sense of humor in certain respects, but it was a lot different than that of the Surrealists.

Q: Of course, one can't merely be a Surrealist today, repeating the work of seventy years ago. Your work isn't purely Surrealism. So what have you taken from the Surrealists movement and what have you left behind?

Morris: I take a lot of the techniques, like collage, decalcomania, and hopefully I introduce my own neurosis into it, subconscious feelings, stuff that I'm not actually aware of. But still, as much as I admire a lot of artists, as great and slick as they are, well, it's as if the Surrealists were the last of the great artists. Not even Giger, I think, has done anything as major as the Surrealists did to change the face of art. And what I've done might be personal, or whatever, but it's not a revolution.

Q: The irony of this is that much cover art in book publishing hasn't gotten that far yet. In the 1950's and 1960's, science fiction art was easing its way into surrealism—the art of the 1920's—but then chickened out and returned to the Brandywine school, the fashion of 1900 or so.

Morris: You're exactly right. At least I see it that way. Richard Powers is a prime example. He is the closest to the abstract Surrealists like Matta and Tanguy. Powers was playing on what they did, relating to the stories, and the result had a unique science-fiction/horror feel. When I was a kid I loved it. Then I grew to, not dislike it, but I got suckered into the more realistic type of stuff for a while. I think that's what happened to a lot of publishers—the realistic swordsmen, etc. But I am going back to appreciating the moody, semi-abstract stuff of Powers, which the Surrealists introduced. Maybe it's the direction that the field is going back to. I'd like to see some more of that happening, rather man the photo-realistic covers that are still popular.

Q: The publishers just want the books to sell. They're not interested in art. Sometimes very good art—like the Ace Special covers of Leo and Diane Dillon—didn't sell nearly as well as those that had, say, Rowena Morrill covers. So it becomes economic Darwinism.

Morris: You're right there. The main objective is to sell the book, and I guess it's just like TV. Go back to *The Twilight Zone* and there's thinking stuff there, but what sells are the sitcoms, which are pretty vacant I'm not saying that all paperback art is vacant but it's immediate; people can relate to it. It may not be fine art; it doesn't have to be. It's what sells the book.

Q: You've been doing some paperback art yourself, so someone must be receptive to a bit more. How have you been doing selling to the big paperback markets?

Morris: I think that Jeanne Cavelos and Phil Rose—the people at Dell—are admittedly taking a chance, which was real lucky for me at the time. They're doing some experimental work with the covers, saying, "This is what has been selling. Let's put something a little bit different out there and see if it will sell better or sell fewer copies." I think it's a great idea.

Q: Getting back to the idea of revolutions in art—are you doing much computer-generated or computer-altered art at this point? Do you think the computer will bring about the next revolution?

Morris: I do quite a bit of it. I am constantly trying to upgrade. It's kind of an expensive trap. The computer I work with, an Amiga, produces some pretty high-end stuff at really low cost It's all relative. You can spend up to $50,000 on a Sun or Silicon Valley Workstation or $5,000 for a souped-up Amiga, which is awfully close. I think that as the technology filters down, more and more people will have the power to do computer art. This is true of both computers and video. There is going to be a revolution coming out of there. Of course, not all of it is going to be great work, but it will become available to more people, financially.

Q: I suppose it's like the new instrument in music. You invent the piano or the violin, and someone eventually learns to do entirely new things on it. Surety there are things you can do on the computer which are not merely faster, but previously impossible.

Morris: You can get close to it in the darkroom, but there is stuff you can do on the computer you just can't do any other way. Of course it's faster. It can be. But there are tricks which are unique to the computer that can't be done without a hell of a lot of work photographically. I don't know about painting. I have always been more of a photographer than a painter. I guess painters can go and emulate what you do on a computer more easily than photographers can.

Q: Bibliophiles probably wince a bit at most collages, suspecting you cut up old books. Is that how you get the images, or are they copied somehow? Will the computer make book-mutilation in the name of art obsolete?

Morris: Not so much anymore. But definitely at first. Back in the 70's, I would go into second-hand bookstores and buy up books published in 1890 with lots of engravings, and I would cut them up. I felt a little bit bad, but it depended on the book. I don't like to cut books up. But after you've cut out one or two images, you might as well do the rest because the book is kind of wrecked. But I would cut the books up. You get the source material in its original state that way without making copies. With a computer, it's easier. If I can get the book to lay flat—I just got a video camera, so I can digitize the page rather than cutting it out. Then the image I want is on the computer screen, and I can cut it without physically hurting the book.

Q: Which gives everyone a clean conscience and probably better results. But, more generally, what techniques do you use most of the time? How is the average Morris picture produced?

Morris: I'm still fluctuating. I tend to favor me computer because it is the newest to me, but I haven't sold out and gone hog-wild on the computer so that I only do computer work. I go back to engraving and collage and cutting up photographs of my own, pasting them, maybe digitizing them, and of course there is a lot of air-brush work. I just combine the new and the old. I haven't given up my old stuff. Maybe I rely on it less. Introducing me computer is just a part of the process.

Q: Other than Famous Artists School, did you have any formal art training?

Morris: None to speak of. I had friends who inspired me a lot, but no formal art training. I didn't go to university. In fact I graduated third from the bottom in my class in high school.

Q: In art or in everything?

Morris: In everything.

Q: Then again, I was just hearing this afternoon how Richard Christian Matheson dropped out of high school because it was getting in the way of his career.

Morris: [Laughs] That's a slightly different case, I think. The guy is at least a semi-genius, ahead of his time. He had the creative ability. He knew what he wanted. I dropped out because I was a rebel and smoked in the bathrooms and hung out with gangs and stuff. It was for different reasons that I dropped out. It took me a while to come to my senses, if that's what it is, and become more creative.

Q: Is art an actual career for you now, or do you have a real job?

Morris: For a long time, from 1970 to about 1980, I was an offset printer. In that time. I bought a lot of my own equipment. During the '80's, and for parts of the '90's, I still had my printing press downstairs. I have a few customers. I'm making enough money from paperback covers now that I can rely on that money to live on. But I don't want to burn my bridges, simply because I don't have any contract I don't know if I'll still have ten paperback covers next year, or zero. So I keep the printing press and the few customers I have as backup. It's a steady source of income. But no, I don't have to go to an 8-to-5 job. I set my own schedule, either printing or doing artwork.

Q: Have you thought of doing more publishing? Lots of people regretted the end of *Nyctalops*.

Morris: I know a lot of people regretted it. But all this stuff was happening at once. J.K. Potter got me started with Scream Press and overwhelmed me for a while. The drive I put into *Nyctalops* I put into these other projects. It's just a matter of time. I don't think I'd ever publish another magazine, because of the commitment. I let a lot of people down. Eight years lapsed between issues. I was holding material. I don't want that to happen. Of course I might do a one-shot sometime in the future. I do have the equipment.

Q: We might mention your other accomplishment as a publisher, being that you published the first edition of Thomas Ligotti's *Songs of a Dead Dreamer*.

Morris: If nothing else, if I'm not remembered for my artwork or for *Nyctalops*—and I hope I am not overrating Ligotti; I hope I am not being too subjective—but just the fact that I kind of discovered him in a way—I'm sure someone else would have if I hadn't—if I do go down in history with my name associated with his, that'll make me happy. He's a great writer.

Q: I don't know if you are going to become Thomas Ligotti's August Derleth, but they're now saying that your edition of *Songs of a Dead Dreamer* is *The Outsider* of the '80's.

Morris: Well, it just has a chance. I published other books that I thought were great and would take off and do well, and they didn't, for whatever reason. Ligotti just knocked me out. He's not like other writers—maybe Sutton Breiding is like that too. I admire him so much. I thought, Ligotti deserves to be published, no matter what. He's so strange. I can appreciate him. Maybe a few other people can. So I'll publish three hundred copies and that'll be it. But instead, I was wrong in this case.

Ramsey Campbell and you and other people recognized him. This is really great stuff. He's taken off. It's kind of by chance. Now, looking with hindsight I wish I'd published a lot more than three hundred copies.

Q: But I guess you have to ultimately focus on one career, rather than several. I think that if I were in your position, I might be thinking that only one person can create your artwork, but someone else can do the publishing.

Morris: I figure that, a little bit, I guess. But I suppose the cliché is I have printer's ink in my veins. I asked Christine once—I was working with the press—"How do I look more natural, as a printer or as an artist?" She said, "You look like a printer." I'm cut out for it, even if it goes wrong. The artwork is so nebulous. But me rewards for the artwork" are much greater than the printing.

Q: What projects have been you working on of late?

Morris: I have a couple of books coming out from Dell, a cover for *Metahorror* edited by Dennis Etchison, a book called *Stitch*, which I haven't read yet, but it's coming out from Dell. I'm not exactly sure when. And possibly a cover for a collection of Richard Christian Matheson stories entitled *Faith*.

Q: Thanks, Harry.

Recorded at the 1992 World Horror Convention, Nashville, TN, where Harry was Artist Guest of Honor.

SEPHERA GIRON

Sephera Giron is the author of *The House of Pain, The Birds and the Bees, Borrowed Flesh, Mistress of the Dark,* etc. She is also a professional Tarot counselor.

Q: We could start by asking how you got to be writing all this perverse stuff. You're noted for writing a rather extreme sort of horror. So, what brings you here?

Giron: When I was little I read a lot of fairy tales, the original fairy tales, and they are actually rather extreme and graphic and gory, and from there I went into animal stories. I distinctly remember reading *Beautiful Joe* and *Old Yeller* and things like that. I found them horrific and terrifying, even though they were animal stories.

Then, when I was about fourteen, Stephen King came on the scene. I'm in my forties, so I was a teenager when Stephen King came around. Before that I was reading a lot of science fiction and mysteries. I was always a voracious reader. So I really got into Stephen King. As I got older, into my twenties, I met a film-maker and he exposed me to all these wonderful B-movies and Italian horror and extreme, violent kinds of things; and I found that my writing started to take a turn towards more extreme, in-your-face kinds of things, especially when Clive Barker came around. I find that Clive Barker a very poetic, yet horrifying writer, and I really admired his style in the way he could lure you in with his prose, but really stick it to you with his gore.

So, for myself, I loved these writers that were doing these extreme things, and I myself wanted to be one of those writers. So I tried to be like those people that I admired.

Q: Isn't the whole problem with extreme horror that once you've shown everything ... you've shown everything?

Giron: That's true too. Sometimes I don't write extreme horror at all. Sometimes I write very quiet kinds of tales. Most of those never get published for some reason. It seems that people do expect extreme from me, and those are the kinds of stories that do get published when I submit them. I have submitted a lot of things that aren't so extreme.

A few have been published. For instance, the piece I had published in *Cemetery Dance* isn't extreme at all. But, for the most part, yeah, I think I am building a reputation as an extreme or erotic horror writer.

Q: I sometimes get the impression from some of Clive Barker's fiction, that some of his characters are basically lunchmeat. They exist to be sliced, not to actually live in the story. There can be a question of making the reader care about such characters.

Giron: I think that's true in this genre, with a lot of our characters, no matter who is writing them, because you do need a certain amount of people who are going to be lunchmeat. For myself I try to introduce characters and not always have a red flag above them that they are going to be the lunchmeat people. I try to keep it a surprise. Sometimes the people that you don't want to die do die, and the ones you want to die don't. Just because I try to keep it fresh and interesting for my readers, I want to take them on a roller-coaster ride and entertain them and not necessarily have them guess the ending before the ending.

Q: Surely the whole point of effective horror is to kill off or otherwise do bad things to somebody that we care about.

Giron: That's true, of course, because we all know the most horrific thing you could ever imagine is having someone you love dearly dying and never being there again.

Q: Is that the most horrific thing? Does horror have to be about death? It could be about the person you love becoming someone else, someone repellent. It seems to me that lot of horror is about the loss or compromise of identity. This includes all those zombies and vampires, who are not entirely dead. So, do you necessarily have to kill the victims?

Giron: It's true. Definitely you don't have to die for things to be horrific. I definitely believe that. As a mother, watching children do things and hoping they make the right choices, it can be horrific watching your child make mistakes.

I can't imagine anything more horrific than being totally paralyzed and still being able to think. That would be to me worse than being dead. I'd rather be dead than be just a head with a brain and not able to move.

Q: Or possibly there's seeing someone you love turn into a psychotic monster.

Giron: Oh yeah, there's that too. [Laughs.] Mental illness, or Alzheimer's, I imagine. That must be very frightening. I had a grandmother who went through that, but I wasn't that close to her, so it was horrific, but we didn't have a close bond to begin with. But yes, she definitely turned into someone who was totally not who she was. It really affected my mother deeply, because she was close to her mother. That would be terrifying, I think, probably worse than someone dying, how they just don't remember you, remember things, and they are just not the person that you once knew or loved.

Q: What about the erotic element? I don't know if we really can intellectualize this. [Giron laughs.] Are we talking about attraction and repulsion at the same time here? After all, sex isn't supposed to be horrifying.

Giron: I have erotic elements in my work because to me, if people didn't have sex we wouldn't be here, so sex is a very human kind of thing. We all do it. We all experience it. People experience it in different ways; and I approach sex in different ways in my work. Sometimes terrible sexual things happen. Like in *Mistress of the Dark*, my latest novel, which is the diary of a serial killer, of a woman who is obsessed with a Johnny Depp look-alike. She gets involved in all these very strange sexual situations. She lives with a man and a woman for a while and they have this bizarre arrangement and they do all this kinky, weird stuff, and eventually people die, but it's mostly because she's insane. It happens, but the sex is a big part of it because that's the world she is living in. She is living in a world of drag-queens and people who work in the sex industry, strippers and people like that. So sex is very involved in her life, but it's not necessarily a "she's a bad girl and people die" kind of thing. It's just the world she is in.

Yet, in another story I have a woman who lures men specifically for sex and then kills them. So I use sex for various reasons in fiction. I am not a one-note person. I try to explore different elements of the sexuality of people, like real sex with real people, and then strange things that happen, and manipulations, power, and all that stuff that sexuality means to us as humans.

Q: One thinks of the vampire as the epitome of seductive evil. I have to admit I don't know if you've ever written anything about vampires ...

Giron: Actually, there is a new line of books coming out called Neon Books coming out of England, and they were looking for twenty-five horror writers to write erotica, or reprints. I know Lucy Taylor is on board with that, Nancy Kilpatrick, a bunch of other people. I found out about it and asked, "Hey, can I do this? What are you looking for?" And they said, "Hey, no one has approached us with a vampire story yet, so do you want to do that?" So I have a book called *Hungarian Rhapsody* coming out in November 2007. I call it a vampire tale, but it's really about a woman in the 1800s who goes to live with this mysterious Transylvanian stranger. She dreams about Gypsies and running away with Gypsies, and it's a very big riff on the "Carmilla" lesbian-vampire kind of thing. But since this is an erotic line rather than a horror line, there is a lot of sex and s&m and that kind of stuff going on. So I don't even know if I would call that horror first, or if it's more of an erotic book, but it's the closest thing to a vampire story that I've done in my own work.

Q: I suppose the comic question at this point would be "How much research do you have to do?"

Giron: [laughs] Well, if you don't include my horror stuff, I do have The Kama Sutra Seductions Deck coming out in June. This is a set of cards with 64 positions from the Kama Sutra. It comes with a little booklet, and it is a set of photographs, a picture of the position on one side and on the back is how to do the position, and little sex tips and stuff like that.

I must say that the *Kama Sutra* does have over 500 positions. I researched the *Kama Sutra* for about a year for a totally different project that I didn't get the green light for, but to make a long story short, with how the publishing industry works, I ended up doing this card deck instead of the book; and, yeah, I researched all 64 positions with my boyfriend. Some were actually possible and some I think you would have to be really good at yoga to actually achieve. They're there just so people can give it a shot if they want, if they're up for that. [Laughs.] But that's probably as much research as I've ever done for anything.

Q: Surely much of the point of writing horror fiction is that you are writing about places you can't go or at least don't want to go if you're in your right mind, and therefore it has to be imagined. Would you agree?

Giron: Oh, for sure. Half the fun of writing fiction is that it is fiction. You do things that you want to do or don't want to do. You just go places you've never thought of. When I co-wrote some of the Darker Passion books with Nancy Kilpatrick, one of them was "The Pit and the Pendulum" by Edgar Allan Poe, and I took that tiny little story and turned it into a huge novel that is totally a science-fiction kind of thing, because I created this whole world where people are bred for s&m experiences, complete with extra flesh on their wrists so they can be tied down, and hermaphrodites and so on—poor Poe—[laughs]. How do you research that? You don't. You just go crazy with your head.

Q: What kind of fan-mail do you get from people who are into this sort of thing?

Giron: [Laughs.] I haven't gotten anything too crazy, luckily. Usually they just ask me out on a date or whatever. It's like "Sorry, I'm taken," so, yeah…I haven't had anything really weird, and I am always waiting for that to happen, because you just never know. [Laughs.] Who's out there who is reading it, and I know sometimes I can be really strange.

Q: If you become famous enough this could become a problem. I know Stephen King has had some problems. I think the dynamic is that if only one person in a million is crazy enough, and you reach 50 million people, that means you have fifty weirdos stalking you.

Giron: That's true. I live for that day in which I have fifty weirdos ... [Laughs.] Or a million people reading me for that matter.

Q: Don't we all? Do you actually write for a living?

Giron: I am a full-time writer. I am lucky in that sense. I must admit that I do other jobs too. I read Tarot as a part-time job. I write a Tarotscope column, which is a combination of Tarot cards and astrology for adultfriendfinder.com and adultpersonals.com. I also work for a publishing company where I evaluate manuscripts. I won't say who it is publicly. That's a freelance thing that brings me bread and butter. I teach online courses of how to write horror at Coursebridge. Sometimes I teach musical theatre at dance studios. I have many fingers in many pies because I love doing so much stuff.

Q: It says here [in the Eeriecon program book] that you teach a course in House Magic and wrote a book on the subject.

Giron: Yes. *House Magic* came out in 2001. Basically, my agent Lori Perkins discovered that I do Tarot reading on the side and me and my friend Julie, who is actually now married to my ex-husband, had a company for a while called Two Stupid Witches, and we'd go to people's houses and do Tarot parties. We discovered that a lot of people have interesting superstitions about how to organize their homes for good luck. So I wrote this book and it's a combination of feng shui, candle magic, witchcraft, astrology, numerology, and all sorts of things. It was a lot of fun to write, because I drew a lot on what people told me, plus research, so now I have this online course. People want to read the book and actually put it to use in their own life.

Q: Is house magic a practice of supernatural activity or is it a theory of interior decorating?

Giron: It's interior decorating. Really it's "The Secret" before the Secret came out. It's basically positive affirmations, clearing out the clutter, making sure your rooms are bright and energetic.

I myself have to say I'm a packrat. I've got piles of crap everywhere. I wrote this book partly as therapy for myself to try and get myself organized. I am more organized, but still it's true. Even Oprah says, "You clean out your closet and you feel like a new person." So it's a lot of that. And I put in people's superstitions. You have citrine for money, turquoise for health. A lot of people like to have these touchstones. It gives them more of a positive feedback and a positive energy. So I think that whatever people want to use to make themselves feel better about themselves, go for it.

Q: How do you actually feel about the supernatural, as in belief in same?

Giron: You mean like God energy?

Q: More like the existence of ghosts.

Giron: [Laughs.]

Q: Curses that really work.

Giron: I think curses are self-fulfilling prophecies. I have to admit I have seen a ghost and it was my grandmother. I never believed in ghosts until it happened to me. How that happened was that I was taking a course in mediumship. I was very skeptical taking this course. That was before I ever did Tarot. I was always afraid of Tarot cards and would never go near them. After my husband and I split up, I took these course. One of the weeks we were trying to do this mind-reading stuff, and I'm bad at it. Even in the Tarot reading I do now I am strangely accurate, but it's not because I can read minds. It's because I read what the cards say.

Anyway what we had to do at this course was write down the name of someone who was dead or the date and we had to put them into a hat and pick the names from other people. So my teacher got me, and I put down my grandmother who had died a couple years before. He didn't know anything about me, and he started going on and on about my grandmother and messages she had for me, and all this stuff I was writing down because it meant *nothing* to me. I went home and asked my mother about things: "He said you had this dog when you were a kid and this house—" He described a house. It was there, because he said my grandmother was there talking to him about it. And my mother said, "Oh my God," this was true and that was true. She confirmed all these weird things that I didn't even know. How did he know?

When I went home that night, even before I talked to my mother, I had this strange feeling, even though I am a big skeptic. I heard some knocking on the walls, whatever. I do believe my grandmother was around for a while. The teacher did say she was around to help me get started with my writing career and get over my divorce and all this sort of thing. I believe she was with me for a while. I asked her not to materialize in front of me because I thought I would freak out and die if I ever saw her ghost or anything. [Laughs.] But, yeah, I do believe in ghosts now, but I do still take it with a grain of salt. I am still very skeptical when people tell me things, but I do understand where it comes from. Even in my own experiences I still wonder if it's some sort of imagination, hallucination, just the want to have something there.

I went to the Lizzie Borden House and I know stuff happened. I know there was a cat licking my head in the middle of the night when no cat was there.

Q: You mean you stayed there overnight?

Giron: I've stayed there overnight three times now.

Q: I merely posed lying down on the sofa.

Giron: I have pictures of me posing on the sofa too. The death position.

Q: Yes, the death position of Mr. Borden.

Giron: [Laughs.] I slept overnight there three times, after NECon[3], last year and the year before and the year before that. There was one year when my transmission blew up. I went to Maine first to drop my kids off. I went to Salem and then between Salem and NECon my transmission died, and I got towed to NECon that year. Then I had to wait for my car to be fixed, so I went to the Lizzie Borden House[4] with other people from the con. I don't know if it was because I was already traumatized from the car blowing up and being a woman alone on the road, and also, too actually, if you want to talk about supernatural. When that car blew up, it was the weirdest thing. I was coming out of Salem. I was stuck in traffic around Boston for hours. I was going really slow. The traffic picked up, and then my transmission popped—the cap popped out or whatever. I saw it fly out of my rearview mirror, and my car lost power instantly, and I was right at an exit. I rolled down a hill and right into a gas station.

You know how New England is. There's nothing for millions of miles, and yet the car blew up at an exit, rolled down a hill, and into a gas station. So I know someone was looking out for me, because I have no cell phone. I was a woman driving alone. It was so bizarre.

Q: How do you feel about using the supernatural in fiction? Do you think that horror needs it?

Giron: I use it and I don't use it. Like in the *Mistress of the Dark* book, *The Diary of a Serial Killer*, she's just insane. Yet in *Borrowed*

---

3   Northeast Regional Fantasy Convention, held in Rhode Island—DS

4   In nearby Fall River, Mass.—DS

Flesh it's a witch and she uses supernatural powers. She battles other witches with supernatural powers. That's more calling on universal energy.

Sometimes I have ghosts. Yeah, I love the supernatural. Why not?

Q: But are they scary? I should think that if a ghost materialized in front of you and began to speak, that would be quite reassuring. It reassures you that there is a survival of intelligence after death.

Giron: That's true.

Q: And I've never heard of anyone being killed by a ghost.

Giron: That's true too. We all hear these horror stories, fiction stories, but that's quite right with the reality. We all saw *Poltergeist*, but that's fiction. You're right. I did find comfort when I thought my grandmother was coming around.

But sometimes things do happen. Sometimes I get the goosebumps when I am doing stuff for other people. And even when I was at the Lizzie Borden house. I think it was Lizzie that was there. I am not even sure it was the parents that were there. There was something at that house, and it was from beyond. I went to the house not knowing all the stories. I just knew Lizzie Borden took an axe, gave her parents forty whacks. That's all I knew about Lizzie Borden before I went there. I went into this one room and I saw children. I was with Trish Cacek and we both kind of like were visioning on these children and we didn't know why. Later when the tour guide gave us the tour, she told us about these children and that they were thrown down a well and their ghosts haunt that room. Meanwhile, we had actually seen them before we actually knew that story. Yeah, there's comfort, and it's creepy, but it's also interesting, because I am a big believer in universal energy. When we die, it has to go somewhere, so where is it going?

Q: M.R. James always insisted that, at least for fiction, ghosts must be malevolent. He didn't like sappy, sentimental ghosts.

Giron: There are the ghosts that are angry that they're ghosts, and the ghosts that don't know they're ghosts, and the ghosts that want revenge. There are all sorts of ways to explore the idea of ghosts and I'd like to play them all before I'm…dead. [Laughs.]

Q: Then you can explore them from the other side.

Giron: [In spooky voice] I'll be ghost-writing, won't I?

Q: Of course if the ghost was really feeling malevolent, could it superimpose itself over someone and smother them in the ectoplasm?

Giron: Yeah. I figure if a ghost really wanted revenge it can figure it out.

Q: If a ghost can manipulate objects, it can throw them.

Giron: Of course. And if they go through electricity like the TV or the phone, they can just electrocute you.

Q: But would this accomplish anything? Then you'd be with them.

Giron: [Laughs.] That's true. Then you get into the whole thing about sometimes there are ghosts and sometimes not, and how come some ghosts are here and some are in Heaven and Hell and other places where people go. You can go crazy trying to think of all the compartments you're supposed to be in once you die.

Q: To get a little bit back to the subject of writing.

Giron: [Laughs.]

Q: Meanwhile, back at the topic…what are your writing methods or habits like? Do you start with character? Do you start with idea? Do you have to outline?

Giron: I do have to outline because I am at the point in my career where I can write a proposal and get a contract. In the old days I was one of those people who would have to write the book first and send it out. Now I can actually outline sometime and send it in, and it will get a yea or a nay. So, yes, I have to outline, and it's hard. I tend to be character-driven. My ex-husband used to complain all the time, "Oh you've got great characters, but they don't do anything." [Laughs.]

So for me the whole issue has always been making plots compelling and modern and fast-paced. Yes, I tend to be character-driven. Today I was on a panel about disgusting things, and I said, "I don't set out to be disgusting. It's what my characters do." Sometimes I even pull back from what they do, because I don't want to be over the top or super-melodramatic. But I tend to be character-driven.

And I also tend to be headline-driven. In *Borrowed Flesh*, when I was writing the book, I kept seeing all these documentaries about these cults of urine-drinkers, so I threw that into the book because I thought it might be an interesting subject to explore. In *The Birds and the Bees* I was watching documentaries on the lost children of Sudan. So I have a character who is one of the lost boys who came over to America. *House of Pain* was directly ripped from the headlines of the Paul Bernardo/Karla Homolka case in Canada, in St. Catherine's, with the bulldozing of the house. My book opens with the bulldozing of the house, and then the couple comes, and what happens if you build your dream-house on the remnants of a serial-killer's house? So it's a combination of character and headlines and things I find fascinating.

Q: How do you explain this to the "normal" people?

Giron: [Laughs.] You mean like your parents?

Q: Start with your parents. How do you explain what you do to normal people?

Giron: Yeah, it's like they pat me on the head and say "Why don't you write romance?" Not my parents. My parents are creative people, so they understand. But, yeah, this is part of what we talk about at panels at conventions. Especially, being a woman horror writer, do you feel a difference because you're a woman? I'll be sitting in a mall doing a signing and someone will say, "Oh, that can't be scary. You're a woman." Or, "Oh this must be romance." Yeah, if you've ever read anything I wrote, you'd know there is not a romantic bone in my body. But, yeah, it's hard to explain to people. You know this yourself, because if you say "horror" people think of *Saw*. They think of Freddy Kreuger. They think of Michael Myers. They don't understand there are a lot of elements and facets to the horror genre. You can point at Mary Shelley or Edgar Allan Poe. There is more quiet horror with horrific ideas. You say, look, there are so many levels. Give it a shot. Give it a try and see.

I know that with myself every book I write is different. I am not like *the* vampire writer, the haunted house writer. I try to do something very different with every book that I do.

Q: Otherwise it would doubtless get monotonous. You'll notice that until about 35 years ago, there was no such thing as a professional horror novelist. The idea that a writer would turn out horror novel after horror novel and nothing else was virtually unheard of. Even Bram Stoker only wrote a couple of them. So I wonder: if you have to produce 25 or 30 horror novels, will that wear out your scare circuits?

Giron: For people who are forced to write the same thing over and over again, certainly it would be boring and dull. Just this week I've been doing workshops at libraries, telling librarians what horror books should be in their libraries. I get paid to do this. It's a great gig.

We had World Horror in Canada just a couple weeks ago, and I had fifty books I'd just picked up, and I pulled some off the shelf, and I said, "Here are different types of horror." You got your small press, large press, magazines. I read them that article that's on the HWA website about what is horror, the Doug Winter idea of horror as an emotion, not a genre, and how the Stephen King phenomenon invented this genre of horror, and then there was the boom and then the glut. Yeah, being a professional horror writer is a new idea.

You see even with my own stuff that I don't do all horror all the time, because I think I would get bored if all I did was horror.

The sad thing is that I don't have the time to read as much as I used to, because I am busy writing or doing the editorial evaluations. I'm doing research on my non-fiction books, and the Tarot, and the astrology, and all this too. I think all of us have to be diverse, or we'd be really boring.

Q: I think that as most professional writers don't get much time to read, all of us are drawing on what we read early in life. The books that you read before you are twenty-five or the ones that are going to matter.

Giron: Exactly. For me it was the fairy tales, and on to science fiction and fantasy short stories—I loved all that stuff—then Enid Blyton, Nancy Drew, Judy Blume. I read everything. *The Exorcist. A Clockwork Orange.* I just read all the time. Yeah, till I was in my twenties, till I got out of university, and then I had babies, and it was writing, writing, writing. Even then I liked reading things like Jackie Collins because they're fun and weird. I read everything when I was young.

Yeah, you're right. It's very hard to find the time now. I try to make the time, of course, to keep up. Even if I don't read a whole book I try to read snippets, or at least be aware of what is going on. Also, too, as a Leisure author, I have to know what my Leisure buddies are doing and try not to be like them, but be kind of like them, for what the line is. It's difficult, because when you're writing, that's when you need to read the most. But where do you find the time?

Q: I've known writers who don't want to read when they are writing. Kate Wilhelm once said that when she is writing a novel, she won't read anything published after about 1900, because she doesn't want to be influenced.

Giron: When I am actively working on a novel, I won't read other people's books. I read non-fiction or magazines, or blogs, message, boards. Now we've got the internet. I won't because if I pick up a Clive Barker book, I'm suddenly writing like Clive Barker, because we all mimic and imitate whatever. That's why I won't read when I am actively working on a novel, because I start taking on the other styles. My thought patterns aren't focusing as intensely as they should be on what I'm doing.

Q: So what are you working on now?

Giron: I just finished doing the galleys for the *Kama Sutra* which is coming out in August. I'm whipping up some proposals. I do my horoscopes. I have some short stories to deliver. I am not working on a specific novel right now, but I have a couple irons in the fire. I am waiting for the green light on that. *The Hungarian Rhapsody* is coming out in August 2007.

Q: Thanks, Sephera.

Recorded at Eeriecon,
April 22, 2007.

S.P. SOMTOW

S.P. Somtow, whose real name is Somtow Papinian Sucharitkul, is a native of Thailand, who began writing science fiction while living in the Washington D.C. area in the middle 1970's. Some of his science fiction books are *Starship and Haiku*, *Mallworld*, and the "Inquestor" and "Aquiliad" sequences. He won the John W. Campbell Award for best new writer in 1981. But this was only one of his many careers. He has also been a leading composer of Thai avant-garde music, a musical ghost-writer, a major horror writer (*Vampire Junction* and sequels and *Moon Dance*), and he has directed two films, *The Laughing Dead* and *Ill Met By Moonlight*.

Q: So, you are not merely a well-established fantasy and horror writer, but, I understand, virtually an ancestral figure.

Somtow: Yes, it was Philip Nutman who first said in *The Twilight Zone Magazine* that I was one of the four ancestral figures of the Splatterpunk genre. Frankly, although I didn't know it at the time, I've exploited it. I admit it. I've used "Grandfather of Splatterpunk" on numerous blurbs. It's amazing to me that such a label is necessary, because actually my work hasn't that much in common with Splatterpunk, except of course for large amounts of gore. And even that—I've mellowed a lot, as far as the large amounts of gore are concerned.

Q: We're talking about *Vampire Junction*, which was a 1984 book. Twelve years ago and you're the grandfather of a literary movement that's already passed its peak?

Somtow: Yes, I would consider the entire movement to be dying in its infancy, probably because there is a limit to what one can achieve in such a narrow interpretation of the horror genre. But many of the things that I tried to do in *Vampire Junction*, like writing a novel that's structurally based on MTV videos—which is really how the novel is put together—those are things that were new to horror writing and were taken up by many people, whether they used that label or not. I think that this is now a common feature of horror writing.

Q: It seems to me that the inherent limitation in the Splatterpunk aesthetic, if we may call it that, is that once you've shown everything, you've shown everything, so there is nothing left to show. It's like bringing on the monster in the first reel, so there are no more shocks later on.

Somtow: Yes, that's why I've stopped showing things. I've shifted from the showing-everything bit to my mainstream novels, because it's a little more new there. In the book that I'm writing now, *Bluebeard's Castle*, which sounds like a horror novel but isn't, there are a couple of very intense serial-killing scenes that are just passed by in a couple of pages. The whole novel is not like that.

Q: Here again you have encompassed an entire trend in a couple of pages.

Somtow: [Laughs]. Well, yeah…One of the reasons that I had to do that is this is a novel being published in weekly installments, and so one doesn't have more than a couple pages to encapsulate entire trends in.

Q: Are you writing this like a 19th century novel, in that you turn each installment in a week before it appears?

Somtow: No, I fax it in two days before it appears, which gives them no chance to change anything. So I've managed to be really out there, and they haven't been able to do anything about it. So it's very exciting. The first novel I wrote in that way was *Jasmine Nights*, and I found myself becoming more and more daring because of the knowledge that they would print it, no matter how daring I was. So it was a real watershed for me in terms of what I dared to write about.

Q: Where is *Bluebeard's Castle* being serialized?

Somtow: It's being serialized in The Nation, an English-language newspaper in Bangkok. Now the English-speaking community in Bangkok is small, but it's frightfully cultural, so I can put in references to really obscure things and it doesn't faze them, which is one of the best things about it.

Q: You could probably slip a horror novel in on them and they'd never know the difference.

Somtow: Well, there are scenes which appear to be horror. The odd thing is that the editor at Hamish Hamilton, who originally bought *Jasmine Nights* after it had been rejected by thirty publishers, had never heard of me, because she didn't read horror or any other genre. She said to me, "I was able to read your novel with an unprejudiced eye because, of course, I don't read genre." Now that the editors at Hamish Hamilton know that I'm a genre writer, they've rejected *Bluebeard's Castle*.

They're seeing all these tiny little genre clues in it, which were also present in *Jasmine Nights*, only they didn't know that I was a genre writer. So it's a double-edged sword.

Q: Have you got a publisher yet?

Somtow: Not yet. I'm going to do what my agent did with *Jasmine Nights*, which is what until it's finished. I seem to do a lot better that way, financially at least.

Q: It sounds like a book someone could publish as horror anyway if they wanted to, like that last Tom Tryon novel, which wasn't really a horror novel at all, but was packaged as one.

Somtow: It was a Boy Scout Camp coming-of-age horror novel. It is horror, but not what you'd think of as horror.

Yes, they may decide that *Bluebeard's Castle* is horror, and if that's the way I have to go in order to pay the mortage, then so be it. But it really isn't.

Q: Apparently horror is absolutely dead as a commercial category right now. So they'll call it "dark suspense" or something like that.

Somtow: The only problem with calling it horror is that this book is hideously funny. All these awful things happen in it, like the heroine has RU-486 administered to her secretly, so her fetus can be aborted and made into a voodoo fetish without her knowledge, and so on and so forth. But she has this cynical sense of humor and is always saying things like, "Yes, it was terrifying, but I was starting to get turned on by it all." This tone is something that might make it a hard sell as a straight horror novel.

Q: Maybe the horror readership is sufficiently jaded that they'll go for it, in the same way that, on one level, Ramsey Campbell's *The Count of Eleven* is a successfully funny serial-killer novel.

Somtow: Yes. That's what I am hoping will happen that people will approach it already jaded, or else it will reach a completely fresh audience that likes to be cynical and likes to satirize itself.

Q: Do you think in terms of being a horror writer or of your work being horror fiction, or do you just let it fly where it may and then let someone else figure this out?

Somtow: I never have thought of myself as a horror writer, and it was only the fact when I did *Vampire Junction* they made me change my name that sort of split me off into a new genre.

Q: Tell the story of why you changed your name.

Somtow: It's a very simple story. Berkley books said that if I changed my name, they'd make me a star. I did and they didn't. But I didn't want to change it too much. It's been a cumulative thing, because, although each edition of *Vampire Junction* has never sold that well, all together it has been quite a large best-seller. It's pretty steady.

Q: I could see it and its sequels as a series of movies. An immortal twelve-year-old vampire rock star has a certain appeal. What a wonderful role for Macaulay Culkin at one point...

Somtow: [Makes sound of distaste.] Mary Lambert, who directed Madonna videos, and then went on to do Stephen King movies, *Pet Sematary* and so on, was very interested in doing the book. We pitched it to Paramount at one point, and the producer there was an ex-starlet. In the middle of the pitching session, she actually asked us if it had vampires in it. So this is about intelligent Hollywood can be at times. She said, "Oh. This book has vampires?" She also asked Mary Lambert who she was. It was very odd. But it seemed to me that someone who had done MTV videos—she is very famous for doing the Madonna videos, which are very erotic and dark at the same time—and was able to infuse eroticism into it, would be perfect. She really wanted to do it. She wanted to have Leonardo DiCaprio play the role of Timmy Valentine—he's a little old, but it might work quite well.

Q: There may be times when it's more important to get a good actor than to get the age precisely right. It would be very difficult to find a twelve-year-old who could play that part, and if you could get a sixteen-year-old instead, who's good, or somebody who just looks sixteen, then go for it.

Somtow: I agree completely. I've done three *Vampire Junction* books, and I am a little worried that it may be my fate to have to produce another, because sometimes I can go to a publisher and say "I have all these great ideas for books," and I start reeling them off, and they're kind of ho-humming, and then I say, "Then I'll just do you a sequel to *Vampire Junction*." Then they just send a contract. This is frightening to me.

Q: If you're successful enough, you could meet the fate of Edgar Rice Burroughs. You could end up writing twenty-five of them, and readers can predict whole chapters in advance. So I guess you need to reinvent yourself every once in a while.

Somtow: As you know, I really hate to repeat myself that much, and this has gotten me into really bad trouble as a writer. I could have written five hundred Aquiliads or five hundred Mallworlds. Or maybe five hundred Inquestor novels. I could have been as big as Stephen R.

Donaldson if I'd written five hundred Inquestor novels, for example. Or I could be like Douglas Adams if I had written five hundred Mallworld books. What can I say? I just can't bring myself to do it. There is always a strong temptation to do so, because it's the only way to make money.

Q: Well, you've had your own flirtations with the movie industry.

Somtow: [Laughs.] You could call them flirtations if you like. *The Laughing Dead*, even though it has never been released in this country, has acquired quite a reputation as a cult item, because of the various well-known science fiction writers who appear in it having their heads crushed, and so on. It seems to show up regularly at every science-fiction convention in the video room. In fact it got a rave review from Michael Weldon of *Psychotronic Film Guide*, which is the imprimatur of greatness among bad horror movies. Then I did the Shakespeare film, because I decided that at that budget I might as well do something relentlessly intellectual instead of just another slasher film, to see what would happen. They didn't go for that either, you know. I made the film and I am still looking for a distributor for it.

Q: You refer to the genre you're working in as "bad horror films," not just horror films.

Somtow: Yes, I have not been working in horror films, per se. I have been working in bad horror films, which is a completely different genre from horror films, okay? Bad horror films contain certain elements which are very important. For example, a mysterious villain who speaks in a British accent. There are certain tropes that are required. Therefore, even though my character in *The Laughing Dead* was a Mayan death god, I still had to speak in a British accent because it was a tradition in the bad horror film that this must occur.

Q: Then we're defining the bad horror film as one which is self-aware and campy, with its own aesthetic, like underground art which may be deliberately ugly and crude. All this is different from the merely inept.

Somtow: Absolutely. I am not using "bad horror film" as a perjorative in any way. It is merely a genre with its own tropes, its own sensibilities. I've tried very hard to make my Roger Corman film a bad horror film. But unfortunately it wasn't quite bad enough when it came out, because they had tinkered with the screenplay too much.

Roger asked me to do an adaptation of Bram Stoker's "The Burial of the Rats" as a film, and he just gave me a list of sets that he had acquired the use of in Moscow. They had things like the Bastille, Versailles, these huge historical sets. He said, "Well you can write anything you want as long as it has this title, and I have to have the first draft next week." This was my job interview. "You must use every single one of the sets on this list."

I thought I would create the ultimate bad horror movie in my script, but it didn't work out that way. For one thing, Roger told me that he wanted it to be really wild. But I didn't know that that was a code Roger Corman word for having a lot of tits. I thought he *really* wanted to be really wild. The script is about the young Bram Stoker being abducted in France by lesbian highwaywomen who are controlled by a mad queen who plays a magic flute and thinks she's Marie Antoinette, played by Andrienne Barbeau. The lesbian highwaywomen induct him into the ways of feminism, while sitting around being scantily-clad at the same time. We have both left-wing liberal indoctrination and hideous male-chauvinism at the same time, which is kind of cool.

Q: But in a self-aware, parodic way.

Somtow: However, most of the hilarious, pseudo-19th century dialog that I created as been replaced by rather stodgy dialog. Only a few lines, like "I am the Pied Piper's twisted sister" remain.

Q: Do you think you could move into the related genre of good horror films?

Somtow: I don't think I'd want to. I think I'd rather move from bad horror films to a completely different genre, like a mainstream film. Well, that's a silly word too. But the film that I just set up was an art film of the most owing caliber. It a cross between *Sleepless in Seattle* and *The Crying Game*, set in Bangkok. Unfortunately for me, Margeaux Hemingway was one of the three stars attached to the film, so, because she committed suicide, I was kind of fucked. I'm still hoping to get it back together again somehow. But this was a film that didn't have a taint of horror to it at all, although it does have a shaman who gets possessed by the god Shiva.

Q: There you go. That's enough. But how to you go about getting a film together. A lot of people would like to be movie moguls and make their own films, but you actually got to do it. So what's the difference?

Somtow: The first time, we were subsidized by Lex Nakashima, a well-known science fiction fan. He simply had the money, so that was great. The second time we did it, I sold five-thousand-dollar shares to my relatives and to many other people, who are now breathing down my neck, so I'd better sell the film fast. I got a $100,000 grant from Mr. Sunti who owns *Buzz* magazine in L.A. He's a Thai guy. Because it was culture, Shakespeare and all that, we were able to get a lot of people who wouldn't otherwise do a hideous low-budget film to work for us. Timothy Bottoms, who is definitely an A-list actor, signed up to do it. Other actors, like Robert Zadar, who is only known for being the maniac cop and other monsters in horror movies, wanted to do it so he can say he's done Shakespeare. So we had actors from both sides agreeing to do it.

Q: To get back to horror fiction, we're talking about all these campy, self-aware horror films, but surely you have to control such tendencies in fiction. I don't think there's such a thing as the bad horror novel.

Somtow: Not at all. I think that my horror novels are about as different from my horror film projects as it is possible for two things with the word "horror" in them to be. But there is one thing that they have in common, in a way, is that both the bad horror film and my novels rely a great deal on the hipness of the viewer or reader to catch numerous references. But in my B-movies, those references are to other bad horror films, but in my novels, they're references to works of literature. So it's a different audience.

Q: What do you think makes good horror fiction?

Somtow: I don't know. At first one ought to say that all fiction deals with love and death, and horror, of course, deals with love and death in a very more visceral way. But I haven't been scared by a horror novel in some time, so that's probably not it anymore. If it brings me even a slight flutter of how I felt as a child reading *Some of Your Blood* or something like that, then I feel that I am reading a really good horror novel.

Q: Can you get this feeling while writing something?

Somtow: I aim for that. It's happened only a few times in my writing, when I've actually become absolutely terrified. It's happening less now, I confess. That's why I'm trying to reach out to something even darker, in some ways. I have been doing a series of extremely blasphemous stories lately. I thought maybe that would work.

Q: It would to believers in whatever you're blaspheming.

Somtow: [Laughs] That's true. But even though I am sort of pan-religious these days, I was still brought up in a strict Buddhist/Anglican environment. Therefore I have two very powerful sets of traditional values working on me.

Q: The readers would be interested, so why don't you say something about your background?

Somtow: When I was six months old, my parents and I left Thailand. My Dad was in the middle of doing his Ph.D. at Oxford, so I grew up in a very dissociative way, because I actually thought I was English. One of my famous statements from my childhood was, "I'm English and you're foreigners," which I said to my parents once. [Laughs.] Then, when I was seven years old, we moved back to Thailand. I spent five years there. I had a tremendous case of culture shock, and I got out of that by retreating into a study of the Greek myths and the classics, and so on. All that is narrated in my semi-autobiographical novel, *Jasmine Nights*. Everything in the book is sort of true, although not in that order or to that extent. Things like the fellating grandmother who removes her false teeth before the act, that, for example, is true.

Q: I know you were educated in Britain, but you have lived in the United States off and on for many years.

Somtow: I grew up in four different countries, but after I started going to school in England, I pretty much stayed there until I was in my twenties. Then I went to Thailand to try to become the Harlan Ellison of avant-garde Thai music. But I got so burned out by that that I came to America and accidentally became a science fiction writer. I actually stayed in America without going anywhere much for about five or six years, but now I have a double life and actually spend a lot of time in Bangkok.

Q: What this must give you is a genuinely unique perspective, by virtue of being an outsider in several cultures at once.

Somtow: Yes, that's right. Wherever I've gone I've always been an alien, which is very frightening, perhaps the most frightening thing about my life. Even when I am with my most intimate family members, I am still culturally a little off from them. I'm the black sheep in both cultures. It's rather scary.

Q: Doesn't this make you observe more, because you take less for granted?

Somtow: Absolutely. I've always said that this is the reason that I've ever acquired skills as a writer at all. I'm spending more time in Thailand, which is really a wild place right now, has caused me to see many more things. As you probably know, Thailand has gone from sort of 1920 to the 21st century in the last ten years. It's amazingly wrenching to see the transformation occur. When I was a child, my house was at the edge of a paddy field, and right now Bangkok is the city with the highest pollution and noise rate in the world, and skyscrapers go up everywhere you look. It's got the world's largest shopping mall, strangely enough. Not only does this mall have a roller-coaster in it, but there's a little water park where you can get into bumper boats—on the eighth floor of the shopping mall. It also has the biggest bookstore in the world, by the way. I believe it is like five hundred thousand square feet.

Q: This has also given you a great sense of the absurd.

Somtow: Very much so. Let me give you an example. The last time I was in Thailand, a woman jumped off a building that my family owned in Bangkok. She jumped off and committed suicide, which is very tragic. So then my family had to have the building exorcized. So they sent a fax to the local shaman. That's how things work there. Of course they had to have a religious ceremony right away, to appease the spirit of the woman who had jumped off the building, so it wouldn't jinx the building. But these are people going around in their Armadi suits and acting very modern, and yet they do these things as a matter of course. It wasn't a special deal to them. Of course shamans have beepers and fax machines. There are astrologers in shopping malls.

Q: Just like in the United States.

Somtow: Yes and no. These astrologers actually do your whole chart. They have all the figures in their heads. They're like idiot savants of astrology.

Q: I see how you can get very powerful horror fiction this way, from the fear of never fitting in anywhere. Do you feel this?

Somtow: I do fear it and I live with it every day, so it provides an undercurrent of unease in my life wherever I am, certainly. Do we have enough material now?

Q: Just about. We have a few minutes of tape left, so we might as well use it. I could ask you the meaning of life. Or is that passé now?

Somtow: Well, it's not forty-two. In my new book *Riverrun*, I try to answer the question of what is truth, which is pretty deep. The hero is writing an essay about truth. Since it goes through lots of alternate universes, the same essay is shown again and again in terms of the latest universe the characters have fallen into. And the answer he comes up to is that everything is true simultaneously.

Q: I suppose the ultimate question then for the writer is how do you write about truth and horror and your deepest fears without laughing? Is it a good idea not to laugh?

Somtow: I always laugh. As you know, Darrell, I've dealt with some of the most profound questions of life by means of comedy in my works, even in my darkest works. Ed Bryant pointed out that scene in *Vampire Junction* where the kid's entire family has been killed and turned into vampires, and they're sitting around feasting on the blood of a corpse in a video arcade, and they say "You must become one of us now." And the kid realizes that this is the first time he's seen his family have a meal together in years. [Laughs.]

Q: Are there also things which are too uncomfortable to be dealt with in any other way except by laughing?

Somtow: Absolutely. Just because you laugh doesn't mean it's funny. Just because you're terrified doesn't mean it's not funny either. The interface between humor and horror is something that *Bluebeard's Castle* really deals with. So I'm afraid nobody is going to buy it because no one will be able to make up their minds as to whether it's a satire or a novel of suspenseful terror.

Q: It could be both.

Somtow: That's what I'm saying. It is both. But they're going to have to decide what it is before they can sell it. Maybe they'll make a funny cover and a scary cover and have them both out at the same time. That would be good.

Q: One cover could have a laughing face and the other could have embossed entrails.

Somtow: Yeah. I could see that. Or they could do it front and back, and it could be one of those display dumps where the books are facing both ways.

Q: Ultimately everything dissolves down to marketing.

Somtow: I hate to think that, but I've become pretty cynical about marketting. I've decided that I'm just going to write whatever the fuck I want to and let them decide how to package it. I've decided I no longer care, as long as I just get to write what I really want to write.

Q: That's probably a good place to stop. Thank you, Somtow.

HUGH B. CAVE

Hugh B. Cave (1910-2004) was born in England but brought up in the United States. He was a successful pulp writer in the 1930s, specializing in horror, mystery, and weird menace fiction, a contributor to *Weird Tales* and occasional correspondent with H.P. Lovecraft. He traveled to the Pacific as a reporter during World War II and lived in Haiti for five years, then managed a coffee plantation in Jamaica for some years. This Caribbean background figures greatly in his fiction, not only in his weird work, but in a bestselling mainstream novel about Haiti, *The Cross and the Drum*. He returned to the horror field late in life. His retrospective collection, *Murgunstrumm and Others* (1978) won a World Fantasy Award.

Q: Did you have any distinct sense that being a "pulp writer" was different from being just "a writer"? Was it really much different than being a writer today?

Cave: I think I can answer that by saying that I, and all the other pulp writers I ever met, learned to write by reading the masters. We read Poe, Ambrose Bierce; we read Stevenson and Kipling and authors of that nature. We wrote an entirely different kind of story than the story that's being written today. Some of the classic fantasy writers of today I find hard to understand, quite frankly, because I'm used to a story that has a beginning, a middle, and an end, and when you get to the end of it you don't have to say to yourself, "What was that all about?"

Q: I wonder if this is so much a matter of it being a different kind of story as much as it is that some of those contemporary examples are actually rather bad.

Cave: Who am I to say who's bad? I can look at a magazine today—I am not naming any names—publishing authors who are well-known today, and I can't understand their stories nearly as clearly as I could understand stories by the old masters. I don't know whether that's better writing today, but I do know this: For years I was a judge in the Scholastic Magazine High School Short Story contests. The prizes were big. They were college scholarships. I was one of three judges who read and evaluated the final twenty stories, out of thousands and thousands that were submitted. And year after year I saw those stories becoming more and more obscure, as teachers who couldn't write worth a damn were teaching their students to write what they thought was arty fiction. When it got to the point where of the twenty final stories you could only understand ten of them, I wrote and gave up the job. I said, "It's hopeless. I can't understand these. How the Hell can I judge them?"

Q: Maybe the thing to do is give the prizes to the ones you understand. I as an editor certainly refuse to let myself be snowed under this way. I think that when an author is obscure, it is frequently to hide the fact that he or she has nothing to say. If you can't understand it, maybe there's nothing there.

Cave: I said that once, when *Necrofile* asked me to do a piece for their "Dark Chamber" feature on what did I think of today's fiction. I called it a ride on the G,G, & O—gimmicks, garbage language, and obscurity. In the course of writing about how I thought those three elements had entered into fiction writing to the detriment of fiction writing, I made the remark that nobody has understood "The Turn of the Screw." There have been dozens of attempts to analyze that story and explain what it is all about. Nobody ever had the guts to say that it wasn't written well enough for to be understood.

By the way, as an addendum to that, James himself said that he wrote the story as a potboiler for *Collier's* magazine back in 1890 or somewhere about that. It was not a classic in his mind.

Well, I got a lot of letters from other writers and from a couple of editors and just a lot of readers, saying that they agreed with me on that article. Only one person wrote and said, "If we could understand 'The Turn of the Screw,' it wouldn't be famous."

Q: In editorial language, the difference is between murkiness and ambiguity. You can tell what is going on, scene by scene. You may not know what it means, but if there's a face at the window, you know there's a face at the window, or whatever. I think that is a very important distinction.

Cave: I agree with you. That's right, Darrell. You can know what's going on, but you have to put your interpretation onto it. But at the end you don't quite know what the author is trying to tell you happened. You have to sort of make up your own ending in your own mind.

Q: I think there's a place for a story which is a great puzzle, like the ambiguities in Hawthorne.

Cave: I agree. All right. I'll back down on that. But there are stories written today that I won't back down on. Here's an example. When *The X-Files* first came on television, most of the plots, almost every episode that I saw, was based on an old pulp-paper plot. They were from science fiction magazines. They were from *Weird Tales*, but they were familiar plots. They were good stories. They had a beginning, a middle, and an end. And *The X-Files* became one of America's top TV programs.

Today, when I see *The X-Files*, I don't understand half the episodes, and I don't think the authors understand half of them, because they are now writing today's type of fiction as a TV show.

Q: I think they turn the logic button off.

Cave: You said it better than I did in fewer words.

Q: One wonders then why so many people look down on pulp fiction. It had considerable virtues, particularly in the areas of clarity and directness. But wasn't it even true that in the '20s and '30s people sneered at pulp fiction? Maybe this is misplaced.

Cave: One mistake that's made about pulp fiction, and I've had it made to me in letters from people, is that people think pulp fiction was written for kids. It wasn't for kids. It was written for grownups at a time when you didn't have National Geographic on television. You didn't get to see any faraway part of the world unless you went to the library and looked at Atlases and travel books. Pulp fiction took you to the jungles of Borneo and it took you to the North Pole, where you never had a chance to go in those days. You traveled by ship if you traveled anywhere, and it took you forever.

Pulp fiction wasn't written for kids. The kids read *American Boy* and *Boy's Life*. I wrote for those, so I know. I certainly didn't write my stories for kids, and I don't know any kids who read them. My other point is that pulp magazines, like any other magazines, had good writers and bad writers. The best of the pulp writers had no problem moving up into magazines like *The Saturday Evening Post* and *Redbook* and *Collier's* and *Liberty* and *Esquire* and *Good Housekeeping* and *Ladies' Home Journal*. A lot of us did that. I moved out of the pulps and sold three hundred and fifty stories to the slicks, and a lot of other writers sold to the slicks. There were other writers who did not move out of the pulps. So I think I make myself clear that there were good writers and bad writers in the pulps, as there are in any magazines.

Q: Did you find the pulps limiting in what they would allow you to do? Someone like Lovecraft or Clark Ashton Smith would have complained a great deal about the limitations of the pulps. Both seem to have felt that there was a limit on how subtle or atmospheric a story was allowed to be. Did you experience anything like this?

Cave: I'm not sure. As a matter of fact, when I take up one of my pulp stories to be reprinted today in an anthology, I like the privilege of being able to go over it and eliminate certain words, certain phrases. You know what I mean. They're not politically correct today. Or not nice today. Or not considered polite. So I think there was a certain freedom in the pulps, simply because of the time that they were published, that we don't have today.

Q: I'm thinking in the sense of subtleties of psychology. We've all read pulp stories in which the hero has to be utterly heroic without doubts or flaws. I'm thinking of, particularly, the very formulaic material in the Clayton *Astounding*. The stories had one-dimensional characters and so much prescribed action that nothing happens. Did you find that sometimes the editors insisted on stories being fast-moving and superficial?

Cave: I didn't. For one thing, I didn't write science fiction, where most of that happened. I got into fantasy, and I wrote a lot of fantasy, and I wrote a lot of—what do they call it?—*Terror Tales*, *Horror Stories*, *Dime Mystery*. There's a name for it.

Q: The weird-menace story.

Cave: I wrote a lot of that, and I wrote adventure stories. But I always tried to get characters that interested me. I wrote stories about people. I learned very quickly when I moved into *The Saturday Evening Post*. I had lunch with Ben Hibbs one day and he said, "One thing you have to be sure of, Hugh Cave, is that your hero, in any story we publish, has to be someone we'd allow in our front door to talk to our family. We don't want stories about people that are not nice, that are not decent, that are not acceptable in our homes."

Now the pulps didn't care about that. They just published action stories with a good plot.

Q: Didn't you find, say, *Terror Tales*, far more limiting than, say, *Argosy* or *Adventure*?

Cave: For that type of story, yes, you're dead right. If you saw in that type of story what appeared to be a mad gorilla chasing a pretty young woman down the street, that mad gorilla had to be Uncle Charlie in a monster suit. Whereas in *Weird Tales* and in *Strange Tales* or any magazine of that nature, he could be a mad gorilla or he could be something weird, something unearthly. In other words, nothing occult, nothing supernatural could be the answer to a story problem in the weird-menace pulps. Everything had to be logically explained. Sometimes they were hilariously explained at the end.

Q: This may be why people today read a lot more material from *Weird Tales* than from the weird-menace pulps.

Cave: I am sure it is. They were a better type of story. And nobody—well I won't say nobody, but very few who wrote for the weird-menace pulps are respected today the way Lovecraft is and the big names from *Weird Tales* are, for instance.

Q: Did you have the sense at the time that *Weird Tales* was a special magazine and not just another pulp?

Cave: Yes, I did. I wrote for many other pulps before I had the courage to attempt to sell anything to Farnsworth Wright.

Q: But you did sell to him relatively early.

Cave: I think it was 1934. I'm not exactly sure. My mind isn't that clear at this moment, in this crowd. I sent Farnsworth Wright a story called "The Brotherhood of Blood." It was a vampire story, one of three that I've ever written of any length. As I remember, he asked me to make one or two very small changes in it, and he bought it, saying he liked it, and the magazine comes out and it's splashed all over the cover. It was my first sale to Farnsworth Wright. He gave me the cover.

Q: So he must have had a great deal of faith in you. What was Farnsworth Wright like to work with as an editor?

Cave: He wrote letters. He asked for changes now and then. Nothing personal ever came out to me in any of his letters. He said, "This is a bit too horrendous for me," or "I like this one very much." Very short letters, and I think that even then he had trouble with Parkinson's Disease. He used to type his signature.

Q: Did you ever find him sometimes arbitrary in what he would buy? What I am thinking of is the depiction of Farnsworth Wright that comes out in Lovecraft's letters, as opposed to what everybody else said about him. Lovecraft does not speak well of Wright, in private. But everybody else I've ever encountered or ever read anything by thinks very well of him. But Lovecraft apparently found Wright to be capricious in what he would buy and what he wouldn't. Did you ever find any of that?

Cave: I didn't send that many stories to Farnsworth Wright to know if that's true or not. I don't remember ever getting a nasty letter from him. I know he rejected three or four stories, but then, in the beginning, I sent him only rejects from *Strange Tales*. Everything that I had published in *Weird Tales*, which was paying a cent a word on publication, had been seen by Harry Bates of *Strange Tales*, which paid two cents a word on acceptance. But that doesn't mean that what Farnsworth Wright bought was a poorer story than what Harry Bates bought. It just means that Harry Bates got first look at almost everything in the field at the time, except from Lovecraft. Lovecraft never tried to sell to him, as far as I know.

But Farnsworth Wright got first look at everything Lovecraft wrote, I think. So he was bound to say, "This isn't as good as you could have done yesterday," or whatever.

Q: Lovecraft made a comment somewhere in his letters that he read an issue of *Strange Tales* and found it to be a formula-action magazine with little allowance for atmosphere, and so he didn't think his work very compatible with it. But some recent scholars have suggested that Lovecraft did submit some work to Harry Bates, and may have even written "The Shadow Over Innsmouth" with *Strange Tales* in mind, because it has a long action sequence. But his perception was that *Weird Tales* and *Strange Tales* were very different magazines.

Cave: Somebody, and I can't remember who, who knew Lovecraft, told me once that Lovecraft would send a Farnsworth Wright reject to *Strange Tales*, with the little red dots that Farnsworth Wright would always put on a manuscript when reading it. He did this, apparently with a red pencil in hand. Lovecraft would sent the manuscript right off to Harry Bates, and it said right across the top of it, "This is a Farnsworth Wright reject."

Q: Did you ever know Lovecraft?

Cave: I never met him, but I wrote to him two or three times, when I was supposed to be the Rhode Island president of the American Fiction Guild, I think it was called. It never came to anything. It was an organization started in New York. They asked me if I would be the Rhode Island president and as such I wrote to H.P. Lovecraft and asked if he would join. He wrote back and said, as I remember, that he wasn't interested. Then we exchanged a couple more letters, that's all. I happened to make the remark that—who was it that said, "Nobody but a fool writes except for money"?

Q: It was Doctor Johnson.

Cave: Yes, Dr. Johnson. And I quoted that remark in a letter, and Lovecraft wrote about me—What did he call me?—a philistine, or something? In other words, just a money-making hack.

Q: I would imagine that after a while that there must have been easier ways to make money, and you wouldn't have stayed with fiction your whole lifetime unless there was more to it.

Cave: You have to remember that in days when I was writing for the pulps in the mid-'30s—at 19 years of age, I was earning five thousand dollars a year as a pulp writer. If college graduates were lucky enough to get a job, they were paid about eighteen or twenty dollars a week. You could buy a brand-new Chevrolet in those days for under six hundred dollars. If you do a little arithmetic, you will realize that today you'd have to earn over a hundred thousand dollars to equal that salary. So pulp writers were not starving to death if they did at all well.

Q: I've done the arithmetic and I conclude that even the lowest-paying pulps paid quite well. If you sold a six-thousand-word story at half a cent a word, the rock-bottom rate, that's thirty dollars, which was a working man's salary for a week. It would be the equivalent of at least five hundred today.

Cave: That's right. You're right. Most people don't realize that.

Q: But then you moved beyond pulps. Did you leave the pulps before they sank under you?

Cave: I left the pulps before they folded, before the field left me. Lurton Blassingame was my agent at the time. Everyone called him "Count." He was selling everything I sent him, by offering them to various magazines. Not every story sold the first time out, but he did sell everything I sent him. I told Lurton that I had been trying slick-paper stories. About every fifth story I had been sending out to slick-paper magazine on my own, because I knew he didn't approve of it. He told me this personally. He said, "You should be content to be a 'big name' in the pulps." But I didn't think the pulps were going to last forever, and besides, there was Collier's and *The Saturday Evening Post* and all those beautiful slicks that were paying better money and were more highly respected. So I was trying to break into the slicks all this time, and I was getting letters from editors, and I was on the verge of selling to the slicks. It just happened that one day the *Post* bought a story and I moved from the pulps to the slicks.

Q: I would think that the other place to move as the pulps were failing would have been straight into books. There was a booming paperback market.

Cave: I did that about the same time. I had made a trip through the Canadian wilderness with Lurton Blassingame, my agent, Ken White, the editor of *Dime Detective Magazine*, and a friend of mine, Larry Dunn. The four of us spent six weeks in the Canadian wilderness, canoeing just under Hudson's Bay. And Lurton Blassingame persuaded Dodd-Mead to let me write a book for young people about that trip. I did. It was called *Fishermen Four* and it was my first book.

On the basis of that, I wrote at least a book a year, to the point I've now written thirty-five of them.

Q: By way of various trips—did you ever go to many of the places described in your pulp stories? You wrote a whole series set in Borneo, for instance. Did you ever go there?

Cave: Not when I was writing those stories. I started writing about Borneo because I had picked up a book at the library all about Borneo, written by a missionary. It was fascinating. It was about British North Borneo, and, being English by birth, I thought it would be fun to write a story about a British outpost in the jungles of Borneo. *Short Stories* magazine bought it right away, and they bought a second one. When those were published, I had a letter from Douglas Dold who was the mastermind at the Clayton magazines. Douglas said he liked those stories of mine. He had personally explored Borneo. Would I like to see his notes on Borneo so I could get my background worked out in a little more detail? So he and I became correspondents. He gave me his notes on Borneo, and I used them as a background for that whole series of Tsiang House stories.

Later, in World War II, as a correspondent, I accompanied the United States Navy and the Australian Army into Borneo, when our people took back Balikpapan. And I got to see some of Borneo at that time. It was wartime, but it was a great adventure just to see what I had been writing about.

Q: Did it seem like what you had been writing about?

Cave: Actually, no. We didn't get into the jungles. We got off the beach around the Paramata Ridge, where I very nearly got killed by a Japanese machine-gunner. I dived under a jeep. He had come up from a spider-hole with a machine-gun. He couldn't quite depress the gun enough to get under the jeep with his bullets. But he made it a trash-heap on top of me, and I was under it for half an hour. So that was a close call, and I didn't want to see much more of Borneo after that.

Q: You've also written a lot of stories about the Caribbean. What was your experience in the Caribbean?

Cave: I had been out to the South Pacific as a war correspondent, and I actually loved it, and wanted to go back with my wife and my two boys, especially because my oldest boy, Ken, was supposed to get away from a Rhode Island winter. He had been suffering some sort of infection. I settled on Haiti, because I had just finished reading *The Magic*

Island by William Seabrook, and I thought it was a fascinating country. I knew its history. It's had a violent, fascinating history. So, I got hold of some people who had been there, and I wrote to them, and I moved to Haiti for the winter.

I was a photographer at the time. Photography was my hobby. I took a lot of pictures as we explored Haiti in a jeep which we took down from the United States. We traveled all over Haiti, got into Voodoo—that's a long, long story, but I had a neighbor who was a writer. He had a wife who was a photographer, and it wasn't until I had been there a while that I also found out that he was a Voodoo *houngan*. I told him that I wanted to get into Voodoo, and he introduced me to the best-known *mambo* in all Haiti, Mama Lorgina, and took me to some services of hers. Then I got to know her, and she invited me to various services. So, I was all over the island.

Q: How much were they willing to tell you, as an outsider? You may have read the book *The Serpent and the Rainbow* by Wade Davis. That seems to have revealed some secrets they never told anybody else.

Cave: I read the book. I even saw the picture. Davis was a botanist. He was a plant man. What he said about the use of various poisonous plants and the puffer-fish poison to make zombies, I tend to agree with him. I know about the plants, because I saw that done with a chicken. One time in a little shop; I was in Jacmel, I was talking to a man beside me—I could speak Creole fluently—and we got to talking about zombies. He said, "You don't believe, M'sieur?"

He went out into the yard and he picked up a chicken. He came back to the counter where we were standing and he put the chicken on the counter, reached into his right-hand pocket, took out a handful of leaves, rubbed them together, and held them over the chicken's head. The chicken sort of staggered around a little bit and fell. It was unconscious. Then he looked at me and said, "You see?"

And he said, "Watch." Then he reached into his other pocket and took out some leaves of another kind, rubbed those together, held them over the chicken's head, and after two or three minutes, the chicken began to stir, got up on its feet, shook itself, flapped its wings, and flew out the door into the yard where he got it from. He said, "You see, M'sieur, there are such things as zombies."

So I believe that. As for Davis, and some of the other things he picked up around St. Mark, the secret societies and so on, I spent a lot of time in St. Mark, and they were just Congo societies. All this mysteriousness that he wrote about, I tend to doubt. He didn't speak Creole. He had an interpreter who was the daughter, I think, of a Port Au Prince Voodoo *houngan*, one who kept his *hounfor* open for tourists. I think she told him what he wanted to hear, and if that isn't so, I think he put it in the book himself, his own thoughts on what might have happened. They were simply harmless, cooperative Coumbite-Congo societies that he was talking about.

Q: I think there's a problem that anthropologists always have, which is that wherever they go, the locals have them on. An anthropologist will seem to believe anything the natives tell him, and it can be great fun to get this strange foreigner to believe all sorts of preposterous things.

Cave: I think that may be the truth there. As I say, I think he may have been dead right about the use of plant poisons, and so on, because he was a botanist, and he was a professor at Harvard, so he would have known what to expect in the way of plants in Haiti. I saw at one time a book made up by a priest who taught at the College St. Martial, and it was about 280 pages, and each page was a poisonous plant of Haiti, with a watercolor drawing he had done himself, and a description of the plant. He told me that there were more than that in the way of poisonous plants in his country. This was a man I knew well, I traveled around Haiti with. He used to get into my jeep and take off his white robe, and we would just be a couple of guys exploring the country together. I believed the book.

Q: How did the Haitians react when they found out that you wrote supernatural fiction?

Cave: I don't think they knew it. I was there to write a book about Haiti. I didn't tell them what else I had written. You didn't have to. You were talking Creole to them anyway. They never would have read any of those books in English. Most of my experience in Haiti and most of my research in Haiti was done in the mountains, by jeep or afoot or on muleback. I walked across Haiti, from one end of the island to the other. I traveled to these places sometimes several days on muleback with this same Father Henry Smith.

Q: You must have encountered a lot of good ghostly lore while you were there.

Cave: I had a lot of fun and I wrote the book. I had a contract for it by that time. After my first year in Haiti, I went back to the United States with the photographs only, handed them to my agent, Lurton Blassingame, and said, "Can you find me a publisher for a book on Haiti on the strength of these pictures?" I had written four very successful war books. They were on the bestseller lists in New York for quite a while. On the strength of those war books, as a correspondent, he got Henry Holt to say, "Yes, go ahead, let him do a book on Haiti." That meant I had to go back there, because I hadn't done all the research I needed to. I spent five winters in Haiti, the best part of five years, actually. Then I wrote that book. It was in print for sixteen years, by the way, that book on Haiti. It was called *Haiti, High Road to Adventure*. Doubleday liked it so much that they asked me to go to Jamaica and do the same thing on Jamaica, and I did. I ended up buying an old, run-down, 550-acre coffee plantation in Jamaica and spending the next fifteen years restoring it.

Q: Have you been back to that area recently?

Cave: I sold the coffee plantation in 1975 and I haven't been back since, because Michael Manley in Jamaica moved in with his Socialism and made a basket-case out of the island.

Q: In recent years you have moved back to writing supernatural stories, the *Weird Tales* sort of thing. Is this a return to a first literary love?

Cave: The first novels that I wrote were about Haiti. They were mainstream novels. *The Cross and the Drum* was a double book-club selection. It was a Literary Guild bonus book and a Doubleday dollar book club book. It went a half a million copies, which in those days, before Stephen King, was very respectable. That was about Haiti. Then I wrote two more mainstream novels about Haiti. Then I got involved in *The Saturday Evening Post* and *Good Housekeeping*, because they were paying wonderful money in those days. When the *Post* finally closed up, when Curtis sold it to that medical company that carried it on, they were paying me over three thousand dollars for a short story. They started me at eight hundred. After forty-three stories, they were paying me close to thirty-five hundred. *Good Housekeeping* was doing the same thing. I was making a very nice living writing for the slicks. But then they folded. The slicks went out as markets for fiction. Like today, these magazines for women, all they're about is how to make your boobs bigger and your butt smaller. They don't use the fiction they did. *Good Housekeeping* used to use five or six stories an issue. *The Saturday Evening Post* every week had five or six stories and a serial. There's nothing like that in the market today. You can't make a living writing short fiction today, at least as far as I know.

So I went back to books, and my first love has always been the *Weird Tales* kind of thing. The first novel was, again, a story about Haiti, *The Legion of the Dead*. It was about zombies. Then I wrote *The Evil*, another book about zombies, and *Shades of Evil*, and an occult story about Florida. I called it *Nebulon's Children*, so they promptly called it *The Nebulon Horror,* because of that book about Long Island with "Horror" in the title—what was that?

Q: *The Amityville Horror?*

Cave: *The Amityville Horror* was a big, big book at that time. So they changed my title from *Nebulon's Children* to *The Nebulon Horror*.

Q: The horror field presently seems to be contracting, if not collapsing. So what do you do now?

Cave: For the past year, I haven't done any writing, because my dear wife Peggy found she had cancer and went under chemotherapy treatment. After a year of my being caretaker, she's just now recovering. I haven't felt like writing for a whole year. So when I do go back to it, I presume I will write some short stories. I have a couple of novels that are screaming to get out. They're not horror novels. Actually, nothing I ever wrote was a horror novel by today's standards. Only two of them were called horror novels. Those are two that Tor published. When I begged them not to call them horror novels in the future, they wouldn't publish me, because horror was hot.

Q: Now you may get your wish, because horror is not hot.

Cave: Now I get my wish. So I don't know what I'll do next, but I have some books I want to write and they're not horror books by today's standards. They'd be more like the mainstream books I wrote on voodoo and zombieism and so on. I don't know yet exactly what I'm going to do. I'm eighty-seven. I don't have to do anything if I don't want to.

Q: You're one of the few writers still active who wrote for the pulps. Do you think you've carried on the good parts of the pulp tradition?

Cave: I've still carried on the sense that a story needs to have a beginning, a middle, and an end, and that when you're through you have said something in that story that is of some value to the reader. I don't want the reader to finish some story of mine and say, "Now why did I waste my time on that and what's it all about?"

Q: Thank you, Hugh B. Cave.

Recorded at the World Fantasy Convention,
London, England, November 1, 1997.

ROBERT WEINBERG

Robert Weinberg, who sold his first story in 1967, is one of the great experts on pulps and pulp fiction, having edited or co-edited many anthologies, such as *Weird Tales: 32 Unearthed Terrors, Lovecraft's Legacy, The Rivals of Dracula, Far Below and Other Horrors,* etc. He has collaborated with Lois Gresh on many books, and on his own written a particularly interesting series of occult adventure novels using Western supernatural lore: *The Devil's Auction, The Armageddon Box, The Black Lodge, The Dead Man's Kiss,* etc. At Chicon 7, the 70th World Science Fiction Convention in 2012, he was given a Special Committee Award for services to the fields of science fiction, fantasy, and horror.

Q: You've obviously come to be a writer from many directions at once. So, could you tell me about some of the things you were doing before you were writing, and what got you interested in fiction?

Weinberg: I think I have always been training to be a writer. At least I hope so. I went to college for nine years and have two degrees in mathematics. I could have gotten my Ph.D. but I finally said, "Enough is enough." Many years ago, when my father was alive, he said to me, "You went to college for nine years in Mathematics and you ended up a book-dealer and a writer. Do you ever think you wasted your time?"

I said, "No, of course not." I've trained all my life to be a writer, but I only spent nine years in Mathematics, but that's part of living. I think being a writer is living and translating what you experience into a story.

Q: Does it matter what you study. There is a school of thought that holds that studying just literature is limiting.

Weinberg: I think the most important thing about any education is that it opens your mind. That's a big problem these days, that a lot of people think they are open minded, but they also think that they know everything. Getting an education used to mean a lot more than just learning to memorize stuff or learning how to do an equation or build an airplane. It meant getting an education, so that you could do anything, because you're open-minded and willing to learn.

Q: So how did you get from nine years of Mathematics to a novel about zombies that ate Chicago? I remember your first novel, which I read in manuscript.

Weinberg: That was my first novel manuscript that you saw. It was never anything beyond that. But, again, I can blame it a lot on Stephen Vincent Benét. I read "The Devil and Daniel Webster" in fifth grade and I said, "Gosh! This is great!" and "I want to write this stuff." From fifth grade on I wanted to be a writer, but the only thing that detoured me along the way as the thought that I wanted to make some money in life as well.

I got into writing. I wrote when I was in college. I wrote when I was in high school. I'm old enough to have rejection slips from a lot of the famous editors: Fred Pohl, but John W. Campbell as well. I have long letters from John W. Campbell telling me what was wrong with my stories. I worked very hard at being a writer. I wanted to do that, but at the same time I wanted to be able to make some money. So I didn't get back into writing until I felt that I had made enough money that I could slide along for a while and not worry that I wasn't making a living writing, so I could just coast and write and see what would happen.

Q: I remember you being involved in Lovecraft fandom and editing *WT 50*, the 50th anniversary *Weird Tales* tribute in 1973, and things like that. We might mention the Morgan Smith adventures. But well before you were selling fiction regularly, you seem to have been keeping a hand in. I assume then that in addition to mathematics texts, you were reading a lot of pulps.

Weinberg: I devoured science fiction. I think I was a typical child of the '50's in the sense of most science-fiction fans of the time. There wasn't much being published compared to now. There were two Ace paperbacks a month in the '50's, and only a few magazines a month by about 1959: *Fantastic, Amazing, Fantasy and Science Fiction* and *Astounding. Galaxy* came out once every two months, because it went bi-monthly in 1959. That was about it. It would take four or five days to read all that stuff. Then I went out and bought everything old that I could find. I became really caught up in it. It was part of my life. Science fiction, fantasy, and horror have been as much a part of my life as eating, sleeping, and drinking for as long as I remember. I can measure things in what I was reading.

So I go way, way back. My first story was actually published in 1967. So I have been writing professionally for about thirty-five years, though not prolifically, at least, in science fiction and fantasy. I did do a lot of writing for tabloid newspapers. I wrote articles for mathematical journals, as well as trying to sell science-fiction short stories.

Q: I remember that you wrote one of Fred Pohl's "*IF* first stories," but I already knew who you were from fandom at that point, because I had read you in *Space and Time*.

Weinberg: I was a *Space and Time* early-on contributor. I think I had stories in numbers 10, 11, and 12, somewhere in there. I was involved in fandom, not terribly, terribly active, but fairly active in fandom from the time I was fifteen. I'd discovered ESFA, which was the Eastern Science Fiction Association. They would have an open meeting every year. It was not a convention. It was just a one-day, afternoon affair, and my parents were reading the Sunday *Newark News* one day and saw, "John W. Campbell to speak at ESFA meeting." I recognized John W. Campbell's name. There were John W. Campbell, Isaac Asimov, Randall Garrett, and three or four other regulars from *Astounding* who were speaking. It was 1963 and the twenty-fifth anniversary of Campbell being editor of *Astounding* from 1938. I persuaded my poor father to take me downtown so we could go see that. I wouldn't just go on my own. I went and I joined ESFA right away, and from there I got immersed in fandom. It was a natural, a marriage made in Heaven. I was president of ESFA for a while, not that long. I founded the science fiction club at the Stevens Institute of Technology. I went to a lot of Lunacons and met a lot of people, a long, long time ago. As I've said, I've never drifted too far away.

Q: Perhaps you were the way I was, you started out trying to write science fiction, but moved into fantasy and horror and found it was your more natural mode, which had been repressed in the '60s because there weren't very many markets. Was that how it was for you?

Weinberg: I think that I could lay the blame in my writing fantasy on Robert A. W. Lowndes, Doc Lowndes. I discovered *The Magazine of Horror* when it was first being published, with issue number One, and I read it. I had already been reading Lovecraft. I discovered him in *The Macabre Reader* edited by Don Wollheim, which had reprinted "The Thing on the Doorstep," and I thought that was one of the greatest stories I had ever read. Then I read "The Colour Out of Space" and I immediately knew that Lovecraft was the greatest writer who had ever set words to paper, including the Bible, the Torah, and every other religious book. Lovecraft was much better than them.

But I never thought about writing fantasy until I read *The Magazine of Horror.* I believe it was issue number 8 that published "Skulls in the Stars" by Robert E. Howard. It was one of the first Solomon Kane stories from *Weird Tales.* It was love at first read. I felt, "I have to write this stuff."

I had been trying to write science fiction since I was in high school. I had actually written some things for the school newspaper when I was in grade school. From about fifteen or sixteen on I was trying to write science fiction, though I didn't have very much of a hand for it. But when I read Robert E. Howard, I knew that science fiction was very passé. I wanted to write fantasy. I wanted to write barbarians. I wanted to write Lovecraftian monsters. I wanted to write the stuff that I wanted to read all the time. I think that is usually how most writers start writing.

Q: I remember you then had a series of stories in fanzines about a character named Morgan Smith, who was kind of Northwest Smith meets Conan.

Weinberg: He was more Northwest Smith meets Solomon Kane, because I was so impressed with Solomon Kane that I wanted to write Solomon Kane stories. I knew I couldn't write new Solomon Kane stories because I would be in a lot of trouble, so I tried to write Solomon Kane stories, but putting in a Lovecraftian setting. So I had poor Morgan Smith in a variety of stories taking place over two or three hundred years. He could be, in one story, in 18th century England, and then in another at an auction in New York City in 1965, but it was all part of this mysterious thing that was connected with Lovecraftian gods and cults of the *Necronomicon* and Nyarlathotep and the three-loped burning eye and so on. Even then I appreciated the thought that when you write a plot, it should be complex. It should be more stuff than just a to b to c. It should be a to h to j and involve the reader, hopefully, in something a little more deep than just going from one spot to another. I tried to do that in everything I wrote. So you got Lovecraft, Robert E. Howard, a dash of Clark Ashton Smith, C.L. Moore, and anybody else I was reading at the time.

Q: Seabury Quinn?

Weinberg: No Seabury Quinn. [Laughs.] As much as I enjoyed the Jules de Grandin stories, and I thought they were a lot of fun, even then I had taken courses in English literature, and also the English language, and Seabury Quinn was one of those writers who was entertaining—like Hopalong Cassidy or a Gene Autrey movie—and he served a purpose in life. I enjoyed reading his stories. But then I also enjoyed eating M&M's, things like that. But I didn't think they were a meal. Robert E. Howard was like a steak, prime rib, and Seabury Quinn was like mashed potatoes.

Q: Well before your fiction career started in earnest, you had edited or written various books—

Weinberg: I was lucky that in college I was still trying to sell some fiction, and I was contacted by Kirby McCauley, as many people were. He was just starting out as an agent, and he said, "Would you like me to try to sell your stuff?" and I said, "Sure." Kirby managed to sell a few stories for me. Again, I was a fan. I was a fan who wanted to be a writer, an editor. I wanted to do a lot of things. I had read so much and I had an exceptional memory and I usually remembered everything I had read. Kirby came to me and said, "We have this series of Jules de Grandin paperbacks. Would you be interested in editing them, because you have all the *Weird Tales* and so on?"

And I said, "Do I have to *pay* to do this?"

He said, "No, no. They'll pay you."

I was astonished. I wasn't *that* naive, but I was so excited by the fact that I could do books collecting Jules de Grandin stories. As much as I could make fun of them, still, it was something to do in paperback. I couldn't turn it down, and one thing led to another. A lot of my career as a writer and editor has come about by happenstance. I was lucky. I was in the right place at the right time. Sometimes I made my own luck in the sense that I read omnivorously, and I didn't forget it, and I was so enthused about it—I will be the first to admit I have always been enthused about this stuff, so that, when I would write articles about it, I think that my enthusiasm showed through. I think enthusiastic people—fans—are the ones who end up *doing* things in this field. We all wrote—at least all of us from that period who loved Lovecraft—articles about Lovecraft just saying how great he was, how terrific he was, and how everybody should read him. I did it too. I've gotten a little more critical as I've gotten older, but that got me into Lovecraft fandom.

Q: But somewhere along the line the zombies ate Chicago and you never looked back. The first horror novel never sold, but then you sold *The Devil's Auction*, which is in some ways an assimilation of all the stuff you'd been a fan of. Can we see it as a more sophisticated version of Seabury Quinn?

Weinberg: In some ways. Probably. I have always been a very meticulous writer in some senses, in that, actually, before I write a novel, I don't write down goals, things I want to do in the novel, but when I think of it, I think in terms of, I want to do this and I want to do that. I always like to write a complicated novel. In the zombie novel, I was just learning to write in the long form, which is something that takes a while to do. When you write short stories, you have to learn how to write 5000 words. When I first started writing short stories, I ended up with a 300 word short story that is actually a novel summarized in 300 words. Writing a novel at 70 or 80 thousand words is more difficult. You usually say, "I'm going to write a novel," and it comes out to be twelve pages. So the first attempt at a novel was the zombie book. But after I had gotten that out of my system, *The Devil's Auction* was an attempt to write a novel where the last sentence of the novel would be somewhat of a surprise. That was my goal in writing *The Devil's Auction*, and that was what I tried very hard to do. In reading it back, I said, "God, there is absolutely no surprise. It is so obvious what the ending of this book is." But over the years I have heard from many, many people who have written to me and said, "I could not guess the ending." I am astonished. I'm pleased, but I'm astonished, because I think it's terribly, terribly obvious. But it was fun to do, and that was actually my goal in it. It was not even to write a novel with a Jules de Grandin type character, or monsters, or cabalistic stuff. It was to write a novel that at the end I had hopefully done enough misdirection that the ending was s surprise, yet made sense.

Q: But somehow, despite all your fan's enthusiasm, *The Devil's Auction* didn't read like a Lin Carter novel, with a scrap of this and a scrap of that pasted every-which-way together and still recognizable. You established an author's voice that was uniquely your own.

Weinberg: Again, I can only say I tried. I am glad that you feel I have. I'd say that reading my novel, people can say, "Oh, that reads like something Bob Weinberg would write." I don't know that I've ever tried a specific sound or style as much as a specific type of novel.

Q: What's fairly unique about *The Devil's Auction* and some of its successors is the use of formal Western occultism. Most modern horror writers might mumble a few lines about the *Necronomicon* but that's about it. Your book must have involved a great deal of research.

Weinberg: I think that was one of the things that I grew up with, reading John W. Campbell's *Astounding* and *Analog*, and of course reading *Fantasy and Science Fiction*, which was wonderfully edited, and reading *Galaxy* when I grew up. It was more magazine fiction than pulp fiction. I got to pulp fiction a little later on and enjoyed it, but the really well-written magazine fiction of the '50s and '60s influenced me a real lot. So in my novels, I usually wrote about subjects that already interested me, like the Kabbalah or the Tarot deck, but I surely didn't want to be writing stuff where people would be writing letters in to the editor and saying, "Well, this guy is absolutely wrong, absolutely stupid." That was one of Campbell's priorities in life. If you wrote a science fiction story, there was going to be some stuff that was going to be just science fiction, but your science, whatever science you actually used in it, had better be right, because Campbell would know that it was wrong, and he made it real clear that he would tell you and he wouldn't buy it. I think it is because of the science fiction influence that I feel that if you're going to write a science fiction novel or a fantasy novel, there has to be a feeling of authenticity in the stuff. If your monsters are eight feet tall, and that's what you want, that's fine. But if you've going to write and say, "I went down to the meat-packing plant early in the morning," you'd better know what a meat-packing plant early in the morning looks like. I think that's the basis of good fiction in general, authenticity.

Q: Well nobody knows what a sorcerers' auction is like. Like a Pulp-Con, only larger . . .?

Weinberg: It just seemed to make sense at the time. Again, it tied in with something—I've taught creative writing since then—that I've always been a very strong advocate of. I feel that the most important thing you learn as a writer is that when you get an idea for a story, something you think will work in a story, you must try to see where you're going. If you know where the end of the story is, what you want to say at the end, and you have that when you begin, then you always have a goal. In every novel I've written, I've always known the end of the story before I set down one word. When I wrote my first trilogy of White Wolf, which was like 275,000 words, the first thing I wrote was the epilogue to the last novel, because that way I knew that the third novel, at the end, was going to have a surprise that I could work for through three books, to lead up to this surprise ending. I also knew exactly where I was going all the time, and that made life just so much easier.

Q: What if they'd suddenly said, "We want four books"…?

Weinberg: They would have had to say they wanted four before the ending of what was to be the end of the trilogy. I am sure I could have put more complication in. I still would have gone for the same ending. If after the third book, they said "We want a fourth book," they would have gotten the second trilogy I did for them, which follows the first trilogy. I'd just take some of the characters and say, "Oh, let's put them in a different situation."

Q: Are you writing fiction now? I haven't seen anything from you in a little while.

Weinberg: About three years ago I got involved, strangely enough, in writing comic books. A couple editors at Marvel read a couple of my novels and said, "We liked your novels and think that you have the pacing to write comic books. Would you be interested?" I'd always been interested in comic books from the time I was a kid on. I'd followed them, and I'd been in the business of running conventions for a long time, so I had been at comic-book conventions. I actually ran the second largest one with several other people for about twenty years. But I had never tried to write a comic book except for one or two short scripts for anthology series.

When I got the opportunity, I said, "Wow, I'd love to try it," and when I did I really fell in love with it. I think it's just the greatest stuff in the world. I have been writing comics ever since. My fiction production has fallen off quite a lot, because it's fun writing comics. I'd rather come up with comic-book proposals than fiction. But as I get older, I don't think I get less creative. I think I get more creative. Hopefully a lot of people feel that way. Lately I have been coming up with ideas that just won't work as comic books. I've been trying to think of good ideas for comic books, and I come up with ideas where I say, "This idea is great, but it won't be a comic book. It might work as a novel." So I did write a story for *Fangoria's* website that Tom Deja edits. I wrote a story called "The Church of Lost Souls." It was the first short story I've written in four or five years. That is the beginning of a novel, the beginning of what I think is a rather unusual take on vampires. I just haven't had a chance to write much more of it. I've been busy writing comics, but sooner or later that's going to be a novel. I also have a trilogy involving Frankenstein's monster, what happened after he was in the Arctic. I don't believe he died. He took Victor's body, but then he wandered off into the ice and snow, and I have a trilogy. The first book is *Frankenstein in Paris,* which my agent has been trying to sell for a while. It involves Frankenstein's monster at the Paris World's Fair of, 1888, if I remember correctly, which was when the Eiffel Tower was first shown. Thomas Edison was there, and Buffalo Bill's Wild West Show with Annie Oakley was there, and some figures from supernatural horror novels were there as well—

Q: You mean, maybe, Dracula?

Weinberg: No, no, the author of a famous novel about Devil-worship—J.K. Huysman. Huysman was there, along with the person he wrote the book—*La Bas* or *Down There*—about, who was a famous Devil-worshipper at the time who ran this cult called the Ways of Mercy, I believe. I took all these real people. Gauguin was there, exhibiting artwork in a tavern, because his stuff wasn't proper art and they wouldn't show it at the world's fair, so he rented a tavern across the street from the World's Fair and ran this huge art show of impressionists, and they did much better business there than they did at the World's Fair art show. It was just a fascinating time, and of course French nationalism and German nationalism were all rising at the time, and I wrote a novel involving

Frankenstein's monster. Unfortunately the horror field is kind of sluggish at the moment, so we haven't been able to find a publisher. Hopefully someday that will appear as well.

Q: Horror does seem to be reviving somewhat...you don't seem to think so?

Weinberg: I think we're going through a revival, but the revival is much more in small press than anywhere else. I think there is some really great stuff being published by a few small publishers who have become mainstream publishers. *Cemetery Dance* publications, for one, is doing books as good as any of the ones that were being done back in the '70s and '80s by the mainstream publishers, and oftentimes a lot better.

A lot of the other small publishers are doing stuff that they feel is worth publishing. Some is and some isn't, but the boundaries of what is considered well written has shifted as we've seen a shift in editorial, and the shift in editorial has gone from editors who actually know something about editing to editors/publishers who don't know much about editing but can afford to publish stuff.

Q: You mean the small press editors.

Weinberg: Yes, definitely. I think that good editors are a necessity for good books, and having somebody whose qualification to be an editor is just the fact that he has some money and has some space on the website is not enough of a qualification. I have worked with a lot of good editors. I've been lucky to work with good editors. A good editor will help a manuscript. Somebody who just says, "I like it" or "I don't like it" probably isn't a good editor. I think that, unfortunately, we're seeing a lot of unedited material being published these days.

Q: I've seen enough unedited material from the mainstream houses, that hasn't even apparently been copy-edited. Some writers, I am sure, just write their books, and there they are, finished. Others have to be nursed along by someone. This is perhaps the Maxwell Perkins fantasy, that somewhere there is an editor who will shape your incoherent mass of prose into a great novel. Is that really the editor's job, or is it the writer's, to shape the book?

Weinberg: I think it's the writer's job. I've had books that come back with two editorial changes and two questions, one being, like, "Really a place?" Is this city a real city, Milwaukee? Something like that. Then I've gotten back manuscripts back that have been somewhat heavily edited, and most of the time I've agreed with most of the editing decisions. Sometimes I say, "No, this isn't right." But I read books now, or short stories especially, where they story seems to be written in a language other than English. Yet all the words are English, but the grammar sure isn't. The people who have edited this seem to have been captivated by an idea. Sometimes the idea is a very good one; sometimes it's not, but in most cases I feel that with some proper editing, this could have been a good story. There are too many "could have beens" now. It used to be I read a lot of stuff and I might have liked the story idea or not, but usually I would feel that the writing was professional. I think it's an editor's job to make sure that the story reads like it's professionally written. That is not always the case these days.

Q: Are we talking about small press magazines or are we talking about anthologies from big publishers, websites, or what?

Weinberg: I think we are talking about some small press magazines, small press publishers, and a number of websites, but by no means all of them. I don't want to paint everybody and say these are all terrible. I think there are some really good websites. I think there are some really good small press magazines and some small press publishers. I do have to say that for twenty-five years I ran a book business that promoted the small press in many ways. I kept a number of small press publishers in business by buying half their print-runs for their small press magazines. When there were a hundred copies, I would buy fifty or sixty of them. If there were two hundred copies, I would buy a hundred of them, and so on, because I had faith and a love of the small press. But those were small press magazines that attempted to be magazines. So the person who was buying the stories or perhaps getting the stuff for free, whether there was money involved or not, the editor, had some sort of standards. Just because someone has a website does not make them an editor. I think that we're seeing somewhat of a dumbing down of America, which I suspect everyone talked about since it was founded. George Washington probably complained about the dumbing down of America. But we are seeing the idea that equality means that you don't change what someone has written. You don't ask them to change it, is what I should say. Instead, we're told, "this is the way they wrote it, so this is the way we're going to publish it."

Most writers can use some editing. I am not saying all writers. Gene Wolfe sure is a better writer than I would be an editor. But there are many writers, particularly newer writers, for whom an editorial comment or two would surely help their manuscripts.

Q: When we talk about any publications on the Web, I think we hastily insert the disclaimer, "Excepting anything edited by Ellen Datlow," whom we take seriously. But there are now hundreds of horror websites and online magazines. Is it possible that it is simply too easy to get into "print," so that there are people out there who think they have made it and become writers when they haven't?

Weinberg: I think you have exactly said what I was circling around. I've talked about this before, that when I started writing and it was only print, and it was mostly a magazine field back in the '50s and '60s, I knew that it was not going to be easy to become a published writer. There were not a lot of markets and there were a lot of exceptionally good writers writing for those few markets. I was competing with people like Randall Garrett, even C.M. Kornbluth, and Fred Pohl, writers who I thought were just spectacular. I was trying to sell stories, and I was very determined. I felt no shame that I had at least a hundred rejections for stories I had written before I was able to sell a story to Fred Pohl. But I worked at it. I have letters from John W. Campbell telling me, "Well you're almost there. I think your story is pretty good, but you should do this, this, and this." I would rewrite and rewrite and rewrite. I would do the stuff over and over again. I would go over it with people I knew who knew something about writing and something about reading a manuscript, and see what I could do better. It was a learning process. I think now, especially with the growth of the Internet, too many people are into instant gratification. They write something down and they want to see it published. That is not always the way to establish a reputation. What that can do is actually harm your career, because if you get a lot of dreadful stuff published, you will establish a reputation early on for being a dreadful writer. You might be a fairly decent writer if you got some experience rewriting and going through your work working on it a little harder. There are a lot of people whose fiction you can read and you say, "This has to be a first draft."

Q: There is a survey of such things in the current *SFWA Bulletin*. They talk of 150 horror websites. Most of them are being described as basically slush-pile level. Excepting something like Chiaroscuro or Sci-Fi.Com and some others that seem to be professionally edited, I wonder if anyone is even reading this stuff. Maybe the writers can be quite bad in complete privacy.

Weinberg: The other thing about the Internet is that it's very easy to get a web-counter. I don't look at them that often, but I do go to websites from time to time, and you'd be surprised how many people are reading them.

Q: Or at least looking.

Weinberg: Yes, looking. Part of the problem is this feeling that criticizing work is bad. I think we see this in schools. We don't want to criticize a child's efforts and grade them, because they'll feel like they're being looked down upon. The thing that I think was realized many years ago, and which we've gone away from, is that equal opportunity—that's part of the American Dream, and when we don't have that, we are being unfair—does not mean that everybody is equal, and everybody is capable of doing equal work. I would never say I can write a book like Gene Wolfe. I am just not capable of writing books with his craftsmanship. I would never think that I could write a humorous fantasy novel as good as something by Sprague de Camp, who I thought was just terrific. But I tried my best and I was happy with what I did. I will read bestsellers and I will say, "Gosh this guy is a great writer," or "This woman is a great writer," and realize that they write better than I do. I don't feel the least bit bad that I write at the level I do, and I want to be better. No one makes you equal just because you want it to be that way. Just because you can write something doesn't mean you can't get better at it or learn to be better. But now we're seeing hundreds upon hundreds of websites and fanzines and anything in-between where people are writing Star Trek stories and comic-book stories and Superman stories. These are fans. It's fine if this is the way they want to express themselves. But when they start saying, "My story is as good as a professional's," well, maybe it is, but just because you publish it doesn't mean that it is. There has to be something more. Too many people feel that just because they can put it on a website, that means it's professional. Professional does not mean that someone can read it. Professional means that it reads like a story.

Q: If all the stories are that bad, I wonder how many people actually read them, rather than just glance at them, which would get the counter up. There are a few writers who have arisen to some prominence out the small press—Thomas Ligotti and Brian Hopkins spring to mind immediately—but there must be many others who have published hundreds or even thousands of stories in these obscure websites, and we have never heard of them, and never will.

Weinberg: This goes back to education. I sound older than the hills when I say this, but when I was growing up in the '50s and '60s, education meant learning, being taught stuff, and not worrying too much about whether we were all equal, but whether we all got opportunities to try our best. I bring is up a lot. Ray Bradbury once wrote a wonderful introduction to Ted Sturgeon's *Without Sorcery*. People would ask Bradbury, "How did you learn to write?" He said, "I learned to write by reading Ted Sturgeon. You read a Ted Sturgeon story and then dissect it, go over it page by page and word by word and line by line." He said, "This guy's a great writer. Let me study his work and learn from him." Ray Bradbury learned very well from reading Ted Sturgeon and from other people. He didn't have to take creative writing classes. But he wasn't afraid of criticism.

Now, it seems to me that an awful lot of people are much more indiscriminate. Our level of what we think of as good writing has gone down. What thirty years ago publishers would not have thought of publishing because the book was so incredibly badly written now is routinely published.

I am not indicting editors of publishers, but we tend to say, "Well, does anybody really care if this guy writes intelligible sentences as long as he has a good idea?" I won't mention any of the bestsellers. How about if we go to non-fiction? How many celebrity bestsellers, tell-all books, are written by somebody with a third-grade education, and yet they're being published now? Years ago, you expected the book to read like it was written by a professional. Now, you don't expect that, or at least a lot of the audience doesn't.

Q: But they are often written by professionals, quite apart from the celebrities whose names are on them.

Weinberg: Well, I think the level of ghost writers has gone down.

Q: We often look down on the pulps as having bad writing. Would you say that the writing in the pulps was better than most contemporary writing?

Weinberg: I won't say it was better, but it was professional. Some years ago I was at a convention with Phil Farmer, a writer whose work I admire tremendously and who I feel is one of the great science fiction writers. Someone asked him a question and said, "You've been writing since 1946, and you've written great stories in the '50s, '60s, and '70s. What's the difference between writing now (in the '80s) and writing back in the '50s and '60s." And Phil Farmer said, "The one thing that's different is that I have to make the stories a lot dumber, because my audience is a lot stupider." It used to be that when I'd put a reference and say, "She sounded like one of the Sirens," I didn't have to put a footnote at the bottom: "The Sirens: characters from the *Odyssey*." Now the editor will cross it out and say, "No, we can't put the Sirens because no one will know what they are."

That's an extreme example, but if you read 1930's and 1940's novels by professional writers, and you start looking at their references, or at least their comparisons or their allusions, and you see that they were writing for an educated audience. Now, in my first comic book, I have the three witches appear, and they say to the hero, "Double, double, toil and trouble, fire burn and cauldron bubble." I had people write and say, "Wow, this sounds like stuff that might come from Shakespeare. Maybe it was inspired by *Macbeth*." I'm thinking, no, it's not inspired by *Macbeth*. It's taken from *Macbeth*. People don't know that. People say things like, "Your story was kind of cool, but it sounded a lot like something I saw on TV last year." I will say, "Well, actually the thing on TV last year was based on the *Inferno* and that was actually from a long, long time ago, and my ideas came from the *Inferno* as well or were at least inspired by it."

We can't assume that our audience knows this stuff. I think that anyone now who writes for an audience in their teens or even in their thirties has come to realize that you can't assume that your audience knows a lot of stuff.

Q: What we see in the horror field is readers or even would-be writers who think it was all invented by Clive Barker or Dean Koontz or fill-in-name. They know nothing about the older writers. I wonder if you couldn't turn this to your advantage and reinvent the wheel and wow them all.

Weinberg: I think you could except for the fact that an awful lot of these people don't want to read the wheel or want to read stuff that you and I found exciting or involving. I don't think too many people really want to read a rewrite of something like *The Ghost Pirates* by William Hope Hodgson, which I think is one of the greatest horror short novels. It's very, very effective. But there's not enough special effects in *The Ghost Pirates*. It would make a very effective horror movie, but I don't think it could be on the big screen anymore. It would have to be on television. It doesn't have enough blood for most horror fans anymore. It doesn't have Freddy Krueger or Jason in it either. Yet, I still think it's a great story, but I don't think that most of the audience that I write for or that most of us write for would feel the same way. It would go right past them. They would say, "Wow, this is really dull."

Q: The question then arises, who are we writing for? Can you make a career out of writing stories that don't satisfy you because you are writing for an audience less sophisticated than you are? This is not what Gene Wolfe does and somehow he's having a good career.

Weinberg: I think that we're writing for the audience that is out there, which is a shrinking audience all the time. No matter what every survey tells us about how many people are reading in America, I wonder how many of them are reading anything other than romance novels or books about how to eat more food but lose weight at the same time. I do not think the fiction market is growing. It is not growing more intelligent, that's for sure. And when we talk about Gene Wolfe, we're talking about an exceptional writer who has a reasonable-sized audience, but not somebody who is going to be a bestselling writer. The number of bestselling writers who are also literary writers is going down and down and down. The only thing that has stopped it from falling is Oprah Winfrey. I wouldn't say that everything she picked by any means was a great novel or great literature, but she tried to pick what she thought were serious novels. Now that she's stopped doing that, I think we're going to see even more of a fall-off of serious fiction selling big numbers. Remember that Oprah's books, before they were Oprah's books, sold twenty thousand copies. They didn't sell six hundred thousand copies until Oprah said, "These are books that you should read" to her audience.

If someone came along of equal popularity and started a science fiction book club, or if Oprah suddenly became a science fiction or horror convert, maybe I'd be a little more optimistic.

Q: Is the object to become a bestseller or is the object to write the best book you can and get it into print? Gene Wolfe, for example, is not a bestseller and never will be, but maybe he is doing the right thing. We might be able to avoid the term "art fiction" and be too snobbish about it, but maybe any fiction that does have its integrity is inherently elitist and we ought to just accept that.

Weinberg: I believe strongly in that you should write what you want to write and what satisfies you. I try. In my comic books, I do not write down to my marketplace, which is probably fourteen and fifteen-year-olds. I try to actually educate them a little, and say, "Look, there are other great writers," or even "Look, maybe you should read Shakespeare, because Shakespeare's themes are even applicable to comic books." But at the same time, I think Gene is one of the exceptions. While his novels are rich and deep and literate and challenging, he is one of the few people who seems to be able to still get away with it and sell such books. I don't think that he has many rivals. I think there are lot of good science fiction and fantasy writers out there, but I think that the number of people who are selling such ambitious fiction is steadily declining, and we are seeing more and more Star Wars novels and Star Trek novels. I ran a book business for twenty-five years, and when I got out of it, one of the reasons I got out of it was that I saw that branded books were becoming more and more the mainstay of the industry. In fifteen years, I'll be very surprised if there are more than three or four new science fiction novels a month that are not branded books, that are not books that are tie-ins to some multi-media entertainment conglomerate. It might be a terrible thing to realize or experience or believe, but I think we're seeing it coming true.

Q: In fifteen years many of our best writers of today—Jonathan Carroll for instance—will still be writing. I wonder if the good stuff will all be in the small press then.

Weinberg: That might happen. Let's remember that back in the 1950's, even though the pulps were somewhat dying, there were twenty-three science fiction magazine, I think, in 1952. Then for a variety of reasons, many of which are misstated, science fiction in the pulps and science fiction just about everywhere just about died out, enough so that in 1956 a well-known fan, Earl Kemp, was circulating a survey, *Who Killed Science Fiction?* People felt that science fiction was just about dead. The small presses were dead, other than for one or two people who were able to publish books fairly cheaply. The magazines were almost dead. We were only seeing three or four magazines. Doubleday Books was publishing one science fiction book a month for libraries. We were close to extinction. The horror field...I don't even want to talk about the horror field of the 1950's, because there hardly was any horror field. I can see that happening all over again.

Q: After we've been talking about how it's too easy to get published in the small press, we might as well put in a good word for the phenomenon. A writer like Thomas Ligotti could not exist anywhere else. All the short story collections of our period, the contents of which will fill the anthologies of a hundred years from now (if there are any) are all small press. Small press publishing then is our life raft.

Weinberg: I don't want to come across as being anti-small press. I feel that if anything, during a time when small press was on the ropes and almost down for the count, I helped keep it alive. Tom Ligotti, in particular, started out as one of my customers. He has mentioned this to me in several letters—this is just nonsense but he says that if it wasn't for me introducing him to the small press, making available to him magazines that he would never have otherwise seen because he did not go to conventions, that he would never have started writing. He would never have realized that there was any place to publish the type of stories that he wanted to write. I helped from my business to get Tom going in life, though I think he would have made it without my business or anything else. I love the small press. I think it can be one of the important factors in genre fiction, especially fantasy, horror, and science fiction. My last book, *Dial Your Dreams*, was a small press book, a collection of my short stories, that I was thrilled that someone wanted to publish as a book. I knew I would never get it sold as a hardcover, maybe not even as a paperback in the mainstream.

We used to complain ten or fifteen years ago about the small press publishing novels by our best writers that we felt weren't up to the quality that they were doing for the mainstream press. Now we are seeing novels in the small press from people we would never have seen in the mainstream press. I just feel that the small press is becoming too much of a vanity press. People that know what they're doing and who are publishing books by good authors are doing a great service to the field. But people who are publishing books by their friends, or are saying, "Wow, this is too extreme or grotesque for mainstream publishers" are actually hurting the field.

Q: Thanks, Bob.

GAHAN WILSON

Gahan Wilson is, next to Charles Addams, surely America's greatest macabre cartoonist of all time. His drawings have appeared in *Playboy* and *The New Yorker* for many years, and used to be an every-issue feature in *The Magazine of Fantasy & Science Fiction*. His cartoon books include *The Man in the Cannibal Pot, Is Nothing Sacred?, And Then We'll Get Him, I Paint What I See, Still Weird, Even Weirder, Monster Party,* and *The Best of Gahan Wilson*. He is also a fiction writer of distinction, the author of *Eddy Deco's Last Caper, Everbody's Favorite Duck, The Cleft and Other Odd Tales,* and more, including several children's books, which he also illustrated. He has received Lifetime Achievement Awards from the World Fantasy Convention and the National Cartoonists' Society.

Q: My guess is, you began drawing well before you began writing. Am I right?

Wilson: Yes. The drawing goes back to when I was a little tiny kid. Everybody I know, from serious painters to cartoonists to whatever, anyone who does any kind of graphic thing at any level of success, has been a doodler since childhood. They always cover their school books and notes and everything else with endless little doodles.

One time, when I held the august office of President of the Cartoonists' Society, and we were engaged in very serious negotiations with a publisher—a very big deal—and there these guys were; they were America's most distinguished cartoonists, a very formidable bunch, dealing with a very weighty matter; and I realized in the middle of this discussion—I looked down on my notes—that I was doodling. I looked around, and, sure enough, everybody else was doodling too. I knew it was hopeless. We weren't going to pull this one off.

But that's specific. Doodling is a must.

Q: You also have to be warped in some way. Presumably you drew skeletons and monsters as a kid.

Wilson: Some drawings were saved. When my parents died, I came across this little trove of drawings my mother had put aside, with loving explanations she'd written in pencil as to what I had prattled as I did these things. There was one thing which I particularly like, which was, "Horrible monster come to kill us all." And that's very creepy. I have since encountered little kids, and if they are creepy little kids, there is a spookiness about their drawing which is formidable.

The most curious one I ever ran into was probably psychotic; he was terrifying, and he did these drawings which were just…The teacher had asked me to see them. She wanted me to comment on the brilliance of these drawings, and I wish I'd conned her into giving them to me, because they were fantastic. There was one I remember of a tree stump, and an axe in it. In the back is a Lovecraftian in-the-woods type house, and it was the most horrifying thing I'd seen in my life, all done with Crayolas.

After that, you say, "Why didn't anyone do anything about it?" I don't know why. I would be very worried, frankly, if I had a kid, and he started doing the sort of stuff I was doing. But, here I am.

Q: Well, there's an American cultural prejudice that says that a kid who likes monsters and coffins and graveyards must be warped and we'd better fix him. But, of course, a lot of very creative people turn out quite well that way.

Wilson: Yeah. It's not a universal, but very often people who manage to take obsessions or fears or whatever it is and turn them into art can take what could be a very negative thing and turn it into a very positive thing. That process, or alchemy, hasn't been looked into much. People who work in this sort of stuff, in the arts, like Goya, and so on, are taking screams and throwing fits and working it into art, which is altogether mysterious; but it is positive. Occasionally, of course, there are mad artists. There's a famous English painter who did these wonderful fairies, and he killed his father and was put in the laughing academy for the rest of his life. So art did not save him, but by and large most artists that you know of who are active in this area are under control. It's work for them. They don't go out and kill people.

Q: The creepy kid who did the drawing of house and the axe will either become a mass murderer or the Gahan Wilson of the next generation…

Wilson: That's the thing. Colin Wilson has gone into the idea that the deviant, the weird person, has sort of a coin-toss as to whether he's going to become a positive or negative factor in society. There's the insistent something that's going on, and the artist turns it into a positive; but it could be very much of a negative. It's very iffy.

There are people here at the Horror Writers of America convention who think dark thoughts constantly, and their minds are working in strange, devious ways. You have these absolutely delightful conversations with them, while you're fantasizing this terrific stuff. You're crossing the street and all these one-liners come out. But you have to be careful when you're with...I don't know what you'd call them, just regular people.

Sometimes you say something, and then you realize, *uh-oh*...They look at you with this funny look.

Q: How serious are we about all this? We joke that horror writers and horror artists are deviants who would otherwise be mass-murderers, but do we really mean this? There is a school of thought that all of this is so unhealthy that what these people really need is psychiatric help, at which point fantasy literature would disappear and everybody would be nice and sane and normal.

Wilson: The big difference is that the fantasy people are not crazy. A serial killer is just a screwed-up ruin who doesn't understand the difference between what's real and what he has imagined. We'll imagine some spooky thing, but we know we're imagining it. Some fantasy writers are very open-minded about occultism or ESP or whatever, but a lot of them absolutely are not. They're very, very down-to-earth. They just don't believe in it at all. So they'll toy with these things, as fiction, whereas somebody who is in trouble doesn't realize it's fiction. This guy makes up something about this woman who is walking down the street, and he doesn't know he's made it up, and he thinks he's got to kill her because whatever he has made up is so offensive and horrible that she needs killing.

But people like that are crazy, pathetic, whereas we will make up some horrible thing and we know we've made it up, and we turn it into a story.

Q: This brings us to the religious fundamentalist's argument that it is better not to entertain these thoughts at all.

Wilson: That's the extremely negative approach. I grew up in the Midwest. I'm very fond of the Midwest, but the great problem with it is that everybody is constantly in denial, and will always say, "It's a nice day," even if it's a horrible day, or "Isn't that a nice man?" They don't really mean he's a nice man. They'll compulsively blurt it out when they've just had a horrible, hateful thought about something. They'll deny it completely. Or the Brits will say, "I'm fine, I'm fine," when they're feeling just awful. You know an English person is in absolutely total depression if they say, "I'm fine, I'm fine," real fast like that.

So, not talking about something which is actually there is stupid. It just continues to fester. So this stuff has to be looked into. In a way, although I wouldn't want to push it too far, the most interesting thing about horror artists and writers is that they have come to terms with horrendous things and handle them rather well. But that is not to say they weren't appalled by them in the beginning. It may be just a sensitivity. As children, they were horrified. They saw, or understood that things were more serious than most of their little contemporaries did, who were too dense to get it. So they had to deal with it.

Mark Twain, when he was a kid, saw his father dissected. There is a good argument that this really shaped little Clemens profoundly. All his anger with God and so on, as well as his humor. So I think trauma or heightened sensitivity is often the basis for humor. S.J. Perelman—he was a humorist, now completely forgotten—once said that the essential requisite for a humorist is an unhappy childhood. To a degree, he's right. The artist is startled into awareness in a way that other people aren't, and is forced to deal with it.

Q: There must also be a matter of degree. Your traumatic childhood can't be so bad it crushes you. No large number of great artists came out of Auschwitz. It has to be more subtle, something which enables to artist to see behind the facade of daily life. And there's something else. You didn't just go on drawing horrible monsters come to kill us all, you made them funny. So where did the transition occur between the straight-horrific and the humorous?

Wilson: I remember I was enormously attracted to Zen before it was fashionable, and still am, because it is enormously un-serious. When a person achieves insight in Zen, instead of going El Greco and looking up heavenward with a saintly, teary-eyed stare into the clouds, they sometimes laugh uproariously and slap their thighs. They get the joke. Which means no disrespect.

One thing that annoys the heck out of me is that humor is treated as a lesser art, or a lesser insight than serious insights. If somebody is unfortunate enough to be humorous, they are enjoyed and admired and that sort of thing, but it's not as important as serious stuff. If a "serious" author does something humorous, this is considered to be one of his or her minor works. There are some who've busted through this. We've mentioned Twain, who forced his way, primarily with *Huckleberry Finn*.

Horror suffers the same way. It's a cliché, but horror and humor are absolutely identical. That's not an original thought, but I think it's true. They're both jokes, of a sort.

The best definition of a joke I ever saw was that a joke is the dispatch and wreckage of the train of thought. You set somebody up to move their minds along a certain path, and then you have this little trick that you do at the end which absolutely derails them, and they laugh because they're startled. A short horror piece has the same structure. You set them up, and then you go "Boo!" at the end; and they jump, or a great revelation comes, or there's a dawning, depending on how subtly it's handled. You realize that things aren't what you thought they were. Humor says things look this way, and that instigates a laugh. Horror—the spooky person—says, no, things aren't that way; they're *this* way. The result is fright..."Oh my *God*..." It's a sudden reevaluation, looking at things under a new light.

But then all art is really that. What for me defines an artist is that the artist is someone who has an insight and is able to communicate that insight to you, so that, having experienced that communication, everything is different for you from then on. Cezanne does his landscape. You see that landscape, and if you really get what he has done, even subliminally, you will never look at a landscape the same way, or tree branches, or apples on a table. He's changed it for you. He's seen something and been able to communicate that insight. That transforms you.

Q: It's more than just a surprise. It seems to me that the best horror stories are the ones which are just as horrific the second time you read them. The way you tell a bad one is that, the second time around, it's like a spent match. So there must be more than a surprise or a joke.

Wilson: Obviously the difference between a joke and humor is the same as the difference between a "Gotcha!" ghost story and a haunting ghost story. Humor gives you this lingering re-evaluation which is always with you. A really good spooky story does the same thing too. It alters your focus. But no, I use the joke to show the basis of both. You switch the mind. In a very crude version, you switch it abruptly.

In Buddhism there is a word they call which is usually translated as "suffering," and it is applied to all of life. It isn't really suffering; it's unsatisfactoriness or not-quite-rightness. It's that you can't quite get it right. No matter what you do, it's always a little bit off. You're trying to force life into a certain channel, and you're never quite there.

In humor, you're pointing that out. Thurber was all about that. You try to do something, and it's always askew. He would just increase the askewedness. The little Thurber man would go wrong. The crudest example is the banana peel. That's the basic joke. You start with that. The fellow wants to cross the sidewalk, and instead, crash, he's on his butt. It's very heavy-handed, but still it's quite a respectable joke. You can go on from there and end with all sorts of wonderful, subtle, cosmic humor.

It's the same with horror. You can start with "Ghaaa!" There's this awful thing that makes you jump by popping out of a closet. But if you turn the rheostat and have this dawning kind of insight, it's still "Ghaaa!" but it's much subtler and more moving. If it's the sort of story you're talking about—Machen, let's suppose—the same chill comes over you every time. Every time you reread somebody of that caliber, you're led a little deeper into his insights. It's a meditational sort of thing. It's inexhaustible. Each time it gets a little scarier.

Q: It may be the absence of realistic pain which makes the difference in this case. The guy with the banana peel slips and does a Laurel-and-Hardy style bounce. That's funny. But if his skull splits open and there's blood and brains everywhere, that's quite another.

Wilson: I did a thing long ago, for *National Lampoon* in its glory days, in which I had the cartoon characters who would get into accidents and be hideously injured. It was quite good. It was very effective graphically. Mickey would fall and his little black skin would split and you could see his skull. He'd be permanently damaged.

Yes. You can have rubber people and you can have real people. That's the thing that the Moral Majority and the like don't seem to understand. When there was such a fuss about these silly little cards which are Serial Killer Cards—Good grief! If our children have these cards they'll turn into serial murderers. They just underestimate pathetically what a serial murderer is, and how awful and how completely different from ordinary people he is. These guys are just incredible. But you don't become a serial murderer because you see some trading cards. Such a claim reduces the phenomenon to a completely silly level.

Q: I am sure there are people out there who believe that all horror writers are in league with the Devil anyway. Well, aren't we?

Wilson: Yes. All artists are dangerous. These people are perfectly right to feel threatened because they can't stand being questioned. So they are always under threat. The great authority-based institutions, be they religious or scientific, are always apprehensive because they cannot stand people who come along and say, "Now actually this is just something you've made up here."

There's no reason why first base should be to the right of home plate. It could well be to the left of home plate. It just worked out that way. Anybody who gets nervous about that kind of insight is going to get nervous if somebody comes along to make a joke about it. Lovecraft scares the bejezus out of them. They want constant assurance. They've live in this fragile little world and they want it to be un-fragile, and they're out of luck.

Q: We're subversive. I think we're rather proud of it too.

Wilson: Yes.

Q: Let's talk about your actual writing. What led you from cartooning to writing fiction?

Wilson: I have always liked the cartooning form. It is essentially very literary. It is a part of a kind of narration. A good panel cartoon has a past and a future implied, rather nicely. It's just a moment in a continuing story, if it has any depth of solidity. When I was in the Art Institute of Chicago and learning my basics, I took a Fine Arts course which was just excellent—but at the time the Fine Arts world was completely dominated by abstract, non-objective art, which was a perfectly tried and valid form of painting and sculpture. But it was interested only the plastic qualities of painting or sculpture. They wanted no subject-matter. You were just to deal with the properties of the flatness of the canvas and the paint on the canvas, and that was that. They tolerated Cezanne and Goya for their painterly qualities, but they did not like any of what they called "literary" aspects. There could be no implied story. It was just paint on canvas. I was in trouble there, with these people. I was tolerated—and I continue to have very good friends among them—because I was a humorist. A humorist can get away with a lot: "He's just kidding around. Ha ha."

But, really, I didn't believe what they were saying. I thought it was malarkey. I continue to think that. I, by nature, prefer painting or sculpture that has literary connotations. I do not maintain that this is the Way or the Truth or the form preferred by God, or anything like that, but, by me, I like it best that way.

Cartooning is very definitely in that bailiwick. So, in the classic panel cartoon with a caption, if you take away the caption, the cartoon doesn't make any sense; and if you take away the carton, the caption doesn't either. It's a two-legged beast. It is a wonderful demonstration of this literary-visual combination working together. It's hardly the unique to the cartoon, but, contemporarily, cartoonists, dadaists, and surrealists make the most obvious, direct use of it.

But the Egyptians were extremely into this sort of association. Their paintings and sculptures were constantly like this. Their language was based on an analog form—it turned digital, but it started out with drawings of things, and then these drawings became vocal effects, but there was still a visual base. The Chinese have the same situation. Their characters are visual puns. You can do all kinds of double-entendres with them. They do it constantly. You'll have a mural which will take a character from a word and blow it up into a full figure. Or in hieroglyphics, they'll have words which are similar phonetically, so to show that one refers to a human quality and the other refers to tables, there will be a tag at the end, to show you that this one is about people and that one is about furniture. They'll take that tag-thing and blow it up as part of the mural.

So, very early I was writing horrible little stories, which were about the level of Lovecraft's juvenilia, but it was always in tandem with art. I'd do little books and illustrate them. And I did a comic strip when I was in grade school somewhere: *Drippy Dan, the Detective*. This is the first time I've ever mentioned this. Drippy Dan would just go on and solve little cases. It was in the school paper. I suppose that was my first published work.

Q: I imagine Drippy Dan oozing like some Lovecraftian horror.

Wilson: No, no connotation like that. It was just like Mickey Mouse or Donald Duck or Horace Horse . . .

Q: No ichor, no tentacles.

Wilson: No, no . . .

Q: Did you grow up reading *Weird Tales* and other pulp magazines and want to write that sort of thing from the start?

Wilson: Yes. The earliest stuff I read was comic strips. An enormous early influence was Dick Tracy by Chester Gould. He was a huge influence, because his stuff was extremely macabre. I was terribly disappointed with the Dick Tracy movie, as were many, because they made it into a Goodie Two-shoes kind of thing; whereas Gould was very scary. He was horrific. People bled and died hideously. There were dead bodies rotting, and all that kind of stuff. I loved it.

And, *Little Orphan Annie*'s Harold Gray was also extremely good. He did horrible stuff. He would do the shock and shudder deals. Daddy Warbucks had two main assistants, Punjab, an Indian fellow, and The Asp, who was a snaky character, vaguely Oriental. At one point Gray brought in another character—I can't think of the name right away—who was a relative of The Asp, and had the same sort of characteristics. But he was the younger version and had a nice little sneakiness of his own.

Through several adventures this character integrated into the whole team. You got used to him. He had fun. There was this business where they were going after these fiendish fellows. Gray had these pursuit panels, where you'd go deeper and deeper into some environment. I think this particular sequence involved a lot of shutters. It was quite good. And suddenly, one of the bad guys pops out and stabs this character in the gut and he falls dead. That's it. It was like Janet Leigh getting killed in *Psycho*. It was very shocking. Gray knew just what he was doing. He brought that guy in there and developed him as he was leading up to—pow!

So that was very heavy, and slowly I came across the written stuff, Poe from early on, and the pulps. I was hooked totally.

Q: When did you start to publish fiction? The earliest I know of was stories in *Playboy* in the early '60s.

Wilson: I did a bunch of stuff for *Fantasy & Science Fiction* before then. Probably that was the earliest.

Q: I can well imagine many of your stories as cartoons. They're short and they built up to some situation you could easily draw.

Wilson: Sure. Some of them are very short. I did fables at one point, and they were very succinct and very cartoony. Again, I have no problem with crossover. When I'm writing, I visualize the scene, but it's perceived via words, so it's a different kind of visualization. But it can flow back and forth.

When *Classics Illustrated* started up again, they hired me to do Poe. They wanted to start off with somebody who was known outside of the comic-book area, so they could get some publicity. So I illustrated some of Poe's poems. I thought I knew poetry quite well—I could recite his poetry as a kid—but not until I gave myself the job of illustrating these poems did I get some insights I had never had before, by the process of turning them into illustrations. When you do an illustration, it's a very interesting effect. When I read, I don't have an inner screen. I just do this mysterious thing of reading. I am not consciously seeing stuff on a mental screen. If I'm to illustrate something, I then activate my visual talents, and bring the material outside, onto a piece of paper. In the process it showed me images in Poe's poems which I didn't know about. I hadn't realized, for example, that in "El Dorado," that the knight is going on after death. I didn't really get that. Poe had him die, then go on undeterred. You know: *over the mountains of the moon, down the valley of shadow.* You boldly ride, if you want to go to El Dorado. That means don't be stopped even by death. You've got to keep right on going.

And when I drew "Annabel Lee" I found myself drawing this man with this corpse of a child, and I realized that what we were dealing with was this grownup who was lying by the side of his darling, his life and his bride, who is a little kid. It's extraordinarily touching, and horrific too. But until I drew it, I didn't know about it. That's another mystery.

But, sometimes when I'm writing, I will look up and make a mental screen. I did this story for *Masques* about a guy who finds out about sea gulls, how they're organized and so on. He goes after them because he feels that birds shouldn't be getting out of their rightful level. He kills his wife and they get back at him. At one point he awakens and opens the window of his hotel window—his wife is this great fat creature, and she's been in the water and now is even huger, and all these gulls are holding her body up and flapping in unison—and he looks out and sees this great, blimp-thing floating in the moonlight. For that, I turned on the internal, mental screen to visualize it. I would constantly describe the thing as I could see it, and I would constantly up the visual. But, very often when I am writing, I don't have a conscious visual image. How about you? Do you have a conscious visual image?

Q: Most of the time, I suppose I do, though I don't draw all that well.

Wilson: But you see something. I see something and I hear something. Hearing the language is as important as the imagery, but I think it's a balance between the two. I think probably the truth is that we are doing more visualizing and audio-fantasizing than we are ordinarily aware of. But I don't see any particular wall between them. In the movie stuff, I'm mixing the same completely. I'm still telling the same story.

Q: What movie stuff?

Wilson: I'm doing a short for Twentieth Century Fox, which is called *Gahan Wilson's Diner*, and it is a Gahan Wilson cartoon. It looks just like one due to the new electronic miracles. I can do all these strange things with color and cross-hatching and so on, so I can produce visual effects which wouldn't have been possible before without—or even with—unbelievable expense. Now I've gotten involved with Disney and with Universal. Whether these things will actually end up being movies is, as always, totally problematical in Hollywood, as I am sure you know. But, so far, so good. But Spielberg and Amblin are negotiating. I designed a project for them which they seem to like very much. I hope they work. I would have a lot of fun with them, I'm sure. But, that's the movies.

Q: Would you have the inclination to write a full-scale horror novel, not an item like *Eddy Deco's Last Caper*, which depended heavily on its graphics, but a three-hundred-page, prose horror novel?

Wilson: Yes. I'm committed to do one, too, for Tor. I have it all worked out, but because of this aforementioned movie stuff I haven't managed to get around to it. I'm going to have to dive into it and just stay with it for a good stretch, at least. I find that if I am to do any writing, I have to get it done at a clip, without interruptions. It's very difficult to do something, then put it away, then haul it out and start it up again, put it away, and so on.

It's a spooky story. It's like these short stories I do which take place in a place called Lakeside, which is really Evanston Illinois in the past. It's a vague past, just childhood, not a date. You are a contemporary and you are remembering back when you were a kid. In these Lakeside stories they encounter various horrific events. In this one it's a big, big super-villain who is historical. I use him in a way I won't go into. He's there, and a kid encounters him, and the kid's mother and father have a conflict between them. Needless to say the forces of good triumph over evil in the end. But it's serious and the whole point of the thing is for me to follow a classic format, an escalating confrontation, and many horrible events occur, and finally the beast is brought down. There will be humor in it. I can't imagine it not having humor in it. But the attempt will be to scare you. It'll be a roller-coaster ride.

Quite nice.

Q: Is there a title for this yet?

Wilson: The working title is *The Child Stalker*.

Q: What else are you working on these days?

Wilson: I have been doing stories for anthologies and continue to do them. I am doing one for an anthology Zelazny is doing, about gambling. It's a nice, sinister, Somerset Maugham kind of story, about a casino, only very spooky and supernatural. It's got some cute interplay with the characters, and it's very visual, because I am constantly evoking mental images of this casino. It's on the coast in Portugal, this ornate, rococo thing. I remember being in such a place and thinking it looked very much like one of those fancy, wedding-cake tombs. So that's part of the feel of the story. And there are these movies, and of course the cartoons for *Playboy* and *The New Yorker*. That goes without saying. But I'll say it.

Q: Thanks, Gahan.

1998 Update:

Q: So, what have you been doing since the 1995 version of this interview?

Wilson: Lately it's been mostly West Coast stuff. As anyone who has tilled those fields knows, everything is purely speculative until the finished product actually appears on the TV or theater screen. After seven years at it I am becoming something of an old hand at pitching and development though, and appear to be moving ever upwards. Just finished a pilot for a live-action fantasy series with elaborate special effects. I had a marvelous time doing it. The whole thing is based on the look and feel of my *Playboy* color cartoons, so I am in charge of plot concept and very active in polishing the script; I sketch and OK all sets and have designed the major elements, ranging from a twelve-foot statue in a park built to destruct just such and such a way when hit by a truck toting a people-blaster (it worked perfectly) down to a "cast iron" rat door-knocker which presently hangs to my left as a souvenir. I particularly enjoyed sculpting a grotesque thing so it could be cast into rubber and floated in a jar. The series may or may not actually run but it was great fun putting it together. I even acted in it. I'm also writing and designing an animated special for cable (which in theory might turn into a series) and am deep into the same for a very splashy animated movie. Same cautionary proviso as above for both of these and for a number of other projects presently at various stages of growth. Whatever eventually happens, it's all made for many a rollicking adventure, many highly educational episodes, and a chance to play in the sandbox I've looked at yearningly all my life.

A couple of new cartoon collections, *Still Weird*, and *Even Weirder*, are out. I am also glad to tell you that at long last I have finally gotten around to putting together a selection of my short stories. I have illustrated it and titled it *The Cleft and Other Odd Tales*. Hopefully it will be out in time for the World Fantasy Convention where, I was delighted and surprised to learn, I'll be guest of honor.

The use of "Odd Tales" was my little way of avoiding the term "horror," since that label has become something of a plague, but I'm damned if I'll use "dark fantasy" or one of those absurdly pussyfootin' terms.

Q: What do you make of the fallen state of the horror field these days? Is it dead?

Wilson: Yes, horror is dead and will likely remain so as long as (and I freely confess this result is totally contrary to my innocent expectations of long ago) it remains genre-obsessed. Of course much of the fault lies in what most publishers have become: slaves of the corporations which own them, which are, in turn, slaves of their financial bottom-liners. Needless to say their major—in most cases their only—question is, "Will it hit The New York Times Best Seller List?" Worse than this, I feel, are the appallingly large numbers of writers who have leapt upon the bandwagon with exactly the same question. They seem to me like obsessed alchemists interested only in dissecting prior (financial) successes, pot-boiling and reboiling them down in an attempt to find and steal the magical formulae concealed therein. They are boring, yawn-provoking hacks with no sense of mystery nor strangeness whatsoever, who could not write a genuinely spooky line if you threatened them with a legion of pits and pendulums; but a smaller, sadder number is made up of real dreamers driven to it by lack of money and by dreary day jobs. Those puppies make me weep.

I have read somewhere your hopeful notion that something along the lines of Carter's "Adult Fantasy" series might reactivate appreciation and production of the real stuff, and approved your cunning move along those lines when you arranged to have White Wolf publish the Crawford collection.[5]

I am also glad you got the *Weird Tales* title back for your ongoing struggle in that quarter. Fight on! Wave the torch over the barricades and encourage the ragged troops! More power to you!

Of course horror stories will survive—it's more than likely that the last human communication will be one! Do by all means keep up your campaign but do not be afeerd, sar, 'twill happen on its own! Concealed under misleading wrappers, convincingly posing as some other sort of thing altogether, it'll sneak back some dark night past the publishers' winnowers and scairdy-cat critics who keep the expectation levels low and the fuddy-duddy readers who are, truth be told, afraid of true scariness—and it'll rip their freaking throats out!!!

Q: Uh, thanks again, Gahan.

---

5   Gahan is referring to a notion I floated, that the horror field could be restarted virtually from scratch, as Fantasy was in the early '70s, with a reprint series to educate both readers and writers to the classics and possibilities of the form, a horror equivalent of the Ballantine Adult Fantasy Series. Alas, I have made little progress with this idea, beyond convincing White Wolf Publishing to issue F. Marion Crawford's *For Blood is the Life and Other Stories*, a reprint of the 1911 collection *Wandering Ghosts* with one story added, which I thought at the time was a splendid accomplishment on White Wolf's part, even if they did misspell my name on the title page. Alas, I later learned that some meddlesome editor at White Wolf has rewritten and dumbed down the text without my knowledge, and also left the last page off the final story. The edition is to be avoided.

RAMSEY CAMPBELL

Ramsey Campbell is an Englishman, whose first book was a collection of Lovecraftian stories, *The Inhabitant of the Lake*, published by Arkham House when he was eighteen, in 1964. Since then he has had one of the most significant careers in the entire history of horror fiction. He quickly broke out of the Lovecraftian mold with his next collection, *Demons By Daylight* (1973) and went on to publish many stories and novels. Some of his other titles include *The Doll Who Ate His Mother*, *Incarnate*, *The Hungry Moon*, *The Influence*, *Ancient Images*, *Midnight Sun*, *The House on Nazareth Hill*, *The Darkest Part of the Woods*, *The Long Way*, *The Kind Folk*, *The Grin of the Dark*, etc.

Q: Your recent novel, *Silent Children*, is a non-supernatural story. I notice you've done some others, but the supernatural element seems to be a persistent and integral part of your work. Any non-supernatural work is, presumably, an occasional departure, not a change in direction.

Campbell: Yes, without any question at all I am going to continue to write supernatural fiction. I have certainly been doing short stories along those lines without stopping. Non-supernatural short stories from me are very rare indeed, novels less so. There was a clump of non-supernatural stuff in the late '90's, starting with *The Last Voice They Hear*, *Silent Children*, and *Pact of the Fathers*, which has a sort of mythic underpinning, but still there is nothing overtly supernatural in it. After this trio I really felt that it was time to get back to the supernatural, and I duly did, with *The Darkest Part of the Woods*. The next one from that will be *The Overnight*, and that too will be very overtly supernatural.

There was a reason for this. In the mid-'90's, my then British agent who is now nobody's agent basically said that nobody was buying supernatural horror fiction anymore in Britain. If they were, they weren't going to buy mine. I would be best advised to write something else. What she actually said was I would be best advised to write in the style of Thomas Harris. I was vulnerable enough to feel that I should do that rather than write like myself. So I did spend some time in coming up with a number of non-supernatural plots which were close to crime fiction. The last one I got at four o'clock in the morning, having turned uneasily in bed, thinking I ought to do what she said.

I began to write, I suppose, under some protest, but that only lasted for the first couple of chapters. After a few thousand words it began to feel like something I would have written anyway.

There have been, scattered throughout the novels—you know, *The Face That Must Die, The Count of Eleven, The One Safe Place,* those could all have published as crime fiction rather than horror fiction. They certainly have no supernatural element in them. At the time they certainly seemed to me to be the next novel that I wanted to write. Before very long, *The Last Voice They Hear* felt like that too. And certainly *Silent Children* did, which was one basic reason why I dedicated it to my good friend Poppy Z. Brite, because there were moments in there where I actually felt, the Hell with this, I will take this farther into the bizarre and the grotesque and the nightmarish, and if that doesn't sell as crime, then so be it. It is what I would like to do with this—to be (as Poppy has been known to quote) "stranger than you thought it was going to be?"

Pact of the Fathers was an attempt to do a pacy suspense novel. Now I am not at all certain that I succeeded very well—but well enough that it has been filmed recently in Spain as *El Segundo Nombre.*

Three non-supernatural books end to end really did feel like quite enough and I wanted to get back to what I liked most about the field which is, for want of a better term, if there is indeed a better term, cosmic terror. And so, *The Darkest Part of the Woods* is my latest shot at that. I've never really felt that I've succeeded, but I think I've probably succeeded more with that than with its predecessors, but I still have a lot to learn.

Q: Cosmic Terror is of course a term we associate with Lovecraft—

Campbell: You bet.

Q: What is the ideal you're reaching for with *Cosmic Terror*?

Campbell: Well I'd like to do something which would be worthy of mention in the same breath with "The Willows," "The White People," "The Colour Out of Space," T. E. D. Klein's *The Ceremonies* and the like. I can't imagine that I will be worthy of that company, but I can try. It's always what I've liked the most about the field, the sort of story that progresses beyond horror and terror to a sort of a sense of awe. That is something that I can appreciate more as a reader than achieve as a writer, it seem to me. But I constantly return to that old quote from Bob Hadji's magazine. Who's the chap who said this? David Aylewood, the Canadian critic, whose quote I constantly cite. His argument was a time when writers of supernatural fiction attempted to achieve awe and achieve only fear, but now they have attempted to achieve fear and achieve only disgust. It is something of an over-simplification, but nevertheless it is the awe that is worth reaching for.

A number of writers have described themselves as attempting this. Machen and Lovecraft would be two obvious examples. Machen's famous bit about "dreaming in fire and working in clay," and Lovecraft also, feeling himself under the influence of the models he was attempting to equal. Some of the best work in the field seems to me to come out of that attempt to reach what you never can quite reach. It's a striving that produces the achievement, even if the author never realizes.

Q: I think what we're talking about here is fiction about the nature of reality itself. I am reminded of another Machen quote, which I am sure you can place, something about "true terror is when a flower begins to speak."

Campbell: It's from "The White People." It's the lead-in to the central section of "The White People," the notebook that we read in its entirety. Yes, that's right. In his sense it's a sense of the ineffable, and of an underlying terror that is revealed, that in Machen's terms, or at least those of his narrator, would blast sanity. This is Lovecraft's position of course, that if we could put all the hints about the universe together, then our poor minds would be unable to cope with it. I'm not altogether certain that that is true. Post-'60's and '70's, maybe I've had a sufficient number of visionary experiences, drug-based, that I've been through the terror and come out the other side. But I still value the terror. I think this may be a crucial thing about continuing to write in the field. To me what separates those who love the field or write in it, from those who don't like this stuff for any reason, is that we value the aesthetic experience of terror. It has taken me a long time to come to that conclusion, but that seems to be the absolute center of why I stay in the field, both as a reader and as a writer.

Q: I am inevitably led to ask, what kind of visionary experiences?

Campbell: Lots of boring stuff as well, lots that didn't fit together in any useful way. But there was an incident in the '70s of going into a church in Gloucestershire, not too far from where I set my early Lovecraftian tales. A crack in the arch over the altar split apart and the entire arch crumbled before my eyes, then lifted itself up like a pair of muscles and put itself back together again. I found that very moving. Similarly in the Lake District, going up into the mountains and seeing the peaks in the distance stir in the mist and become restless. They began to wake like very old gods. Then they'd go back to sleep again, just lying there reminding me that they were there. We're talking about LSD, here, you understand. That doesn't make it invalid.

Q: This is an imaginative or metaphorical approach to reality itself. The mountains don't truly wake up. I recall another quote from Machen, criticizing Blackwood, to the effect that he (Machen) wrote of fantastic things as a kind of metaphor, while Blackwood actually believed it. At least I think it was Machen about Blackwood and not the other way around.

Campbell: I don't know....Well, yes, there are levels of belief, aren't there? Machen has this sense, I suspect, of reality being a veil over the infinite and the numinous. Blackwood was perhaps more mystical and less inclined to specify. More recently Robert Aickman regarded the supernatural as being routinely present behind or even within mundane existence. I can't pretend that I have these visions. I tend to find these things imaginatively appealing, certainly.

Q: It seems to me that in any kind of fantasy we are pretending to believe in something we know is not true in the pursuit of some deeper truth.

Campbell: Yes, that's exactly right. I have to say that for me the supernatural in the stuff that I write is more often metaphorical or some kind of embodiment of a psychological state. What is extremely important to me is that you can't explain it away by simply saying that it is a psychological projection. I've had lots of disagreements with friends, not necessarily over my stuff. I can give you some specific examples. I remember two instances. The original *Cat People* (1942) and the film *Rosemary's Baby*. I had a friend who felt that once it was apparent that *Cat People* was not just a psychological case-history, and equally that *Rosemary's Baby* was not just about pre-natal paranoia, then somehow these stories became undermined by the presence of the supernatural. As far as I am concerned, exactly the opposite is true. They have already functioned as a detailed psychological study, but, for me, the supernatural enriches them. I hope the same is true of my stuff.

Q: Do you personally believe in the supernatural in any sense?

Campbell: I am deeply skeptical. At the same time I've occasionally had the odd experience which seemed to me, at the very least, to undermine my skepticism. There's a place in Wales called Plas Teg, out in Machen territory. It is a Jacobean mansion, where I have certainly had very curious experiences. The place is open to the public and you can wander around it without a guide, usually. There are whole sections of it where I feel very uneasy. There is one particular set of apartments where in February there were dozens of dead flies lying around on the windowsills, which is not something you ordinarily find. If you assume that the owner didn't collect them together and put them up there for the benefit of atmosphere, then there indeed seemed to be something very odd. There are paintings on the wall by one of the members of the family who used to own it for many generations, which again seem to have something very unpleasant but difficult to define about them. They seem to be mainly studies of the human form. There was a sketch of a male body up to the neck, which then stopped. That's very common. There was a sketch of the inverted head next to it. The inverted head looked very unhappy about it. That's not usual. We then went down into the basement of the building because we were allowed to do that. There was a storeroom of stuff that was too shabby to be put on show, I suppose, was kept. Luckily I have this on video, because I was filming, so we have the evidence. I think J.K. Potter was with us as well that day. In a corner of the room there was a framed sampler, the sort of thing that would normally say something like THOU GOD SEEST ME, but the motto on this one was DO WHAT THOU WILT, Aleister Crowley's old dictum. I commend Plas Teg it to anybody who needs to be persuaded that perhaps haunted houses do exist after all.

Q: I've always had the feeling about English inns that if there isn't a ghost in residence, you should ask for a discount. They usually have one. Do you think that in some sense we wish they do? Would you prefer to stay in an inn that has a ghost?

Campbell: Yes, absolutely. I think it would be more fun. I'm more than willing to have the occasional odd haunting. And certainly we're happy to believe that our house, a big Victorian edifice, is haunted. All I can tell you is this. My sister-in-law had the experience of thinking that the kids, when they were young, had come up behind her in the guest room on the third floor next to my work room, when there was nobody there. Not long after that the house was burgled, and the thieves took Jenny's jewelry out of our bedroom which is on the middle floor to the top floor, and abandoned all the jewelry in the very room where her sister had this experience. More recently I spent a night in there myself, and something came and sat next to me on the bed twice. It was too lightweight for an adult - I'd have thought it was a cat if we had pets. So if indeed there is some kind of intimately benevolent and intimately terrifying specter in there, I think we're rather grateful. It saves on the burglar alarm.

Q: The thing that would be reassuring about the existence of ghosts would be that if ghosts are not just recordings of some kind, then that would be proof of an afterlife—which most people would find reassuring. This starts to suggest that the traditional theologies might be valid. But then we are always afraid of ghosts. So I wonder if the core of supernatural fiction is the comfort of the idea of survival beyond death, or is it the fear of forces we do not control? I mean this in the sense that the Victorian specter is in some way reassuring, but the Lovecraftian monster is not. So, what do you think these stories are really about?

Campbell: It depends on the story. There is the kind of supernatural fiction that seeks to reassure in all sorts of different ways, though I am not certain that all Victorian fiction of the kind does. Where do we start? Le Fanu is certainly not remotely reassuring. Edith Wharton is not. Later still, M.R. James surely intends to be as frightening as possible. Dean Koontz makes this argument that all ghost stories are fundamentally reassuring because they involve the notion of an afterlife. That strikes me as a remarkable over-simplification. In M.R. James, once you're dead, you turn into this hideous, scrawny thing that scrabbles about a lot and is certainly not very happy about it.

On the whole, in my own stuff, for what it's worth, I have occasionally tried to come up with an idea of the afterlife that satisfies me. The one that I tend to come up with is that the last dream never ends. If you don't wake up, you have a sense that this goes on forever. Therefore, if you die while you are dreaming, that is the way you do die, then that will be your heaven or your hell.

I used to have recurring dreams about an immense bookshop, which turned up in various familiar locations from my childhood, and I would find all sorts of things that I didn't know existed but which I wanted. I never actually left the bookshop. I never got to the cash desk and paid for what I'd got. It was simply the experience of finding this stuff that I still had to read and really wanted to. I used to feel that maybe this was where I'd spend my eternity. It's gone away for a while, but nothing has replaced it, so maybe it will come back again.

Q: In the traditional ghost story, even the most malevolent or perturbed spirit is the exception. These are the ones that didn't go on. But by implication, the rest of them do, so that there is order in the universe, and possibly even a God overseeing it all. This is the very view that Lovecraft rejected.

Campbell: Me too. There is very little sense of reassuring order underlying my ghosts. On the whole I think they tend to be embodiments of the aberrations within us all. I tend to feel that everybody's got them, and most of them are not at all reassuring. But then I am not in the business of reassurance.

Q: Do you feel a difference in approach between writing a story with a fantastic element in it and one without? Is it a different game with different rules?

Campbell: I certainly don't feel in terms of writing them any very considerable difference. It isn't so much that my psychological stories are like my supernatural stories with the supernatural element taken out as that the ghost stories or the supernatural stories are the psychological tales with the psychology taken one level further. So the something out there reflects the situation of the central character. But then again, I don't altogether admit those distinctions anyway. I've never really felt the need to make that distinction all that apparent. If the story itself makes it apparent, that's fine. Obviously I have written some pretty traditional ghost stories in my time, traditional supernatural stories of various kinds, where the distinction is overt. There clearly is something embodied out there. If the story makes an issue of the distinction, that's fine, but otherwise, no. Effectively, they're two aspects of the same thing.

Q: So it doesn't feel any different, writing one or the other?

Campbell: Well, it does in a way. If it's a supernatural story, then it begins to engage that level of my imagination, and it is something that I have found very imaginatively appealing. I've felt that the aesthetic experience of terror is what I find so appealing about the field. It is what I greatly value. It's why I stay in the field as a reader, and not merely a reader, but as a watcher of films, a listener to music, a viewer of paintings, for that matter. So, yes, the supernatural element does strike me as being one level further up, that one level closer to awe. We're coming back to this, aren't we? That is what I am always trying to get to.

Q: There are many people—Douglas Winter, for example—who define the horror story in terms of an emotion rather than content. Therefore it's a horror story, regardless of how that emotion is evoked. But you're suggesting that if it is evoked imaginatively through the supernatural, it reaches a different level.

Campbell: It does for me. I wouldn't want to impose that on anybody else. Yes, I suppose, if it is reaching to that visionary level. I do think that such visionary horror is useful. I think that it does give us a particular experience. Then that is what I most value. This is not by any means to denigrate the great psychological horror stories from Poe onward to "A Rose for Emily," to cite some of the classics. But if I had to choose, if I had to indicate where my imagination is drawn to more, then, yes, it would be supernatural terror. That is what I love best.

Q: Were you then dismayed when the field tried to steer away from the supernatural and call itself Dark Suspense or somesuch? You mentioned that at one point your agent told you that supernatural stories weren't selling anymore. You must be glad that they are again.

Campbell: Yes. But I never really gave it up, because at the very least I could go on with short stories, as I certainly did during that period. Most of them are in my new collection, *Told by the Dead*. But, yes, I would prefer to have at least the sense of the supernatural. The novel I am about to commit myself to (*Secret Stories*) isn't supernatural, but the next one may well be. There is still always underlying the sense that after that I can get back to the supernatural. But if I say there are stories I like best, this implies that the one in the middle is second best. I don't feel that way when I am writing it. I think I perhaps need that kind of the swing of the pendulum, that I am able to write both. I certainly find intense psychological detail appealing enough that I am willing to spend a year or longer at writing a novel. But I always want that supernatural light at the end of the tunnel. Maybe that's it.

Q: After all this time to you still find yourself looking back to Lovecraft, either to write a Cthulhu Mythos story or to embrace his view of cosmic horror? Is he still with you?

Campbell: Yes he is still here, yes, with me. And, yes, I still find his work something I'd like to touch, if not to match. *The Darkest Part of the Woods* is certainly my latest attempt to do what I like the most about Lovecraft. There is a necromancer from centuries ago in it called Nathaniel Selcouth, and his journals. We get fragments of them and glimpses of what he evoked, and we get more than glimpses of the way that what he did altered the landscape around him, where the characters of the story are now living. Yes, that was an attempt to get back to Lovecraft. It was also an attempt get back to Lovecraft's first principles, so there is the smallest reference to Lovecraft's mythos, or actually to the bits that I added myself. But what there mostly is, I suppose, is an attempt to get back even further to Machen and Blackwood and the kind of tradition on which was Lovecraft was drawing. I actually think it is very important that that tradition is not lost. I am not sure that it has been by any means, but it does no harm to remind people of it. I suppose this is the dispiriting business about the collapse of the field, or the reasons why it collapsed. It seems there are so many people around who actually had no sense of where the field had come from, who were only reading what was current.

When I thought that Lovecraft was the essence of the field—in my early to mid-teens—at least that was reaching back to a tradition several decades before where I was. For a while there was a period where it seemed that no one did even that. So I think it is good to remind people that there is a very vital tradition, without which the field wouldn't exist.

Q: Editors now receive a lot of stories which are bad retellings of horror movies—not even good movies. These writers haven't seen the classic horror movies, much less read anything. So there is this general perception in the public at large that horror is simply the shock of a guy with a knife, and there's nothing more to it. It's all being dumbed down. So, how do we avoid our reader base being eroded by people with such very limited expectations?

Campbell: All we can do is write as well as we possibly can. I don't think there's any other way to address it. I don't think you can write didactically in that sense. You can't address the reader and say, "Well, look—what you think about this field is wrong." It wouldn't interest me to do that in a piece of fiction—I'd rather try and show what I love about the field.

Q: A guess what you can do is write the kind of story which, on the surface at least does not require any knowledge of the field—at least until you have seduced the reader. Then you can lay it on.

Campbell: You could do that.

Q: Otherwise, isn't there the possibility that the audience for more sophisticated horror will just disappear? Do you worry about that?

Campbell: I do and I don't. I greatly admire (for instance) the work of Peter Ackroyd and M. John Harrison in Britain and in America, I was very impressed not very long ago by Mark Danielewski and *House of Leaves*, and by several fine ghost stories by a new writer, Glen Hirshberg. These are all literate and demanding novels and stories. Mike Harrison goes for short stories, mainly, which certainly do not flatter the reader in the sense of requiring too little of them, of their intelligence, their erudition. As long as I see such fiction being published, I think the field will still remain vital. It may be that some of the best work in the moment is being published without the horror label, but then that has often been the case in the past. It may be that periods in which horror is labeled and marketed as horror and put in the Horror section of the bookstore are a kind of a temporary aberration, and what we are actually seeing at the moment is that the field is returning to its natural state.

Q: I wonder if the existence of the category effects the way the books are written, in the sense that a mainstream literary novel, which also happens to be a supernatural horror novel, doesn't have to have an apparition or a splat of blood on page one so that the casual browser will know what sort of novel this is.

Campbell: Neither do mine.

Q: But a lot of the more commercial horror novels seem to be written that way.

Campbell: Oh yes, I understand. I know what you mean. There is this generic branding that comes with a need to reassure the reader. I think some writers feel the need to do that, and if they do, good luck to them. But, I don't think the field is ever going to die. It's always going to claw its way up over its own corpse, because, even if they don't call it horror, the human imagination still needs that macabre element. The darker side of the imagination is not going to go away, and the best way we can celebrate it is in fiction.

Recorded at the World Fantasy Convention,
Minneapolis, MN, Nov 3, 2003.

DAVID J. SCHOW

David J. Schow was somewhat reluctantly associated with the Splatterpunk movement for several minutes in 1989, but he got over it. He is a strikingly original, darkly sardonic writer (the author of the funniest necrophilia story I know, which I published in *Weird Tales*), whose books include *The Kill Riff, The Shaft, Seeing Red, Lost Angels, Black Leather Required, Crypt Orchids, Gunwork, Upgunned,* and more. He has also done considerable work as a screenwriter.

Q: I was particularly amused by your recent comment that vampires "have become the *Star Trek* of horror—

Schow: It got me into the *New York Times Review of Books*, that quote did.

Q: I suppose this leads to the more general question of how you escape the image of the horror writer. Everybody now seems to have a very precise idea of what horror is and what a horror writer is.

Schow: And the kind of horror they're talking about is extremely traditional, and there will always be a lot of writers who are content to write traditionally. I won't want to, unless—as was the case with Ellen Datlow's *A Whisper of Blood*—I can write a "vampire" story with no vampires in it for a vampire anthology. Vampire stories are very popular. I don't want to write them. How can I maintain my moral position? Easy—I write about someone who preys on people more than willing to believe in vampires, fanatics, the very audience for vampire fiction.

But to get back to the question, I never had to escape any image. I never expected or wanted to become a traditional sort of writer. If I was ever in danger of that, it was a long time ago. Traditions try to cripple you, they lean on you as a writer. But they're fun to "goon," if you can play them well. There's no image to escape. So far.

Q: Well, there was the Splatterpunk image.

Schow: Oh, yeah, the "image" summed up in that brilliant anthology by that editor everyone has forgotten. The image that's one channel on the dial. If that's all you're going to see in the landscape of someone's literary work, then I guess it means you have a severely limited horizon for reading matter.

I detest doing the same thing over and over, even within the range of explicit stuff or violent stuff or loud stuff. I'm trying to vary my dynamic range. Mostly it all boils down to the battle between what you want to write, versus marketing distinctions. Most of the "problems" writers have with categorization or image can be dispelled by sampling emotional tones on the palette—go out there and show 'em different. Maybe that's how I got asked to collaborate on a *children's* book of all things—by people who relish the different.

Q: We're in a unique position now because maybe for the first time we have career horror writers, who are expected by their publishers to write nothing else. The great names of the past, even someone like Algernon Blackwood or E.F. Benson, wrote a lot of other sorts of things. They were general writers who happened to turn out a lot of horror. But now we have a writer like Stephen King who's spent decades writing virtually nothing but horror. Eventually most of us are going to have to escape this.

Schow: It's easy to do, though, because as soon as somebody types you as a horror writer or a suspense writer or a mystery writer, that's a box. It may be a welcome box, but a box is a line they're drawing around you. Once I see the line I'll do everything I can to escape the box, to break that safe little sanitary cordon. You don't draw a line around a body until it's dead.

Writers will write strictly short stories, or novels, or just screenplays—that's another box. I'm trying hard not to stay in any of those boxes…which is one reason my third novel has been so long in coming. I've attempted to take the lessons I'd learned or taught myself in my first two novels and apply them to a bigger canvas—not an inflated, "epic" thing, but a trip down some road to which those first two books are side streets. For example, if you wrote a vampire novel that was a big hit, the powers-that-be would jump right on your back to do *another* vampire novel as quickly as possible. You could choose to build an entire career on big-hit vampire novels and almost no one would stop you. But don't delude yourself you've written 20 novels when what you've really done is write *one* novel, 20 times. I've done that, too, having written series novels and stuff like that; it's something I don't want to keep doing if it is *my* name suddenly on the spine. By that I mean I value my "David Schow" novels pretty highly, and I don't want to repeat myself, at least as far as those go.

Q: What I see is people who have become professional, full-time horror books, having written twenty horror novels, are going to be getting awfully tired. This was my point about Benson and Blackwood and so on. The great masters of the form in the past, none of them ever wrote twenty horror novels.

Schow: Also, the guys who were "career" horror writers before are now more visible as "brand-name" career horror writers. Writers came from other places, and the occasional "horror" books they wrote were much further apart—not two or three of the same flavor per year. Ray Bradbury is venerated as a science fiction writer to this day, but his first collection, *Dark Carnival*, was essentially a book of horrors. I've always seen Bradbury as a horror writer foremost. What he writes doesn't change so much as the categorizations and labels other people apply to his writing. "Horror," right now, is different from what "horror" was even five years ago. It has encompassed what Bob Bloch called psychological suspense. But "psychological suspense" was just an upscale marketing distinction, and gave birth to "psychological horror," another genre marketing nook. What's the difference? Well, if you want to give an Academy Award to *The Silence of the Lambs*, it's psychological suspense or a "thriller;" if you want to give it a Fangoria Chainsaw Award, it's a horror movie.

So unless you let an editor or publisher strictly dictate what you do next, you *just have to do something different*—not just a half-twist on an old theme, like, *They're vampires but they're gay!* or *They're vampires but they're really MUMMIES!* That's category writing; that's writing "underwater Nazi cheerleader" books, as Michael McDowell said. If a writer produces a great many books in the same category, in a short period of time, how many of those books are really the *same* book? Was the impetus for the books a success ratio that mandated an ever-increasing amount of product? Thus do ideas that should have been short stories become novels, and ideas that should never have gotten full production become finished, mediocre books because the writer had a four-book contract to fulfill. That's not the way I want to approach writing my novels, ever.

Categories are zeroing-in, from the specialization of the 1970s through the hyper-specialization of the 1980s, and more than ever people are convinced that if you write, you only write one thing, over and over and over, which is why people ask writers, *"What* do you write?" No matter what dress jacket the writing goes out in, the best you and I can do is not write that "what," over and over.

Q: So, how's your eagerly-awaited third novel going to fit into all this?

Schow: Not enough of it is really there to talk about yet. But I can demonstrate, I think, how forms suddenly cross over. While we were on hiatus (from location production) on *The Crow*, I wrote out the idea for the third novel as a screenplay. I've never done that before. When I went to New York to scare up interest for the book, editors reacted very well, but couldn't resist asking, "What happens next?" Which is a sneaky way of asking you for an outline. At which point i could drop the script on the desk—bang! There you go—a 110-page outline!

So I could be novelizing my own screenplay—back to category writing, again! It sucks everyone in, it's loose, it's ready for dinner, and dinner is you.

Whereas the prose came slowly, the script came quickly. It's like a memo to complete the novel, and in screenwritten form it coalesced very fast. Now, to generate the sort of prose I want to surround this skeleton with—that takes time. Plus, there's a lot of research involved. Stuff you could cover with a time-cut in a film is not glossed over so easily in prose. For one thing, I need to check constantly to make sure my Second World War guys don't use ballpoint pens, stuff like that. So the book is *there*…but it's not there yet.

Q: What is the screenplay about? Is there any element of the supernatural?

Schow: Yes, there's an element of the supernatural in that it is the only explanation—other than insanity—for what befalls the characters. Eight guys who were all on the same B-24 crew in World War II realize, 50 years later, that the war has come back to get them. Each of them develops a theory about what is happening and why and none of them agree. In turning it into manuscript, one of the things I'm trying to leaven is how much explanation of their predicament is necessary. Are things plausibly weird or do they need more backup, more incident to support the supernatural stuff? Should it all be wrapped up with a bow of explanation, nice and linear, or should some mystery be left, and if so, how much? The usual torment you go through when doping out a book line-by-line, as opposed to waving your arms and talking it out as a thrilling one-liner with a terrific punchline.

Q: We can backtrack a bit from here. Why did you start writing and when?

Schow: Unlike most people, I had very few straight-up wage jobs. I'm a university drop-out. I just sat down and started writing things which I then mailed to people who could potentially give me checks for them. I thought that was a better system than paying people money to go to their workshops to learn how to do it their way. Eventually someone would buy something, or I would die. Somebody bought something.

I wrote for free papers and did journalism in Arizona. My first non-fiction sale and my first fiction sale came about six months apart. With almost no backsliding—that is to say, legitimate employment—I have been writing for a living steadily since the late 1970's. So, once Charlie Ryan cut me that check for *Galileo*, the world was doomed.

Q: You moved rapidly from science fiction for *Galileo* to writing horror. I first noticed your name in *Twilight Zone Magazine*.

Schow: Yeah. I saw the very first issue of *Twilight Zone* in 1981, I thought I MUST be in this magazine! But I got in not with fiction, but journalism—a long series of articles on *The Outer Limits* which ran in the magazine for a year and a half. By the time the third installment of the series was published, I had a contract to do *The Outer Limits* all over again as a non-fiction book, which was the first book with my real name on it.

While doing those articles for Ted Klein, I was constantly trying to sell fiction to him. The first story in which he was interested got bounced back from him twice and eventually wound up in *Night Cry* when he decided he liked it after all. While *TZ*—the magazine—was still running the *Outer Limits* pieces, Ted and I invented pseudonyms for some of my stories because Ted didn't want to make it look like I was writing too much for the magazine at once, and I didn't want to wait until *The Outer Limits* had run its course to see the stories in print. I finally got a short story into *TZ* in 1982 and I was in that magazine in some form until it folded in 1989, including the mystery period where Michael Blaine was the editor. Fortunately Tappan King came along and published stories for which I guess I'm even more notorious, even now.

I miss *Twilight Zone*. If there's one reason for the Eighties to live, so we don't have to flush the whole decade in retrospect, in horror, *Twilight Zone Magazine* summed up everything that was going on. Somebody should assemble a big anthology of all the important and interesting stuff that passed through that magazine. Ted Klein was a hell of an editor, the first and best the magazine had. In publishing, there should be more like him—people who understand editing, rather than people who merely have the *title* of editor.

Q: You've done a bit of anthology editing yourself. How would you define "know how to do it"?

Schow: I'm not good at it. When I finished *Silver Scream*, I felt excoriated. I said, maybe five years from now, if someone wants me to do another anthology, I'll be ready to dive in again. Well…more than five years have passed and I am not interested in the least. Editing became too political for me, and I am not politically patient. Nine times out of ten, when presented with an editorial problem by a writer, the solution that leaps most immediately to mind is to go to the writer's house and throttle him or her until he or she does what I (or me) want.

I enjoy working with editors who know basic stuff. For one thing, they have to know how to read. For another, they have to *have read*. They have to like the editing process. A very familiar case is the writer who hates writing but likes having written; there are a lot of so-called editors who don't know dick about editing, but enjoy "having edited"— mostly so they can lay claim to a book they had no hand in creating. It all boils down to how you react when an editor says, "Well, we like it but we'd also like to talk about some things." If the comments strike you as thoughtful, the editor will have observed some nuance or reacted to some character you have created. If the commentary is gratuitous, it'll be based on statistics or arbitrary, sweeping generalities, such as an editorial comment I got on *The Shaft*: "Drop the first 150 pages and take out all the drug references."

It's like being a "no" man in Hollywood. Everybody has heard of "yes" men. You have seventeen guys sitting around a table. Sixteen guys have made reams of notes on your script.

The seventeenth guy says, "This script is fine. There's nothing wrong with it. We should do this exactly as written." Then another script passes around; same story. The seventeenth guy says, "I know it's against all odds, but this script is pretty good too. I don't think we should mess with it either." Pretty soon the boss is glaring the last guy and saying, "You're not doing your job! I want to see *notes* on this script!" Development executives have no power other than the power to say "no," because "yes" has to be cleared with sixteen other executives, all of whom need to keep their jobs...which is now a yes-man becomes a no-man.

Publishing has always prided itself on being gentlemanly, not a snake-pit like Hollywood, right? Except publishing has become enslaved to the Hollywood model—it's now *exactly the same* as the film industry, except that in movies the pay is better. In publishing you have buildings-full of people throwing out "editorial" comments they're not qualified to make. They don't have the balance that truly good editors have. One example is Bill Thompson who almost bought my first novel for Arbor House. Bill Thompson was the guy who gave the world *Carrie*, buying it when he was back at Doubleday. He sent me back a letter saying, "I think the back third of your book needs these things." Once you get over the initial anger—that anyone would say *anything* about your manuscript— you realize that some of these outside ideas aren't so bad. In fact, you say to yourself, they are *really smart*. And Bill Thompson became a man who contributed substantially—because he's a good editor—and he's a totally invisible part of the process. Melissa Singer eventually edited that novel for Tor Books. She impacted that same part of the book, the third act, but in an intriguing editorial way—she made a series of "what if" suggestions instead of outright orders to change things. And once again, once I could decide for myself that the changes made the book better, Melissa contributed substantially from behind the curtain.

Q: This is *The Kill Riff* we're talking about here.

Schow: Yes.

Q: What about your second novel, *The Shaft*? Why didn't that get published in the United States?

Schow: *The Shaft* was part of my Tor deal, originally. It met with massive editorial indifference there. I let my agent persuade me to pull the book. It sold immediately in England where no editorial problems arose, no strings or conditions. People have suggested that the book has been suppressed, but I've never seen evidence to support this. Then again, I wouldn't see such evidence, would I? It was sabotaged at one house by a little piss-ant who doesn't deserve the immortality of being named in print. But we've had no difficulty making deals for it all over Europe; it just sold in Russia. Not the USA. Think about that.

Some small press will eventually do an American edition. Right now it's part of my back-list package of about six books. Some of the offers for the new novel contain provisions for the backlist. I hope it'll be included.

Q: If you don't have much patience for the political compromises of editing anthologies, surely the situation in Hollywood is a lot worse. How do you cope?

Schow: It's really schizophrenic as in dementia praecox—and disordered, as in multiple personality. You must occupy several insane heads simultaneously. Part of the way I survive the process is that I always have the printed word to return to, as opposed to the filmed word. If you acknowledge, going in, that your script will be miss-marked by every monkey around the table, then the changes don't come as such a shock. Then you link up with a director as crazy as you are, and it becomes the two of you against the guys with the note-pads.

One of the things I like about screenwriting is that by shooting a movie on a set you get to observe an entire created community of craftspeople all laboring toward the common end of filming something you *made up*. You said it and seventy people did it, got it, built it. But doing movies is so much a compromise on a day-to-day basis that eventually, if you have the option, you'll long for more control, which is what writing novels and short stories gives you. While solitary writing does *not* give you the community, it can evoke the feeling you're speaking to a diminished audience, because the chances are that more people will see the worst movie you ever make than will read the best book you ever write. Unless you're already a director, novels are the only place a writer can wield directorial control. It's just you and the words. So I put prose and movies at opposite ends of the same see-saw, and dash back and forth between the extremes depending on how much company I want around me.

Q: In the scripts, do you get enough of what you wrote on the screen to make it worthwhile?

Schow: That's another gradated scale as. So far, the movies on which I've worked have been subject to the whims of everyone from producers' wives, daughters, boyfriends, to the producers themselves who are frequently less talented than their wives, daughters, or boyfriends. Each film you do, you try to get the end result a little closer to what you actually wrote down. If it's not verbatim, then you try to retain the spirit of the words. This has worked to the extent that *The Crow* is a definite step up from *Leatherface*. If the trend continues, it has one of two inevitable results. One is you hook up with directors who ask for you because they're already on your frequency. The other is that sooner or later somebody will ask you to direct something. Film, as they say is a "director's medium," just as TV is a "producer's medium." By job definition, that producer and that director are writers—because they have more power than anyone else in the film or TV food chain to determine the POV and attitude of a movie or TV show. So if you can control what you're presenting a little more with each project, I define that as progress.

Q: How many screenplays have you done that have been produced?

Schow: My written-to-produced ratio runs about 5-to-4. To date I've done four TV scripts and five features; I wrote a spec script that's been optioned a lot and is a great calling card, but which was never filmed. I've written two more features for Alex Proyas which will be shot in Australia sometime in the distant future. Then there are rewrite gigs, commonly known as "script doctoring." You swing in on a vine like Tarzan, make them think you "saved" their movie, and go away. Sometimes you even get credit. The downside is what Sterling Silliphant said about Hollywood: "When I got there, I heard the siren call: 'Oh God, you can save us! Can you write this in two weeks?' And suddenly it was 30 years later."

Q: When you fix up a script like that, do you find yourself in conflict with the original author?

Schow: Not really, because the majority of the time what you're really doing is not a makeover, but starting again at ground zero with the same raw material. Have ten writers write their "take" on, say, "three generations of a vampire family," and if the writers are any good, you'll get ten different but superficially similar novels.

When the producers give you a bottom line on a rewrite, when they start by saying, "Keep this, this, and this; change that, and we *hate* that," then you're to a certain extent plugging in ingredients to something that is prefabricated. You're trying to address the problems that they've asked you to solve; that's why they hired you. Maybe they just want peppier dialogue, or mote action, or they want a "budget rewrite" to address the exigencies of production—how to shave five location days down to two, re-do exteriors to shoot as interiors, that sort of thing.

So, the frequent result is that a rewrite looks very similar to the original because they are both derived from the same source material. But in every such gig that I've worked on so far, any similarities came solely from that common source material. It's not like the first eight writers left too many footprints, because the producers and directors know what changes they want worked, and you can always say to a producer, "You know, I really hate this thing here," and almost every time the producer will say, "Really? Then lose it. I didn't like it either."

Q: How would you feel if someone else were called in to rewrite your script?

Schow: It's happened. I've been on both sides of the Writer's Guild's so-called "arbitration" process several times, too, and I've arbitrated credits on scripts written by other writers. How I'd feel all depends on the individual circumstance. Were you credited unfairly? Was it a rewrite, an original, a polish, an adaptation? In one case I wasn't credited at all, but I didn't mind. In another, I was credited fairly, I thought, while others got credit they had not earned.

Sometimes they want you to rewrite your friends. Example: Warner Brothers asked me to rewrite a script by the Mathesons. I thought, *Why?* The Mathesons know how to write scripts and they've been doing it for a lot longer than me. Before I went to the meetings, I called Richard and Richard Christian up to ask, "Are you guys okay with this?" Their answer, which, I think, was an excellent answer, went something like this: "We sold the studio an idea many years ago. We wrote them a script. They paid us. We thanked them and went away. If they want to bring it back to life with another writer, that's fine with us."

Of course, the punch line is that they wrote it as a comedy and Warner Bros. wanted me to bring it back to life as a straight horror movie. It never got done. But if it does, the Mathesons will get residuals. I think theirs is the most comfortable and sane attitude to have.

Q: What are the five movies you did? You've mentioned two of them, *The Crow* and *Texas Chainsaw Massacre III*.

Schow: I did a couple of made-for-cable *Critters* sequels and a production rewrite on *Nightmare on Elm St., Part 5: The Dream Child*. Frank Darabont and I wrote a terrific sequel to *The Hitcher* which died in-utero.

Nightmare 5 would have been the first screenplay I'd ever written but for the fact that I'd never written a script prior to Christmas, 1988. That year, New Line Cinema contacted a bunch of horror writers to transfuse their blood into the Freddy Krueger films. One writer gave such a good pitch that he later ran all over town claiming he was writing the next *Nightmare* film...while two *other* writers were busy on the first draft! New Line asked me if I wanted it and I worked up a treatment titled *Freddy Rules*. We were all set to sign on the line. Just one thing: Could they see another script I'd written?

I rather lamely said, "I do not have one," and I did not get the gig. Later, after the screenplay had gone through four other writers, *Nightmare 5* came back to me. During that time, Mike De Luca, who is now the exec in charge of production for the entire company, got me an episode of the Freddy TV series. My teleplay for that was the first thing I ever wrote in script form. The day I delivered the teleplay was Friday the 13th, January of 1989. Within 24 hours reading it, New Line hired me to do their next horror feature after *Nightmare 5,* which is how *Leatherface: Texas Chainsaw Massacre III* came into the world. When I completed the first draft of that, Mike asked me to pump up the dialogue for *Nightmare 5*. My assignment was to help salvage the script I could not get hired to *write*. This was during shooting, incidentally; they had a man coming to my house, literally taking pages out of the typewriter and down to the set.

Q: What do you think a good horror story needs, either for screen or print, if it's to do more than just say "Boo!" and resonate for more than a minute?

Schow: It needs not to go where you, the reader, expect it to go. Adept at this are many writers probably nobody but you and I have heard of, people I admire, who wrote classics. Jane Rice—no relation to Anne—is one; Gerald Kersh is another.

Charles Beaumont is another. Today, horror readers may know him, but the public at large won't, even though Beaumont was a mainstay of *Playboy* and other highest-paying fiction markets in the 1960's. *Playboy* even kept Beaumont on a first-look retainer, paid annually.

Here's the trick. They all could do it, and I like to attempt it when I can. You are putting a story down on paper. You ask, "Where is this going?" You venture to the obvious destination of the story; perhaps you even write it. *Then* you go somewhere else. In essence, you "invent" the story past its predictable ending just to reach the unusual ending. You puzzle out what would happen in that conventional denouement...then you *don't do that*. And any mechanism you use to drive the story to the hidden conclusion—subtle, explicit, red, wet, gauzy, whatever—is fine. The single most important thing is not to go where the story would go if it were a run-of-the-mill page filler, dull, boring, and predictable, taking more from you than it leaves. You go to the obvious place first, so you'll recognize it and therefore avoid it for the rest of the writing process.

Q: The only use you can get out of the really traditional plot—like the one about the nasty skeptic who offends the native gods and meets his doom thereby—is to stretch something really incongruous over that familiar framework. The result is comedy more often than horror, though.

Schow: That's like the Adam-and-Eve plot in science fiction. If I get to the end of yet another Adam-and-Eve story and all you have for me is it's really the Garden of Eden, see?...you die. The challenge is to do the best, most outrageous twist possible on the hoary idea. You have to do the best story ever twisted from I'm a nasty skeptic who offended the gods and it's all silly native superstition and it's probably nothing but we'll check it out anyway. Clichés exist to be blown apart. You get people to swallow stuff with a laugh they would never swallow with a scream, and vice-versa, which maybe explains that Matheson script. As our patron saint, Bob Bloch, told us, comedy and horror are flip sides of the same coin. We should never forget that. Ultimate-stress circumstances have an inherent absurdity that cannot be ignored. You must not devote yourself to taking readers to the usual destinations. You do not want the reader to get there ahead of you, and you need to keep the reader awake, or the journey will not be fulfilling.

Q: The test of a good mystery story is whether or not you can read it twice, once after you already know whodunit. Is it still an interesting story, or like a spent match? It seems to me that the test of a good horror story is similar, and novelty and surprise are the most transient of fictional virtues. Something has to resonate after the reader knows where the story went.

Schow: This has to do with the approach you take, the style, the structure—all personally yours. Good mysteries can be read twenty or thirty times, and I read at different times for different values. On first reading, what grabs you first is the "how," then the "why." How is sheer method and why is assorted motivations. *Mission: Impossible* was a TV show entirely about the how, the primary level of storytelling—how are they going to pull this off? After that, read for the subtleties, for character, for language, for insight.

If you do this often enough as a writer, readers will come back to you no matter what you've just written. The Categories don't matter, the "how" and "why" no longer matter. What matters is the who—the you, the writer and the way you write, which can, in the best of times, win you a very faithful audience.

Doug Winter just read a brand-new story, called "Loop." It was staggeringly good writing, very layered, like a torte of gore and awfulness and sadness and things lost. I would go back and re-read that story several times just to admire the architecture It's put together very skillfully and does its tricks very subtly. And it's interesting to think that people may be reading *your* stuff, looking for and finding the same qualities. Then one day you turn around and say, "Damn! I have a style." As I'm sure you have.

Q: Someone commented that you write for several years, and then you look back and see that you write in a certain way, and that's your style.

Schow: Basically, yeah, that's it. If you try to consciously generate it, it smells artificial—if you take bits and pieces of other writers' styles and make them into this tinfoil sham and then yell really loudly, "Look, I'm being stylish!" It's not a style; its more of a captured voice you stole, and horror writing has its share of absurd thieves. Maybe styles per se are fated to remain the province of critics, of the autopsists of literature who determine shit about you after you're gone. "Hey, look at that—it's dead." "Yeah, but it sure had style!" Those guys who draw the line around the corpse are back, aren't they?

Q: There are certainly a variety of voices a writer deliberately assumes. Certainly if your first-person narrator were an aristocrat of the 19th century, you, the author would assume a very different voice than if you were writing about a street punk. So I'd guess you have a repertoire of styles you accumulate.

Schow: The recurrent thing critics have noticed, especially about my short fiction, that it jumps around between arenas. Their misconception is that one writer writes one sort of thing, and I like to be chameleonic.

Q: How much of your writing is a matter of deliberation, even a consciously assumed technique or manner, and how much is just an emotional outburst?

Schow: It's a really slimy string connecting the two, with a lit cherry bomb in the middle. I don't know. I wrote very intuitively. I hate outlines. I hate structured beats. Sometimes you can coax the words out, and sometimes coaxing makes them run away. The words come out when they're ready, sometimes in a rush, but a methodical rush. Once they're on the page you must deliberately take the time to sweat the details… which is another reason it takes me so long to do novels. I devote to novels the same attention I do to short stories, and sometimes stories take a year or more just to mellow or make sense. So don't hold your breath for my so-called "new" novel.

Q: Does this new novel have a title?

Schow: Not yet.

Q: I understand that need for deliberate, hands-on working of the material, no matter how much it comes out in a rush. I at least find the idea of dictating fiction, rather than writing it down yourself, to be fairly incomprehensible.

Schow: I get dictated letters from publishers and producers. I can't see how they do it. It's tempting as a discipline, but I don't think I could do two lines. Rod Serling was a big proponent of dictation. When Richard Matheson wrote "A World of His Own" for TV, for *Twilight Zone*, he wrote a comedy about a guy who dictated his plays, based on his own experience of dictating to a secretary. Bob Bloch hired a secretary, and through dictation, he did four books in the time it would have taken him to do two. Now the thought of standing around and orally representing this stuff in one draft right out of your head and onto the page doesn't make much sense to me—as you can tell from my labyrinthine, grammatically disastrous answers to your questions. I suppose you can always clean up the text later, But I have to twist and turn and torture it too much for it to ever look good naked, first time out.

Q: Call it practiced spontaneity, like what you see when a cartoonist whips off a cartoon almost as freely as conversation. He's done that thousands of times.

Schow: You have to do it a thousand times, develop a facility for it. It's like signing autographs, to cite something I'm sure you've experienced. The first time someone asks you to sign your name to something you wrote—the most natural thing in the world—you stammer and stomp about. The initial reaction is incredulity: "You want me to sign that?" Then: "Uh, yeah, I'm him." Then you brace to get punched. Then you realize it's a compliment. Then you realize you are absolutely unprepared to deal with a compliment. Then you must write something cool. Then you must not scribble the wrong name into some $60 book. Then you must remember how to write your own name. Is your signature cool enough, or do you write like a dork? Readers: This is the sort of deep, psychological crap writers torment themselves with constantly.

Q: I think what we ultimately torture ourselves with is the prospect of becoming the nominal head of a factory system, where you're such a brand-name that publishers hire whole assembly-lines of hack writers to write your work. They want you, but they don't really, because the hacks are more reliable. You're just supposed to lay your hands on the product and bless it.

Schow: I have a friend of long standing who is in exactly that position right now. He has been on *The New York Times* bestseller list as someone else. Extrapolate this phenomenon. Any writer who is perceived as a brand name could eventually wind up with a factory of anonymous writers behind him, because the market is limitless. If they could do a book a month, they would sell four million copies if it has so-and-so's name on it. This gets back to what we were talking about earlier. The ceiling for this sort of thing is unlimited. That's why it seems you have people who have become successful in the field writing so many books in so little time. If it were me, the little guy inside my head would say "You're writing too fast and you need to take more time with these if they're going to mean anything." On the other hand, given that kind of fame and position, wouldn't you do the same thing?

Q: I don't think anybody knows how he would respond to having five million bucks thrown at him until it happens. The rest is self-righteous posturing.

Schow: Yeah. Like the people who crap and carp and bitch about Stephen King. I don't know Stephen King. I've never met Stephen King. But were I in his position, would I write as voluminously as he seems to enjoy? Why not?

Q: We could spin it out into the ultimate paranoid writer's fantasy. You're as famous and as in-demand as Stephen King, only you're sick of writing the same thing over and over again, and you start to resist what the publishers and movie-producers want you to do. But they don't need you anymore. They can merely have you killed and let the factory go on without you.

Schow: It's not an exaggeration to say it's happening now, just without the murder part. The man or woman bearing the brand name has already become utterly unnecessary to the whole process. It's much easier than you think. Having written my share of pseudonym novels, God knows, I'm aware. Although it couldn't last because no one in America seems constitutionally capable of keeping a goddamn secret, anymore. The size of those tabloid TV checks has made the US into a nation of finks and squealers. All you need to get away with this deception is a couple of extremely hungry writers who are competent mimics. Murder the brand-name person, and swear an agent or two into secrecy. That's it. It could happen to us, sitting here, right now.

Q: They could end up hiring me to write your books and you to write mine.

Schow: And both of us could wind up tomorrow with some cushy gig to write something that goes out under a famous guy's name, and you out there in Readerland will never know the difference because we've trained at the Mission Impossible School.

Q: I think that ultimately the readers can tell the difference. The book that comes out of the author's contract first, and out of his heart and mind only very secondarily, are going to seem superficial and hollow.

Schow: Yeah, they have generic qualities going in, and therefore generic similarities are not going to be noticed. They have a certain job to perform and that's all. Someone on a radio show said once that they thought Trevanian was an umbrella pseudonym for a gang of writers, á la Michael Slade (being the three lawyers). I remember writing in a long letter in which I said, no, if you read the work it was clear that it was the other way around. One person was working under a variety of pseudonyms. But there were common elements to all the works, the Trevanian books, the work he did as Rod Whitaker, which is his real name, and the work he did as Nicholas Seare, the name under which he wrote *1349 or So, Being an Apology for a Pedlar*, and the better-known *Rude Tales and Glorious*, the risqué retelling of Arthurian myth. This is a trick that I admire greatly: He had assigned a genre to one of his pseudonyms. Then he took another genre, the action-spy genre, and assigned it to the pseudonym Trevanian. I think that if we're unable to resist being walled up in genre, then put another name on it. Eventually the people who give a damn will know it is all by the same person. But if you're going to meet such resistance from people who rigidly categorize everything, you have to attack the problem obliquely.

Q: This brings up my favorite theoretical question about genre. What would happen if Stephen King suddenly wrote *The Sound of Music*? That is, he writes something that's good for what it is, but totally far afield from what people think of as a Stephen King book. What does the publisher do?

Schow: It would be like Tobe Hooper directing a Harlequin Romance as a movie.

Q: And doing it well.

Schow: They might go for it. But they might go for it faster if they didn't have preconceptions of genre and brand-name going in. So what would happen if Darrell Schweitzer wrote a straightforward mainstream fiction novel?

Q: The honest answer is that I am probably not well enough established in the book market for anyone to care. It would be treated like a first novel.

Schow: If you look at genres as markets, you can have an infinite number of first novels. You can have people who come back to you and say, "We don't want to publish this book because your last novel didn't sell enough copies." If you put a pseudonym on it, you don't have that problem. You have another problem, which is that they might try to bone you with a low advance, but you have to surf around these extremes. The way you win is by continuing to be published and continuing to make a living being published. Who knows? I might write a pseudonym novel tomorrow. I might have already written one.

Q: You might already be several famous writers.

Schow: I am in fact several people. I registered my pseudonym with the Writer's Guild, though. If you want to change your name on a movie, you have to have your pseudonym registered, which I find to be a real laugh. I was thinking Lemmy Lone might be a good pseudonym. Or Chastity Gulch.

Q: Or Harlan Ellison's Cordwainer Bird.

Schow: My favorite of those was one registered by David Gerrold, Noah Ward.

[Much informal chatter follows.]

Schow: This is getting more like a conversation and less like an interview, which is what I like.

Q: And I haven't even asked you where you get your ideas.

Schow: The best answer that I ever came up with stemmed from the fact that I used to work on a Smith Corona manual portable. I had four of them, because I would strike the keys so hard that the letters would break. If you're trying to write a novel in a week (four days in one case), you just have to switch to the next typewriter in the stack.

These machines had a little V-shaped paper guide that popped up. This was the antenna. I was just the operator of the device and had no say in determining what signals were received. This was a serviceable answer until word-processors came along and screwed everything up for people like me. Now I have to think of another answer.

Q: It's all in the software.

Schow: It's a glitch. My entire career is a glitch because I jacked into the wrong port.

GRAHAM JOYCE

Graham Joyce is an English writer, who describes his work as "Old Peculiar" akin to Arthur Machen and Algernon Blackwood, and other masters of the English weird tale, though some critics have tried to link him with the magic realists. His novels include *Dreamside, Dark Sister, Requiem, House of Lost Dreams, The Tooth Fairy, Indigo, Smoking Poppy, The Facts of Life, The Kind of Fairy Tale, The Year of the Ladybird, The Ghost in the Electric Blue Suit*, and others. He has also published a good deal of very fine short fiction. He has a Ph. D. in English Literature and teaches creative writing at Nottingham Trent University.

Q: Some of your relatives have doubtless asked you, "Why do you write this weird stuff?" A better way to phrase that might be to ask "What is the appeal of putting the fantastic into your work?" You went to the Middle East and the result was *Requiem*, where someone else might have written a travel book or a realistic novel with an exotic setting. So, why the supernatural?

Joyce: I think the answer to that is that I don't trust rationality. Rationality is a construct that is helpful, and it helps us in analyzing the world. It gets us a lot of science and technology and it's very practical and useful, but there's an awful lot of stuff that can't be addressed by rationality.

What I'm trying to do by including the fantastic in my narratives is to try to find some sort of metaphor for responding to the overwhelming experiences of life.

Q: But you're basically following the emotional texture of the story to get characters into extreme states.

Joyce: Yeah, that's right. When you've got somebody in a state of psychic distress or emotional meltdown, it doesn't seem to adequately capture it just to report the external emotions, or the emotions externally viewed. So I often use psychic distress or hallucinogenic states as a kind of metaphor for what people are feeling inside themselves.

Q: Do you start with a character, or an image, or an idea?

Joyce: I always start with a particular scene I have in mind, a character in a location. The two things arrive together, usually. It's a picture of somebody in a situation. That situation might not necessarily be remarkable, but it's the question of working out how the character came to be in that situation and what they're going to do next.

Now the scene I start with—that trigger scene—may actually drop away once I have developed a novel. It might not have anything to do with the story later. It's a bit like a potato root. The original potato that you plant drops away. That's often been the case with my stories. With *The Tooth Fairy,* the very first scene I saw in my mind, I never used in the book.

Q: You're certainly the only writer I know who could write a straight, serious horror novel with a title like *The Tooth Fairy* and get away with it. From anyone else, that would be a joke. How did that one come about?

Joyce: It does sound like a joke. Everybody thinks it's either a joke or a kids' book when I tell them the title of that book. But how it came about was that I remembered some incident from when I was about five years old. My aunt and uncle had taken me to a restaurant, and I fell in love with the waitress, and I wanted to show her this tooth that had just dropped out the night before. I'd got it wrapped up in my pocket. I remember falling in love with this waitress and I wanted to show her. Yeah, it's sort of sick, but there it is. I remember the exchange, and that whole scene started the novel off. But I never used it. So it was just something that generated all that came to be the novel. It has its purpose, but it was just a piece of waste material at the end of the process.

Q: Do you have any awareness of working in a genre, in the sense of deciding, "This will be a horror novel," or do you avoid that and just see how things turn out?

Joyce: I am very aware of the genre and I am a fan of the genre. The thing is, I work on the edge of the genre. I don't go down the main stream. I am pretty much familiar with the main stream of both fantasy and horror, and I cut my teeth on it in my teenage years. I used to read loads of fantasy and horror. But the fact is that I am not playing in the middle of the genre, because I want to create a different kind of tension. It's more about the tension of whether this, say, supernatural event is really happening or not. If there is a ghost or a monster, I am less interested in looking at the ghost or monster and more interested in looking at the person who is seeing the ghost or the monster.

Q: This is more in the direction of Robert Aickman or Henry James than, say, Lovecraft.

Joyce: Aickman, definitely. Henry James, I'm not a great fan of. Less Lovecraft, more Arthur Machen, and, yes, Robert Aickman.

Q: One thing these writers—Machen and Aickman in particular—have in common is that in their stories you never come to full comprehension of what is going on. Their fiction is about ambiguity. Is this what draws you to them?

Joyce: I think that I live with ambiguity, with the things I was talking about earlier, about the nature of irrationally apprehended material. It goes back to the fact that I had a grandmother who herself had numerous prophetic dreams and visions. I heard stories from my mother and her sisters about my grandmother's experiences. My own skepticism kicks in immediately and my own credulity answers that. I shuttle between skepticism and credulity and I always have done. So I guess what I am working out in the novels is some point between those two things where I can actually carry on and not feel too muddle-headed about it.

Q: Isn't writing also a consciously visionary experience or dreaming, in the sense that other people have visions, but you can make this up?

Joyce: Yeah, I think it is a kind of dreaming. It's dreaming with a controlled focus, and like a dream, I don't want it to be fully interpreted, because somehow that dream is punctured, and it deflates, once it is fully interpreted. It doesn't have its power over you anymore. I do resist ending up with the rational explanation for these things. But even if I were to go further into the middle of the horror genre and say, "Ah, yes, it was a monster," that puts it in a box and explains it away in a different manner. I avoid that too.

Q: Think of any number of Aickman stories, or "The Turn of the Screw," which cannot really resolve beyond inexplicable mystery. Maybe this is the strength of this sort of fiction, that it stays with you, like the last shiver of a bell ringing, forever.

Joyce: Yes. The point is that what I like to aim for, and what I like reading, is that kind of fiction that detonates after you've reached the last page, so that you walk away carrying some of that stuff with you. That's the exemplar for me.

One of my favorite books is *Perfume* by Patrick Suskind. An extraordinary book. I went away from that book for days just smelling new things and feeling like my nostril cavities had been opened wider. If that sort of thing can happen after fiction, I feel that's a great realization.

Q: I guess you'd only find out from your readers if you've accomplished this yourself.

Joyce: I'd like to get there! Let's put it that way.

Q: Can you think of other books that you thought did the same thing, or even influenced you, or just made you wish you could write that well?

Joyce: British fantasist M. John Harrison is an exemplar in this field. I don't know how well known he is in the States, but he is just superb, and pretty much any of his stuff has this effect on me. His writing has been a tremendous influence. But I have a Master's Degree in English and I have pretty much studied the canonical literature, so it's too wide to say who has been an influence from that sort of background. It all gets trampled in the barrel, and I am sure there is a bit of something everywhere.

Q: I will posit a theory, that the way you deal with the matter of influences is by having so many of them that they blend together into something new. If you were just obsessed with one or two writers, you would end up writing imitations. So Ramsey Campbell had to move beyond Lovecraft, even as Lovecraft had to move beyond Dunsany. Was there ever any writer you had to move beyond?

Joyce: When I was in my twenties I did have a big fix on Thomas Pynchon. At the time I thought he was the greatest writer who had ever emerged from the planet. I don't think that now. It seems to me that there are books that are appropriate for you at different times in your life. Some things you read and have enjoyed immensely, they won't stand up later to any rigorous examination. But I did have a time when I was just trying to write stuff like Thomas Pynchon. That had to stop. It did stop.

But there are other people. I mean, ridiculously, I had a period where I was trying to write like Jonathan Swift, because I am an enormous admirer of Jonathan Swift's stuff. I was writing this circumlocutory, mandarin, 18th century English for some reason. But it all helped at the end of the day, in doing that thing of writing lots of stuff to try and develop my own voice.

Q: How did you go from writing imitations of Jonathan Swift to publication.

Joyce: [Laughs.] Well, I stopped, is the short answer to that. I quickly realized that this very masculine, long-winded prose wasn't really what I wanted to write at all. I think that after I had thrown off these shackles, of people as diverse as Swift and Pynchon, I just began to write more in the vernacular, in the way that I speak myself and the way that people around me speak. It was a big realization, that you don't have to sound like some big cheese writer from the canon.

Q: Did you then just write a novel and sell it?

Joyce: I wrote a novel and sold it. I didn't go the short-story route. In fact I wasn't very much aware of the short-story market within this genre. I quit my job. I went to live on a Greek island, and I just got my head down and I wrote what was effectively my second novel. The first novel is still rotting in a drawer somewhere. (The best place for it.) But this second novel, that I wrote while I was in Greece, that's the one that sold, and it was published as *Dreamside*.

Q: Once you got going, you don't seem to have had a discernable apprenticeship. Was this because you started writing seriously later in life?

Joyce: No, not at all. I didn't mean to give that impression. I started writing when I was a kid, but it was mostly just that, kiddie stuff. I think the very first complete story that I wrote was when I was about eleven years old and my school team won the Soccer League in my town. This passionate event was recorded in a story that I wrote. I kind of liked making up stories from that point, and I continued to do it. Throughout my teenage years, I was scribbling stuff. But I never got serious about a full novel until I was seventeen years old, and I got seven chapters into a fantasy novel, which I abandoned. But it wasn't many years later until I completed a novel proper.

Q: I always admire the stamina of people who write novel after novel before they sell anything. We hear about writers who have twenty or so unpublished novels in a closet. I know I couldn't do that.

Joyce: The other thing I was doing in my early twenties was writing a lot of poetry. I won a prize for poetry at the time, so I had an image of myself as a poet or a would-be poet. I don't know what happened, but I think I got to the age twenty-eight, yeah it was exactly twenty-eight; I think it might have been on my twenty-eighth birthday. I looked at all these poems I'd written and realized what dross it was.

Poetry and I just fell out. The Muse left me, or I left the Muse; I don't know. But I just switched all my energies to writing novels. So there was an awful lot of writing going on, in a lot of ways, and it was good in that it was always helping me to find out how to push words about on the page. So the quantity was being turned out, even if it was drivel. I was developing the capacity to find out how words worked, in all that bad poetry and those kiddie stories and the rest of it. I think it helped me later.

Q: How did you develop the critical sense to realize that the early stories were not masterpieces? Were you in contact with any kind of writing community?

Joyce: I wasn't in contact with writers, but remember I was studying English at university. I did a master's degree, studying English. [Laughs.] So, it was painfully apparent how woefully inadequate that this stuff I'd written. I didn't need to be a genius to work out that this was not great stuff.

Q: Did you ever have professors tell you, "No, no, this horror and fantasy stuff isn't Literature, you just write Serious work."

Joyce: We didn't have creative writing modules in my day. Today a young person wanting to write is quite lucky, because they can go to a university and take a creative writing module and often be taught by practicing writer. But it wasn't available in my time. Writing was something furtive you did alone in your room, and that you kept quiet about.

Q: I understand that your new novel, *Smoking Poppy*, is something of a departure, and based on your travel experiences. Could you tell it came about?

Joyce: Well, first let me say that I don't think it's that much of a departure. It's just that the supernatural and fantasy element is very thin. But it's still there in a very thin line, the way it has been with some of my previous novels. I guess the thickening or the thinning of the supernatural or horror line is what distinguishes my novels, but it's certainly still there.

The whole thing came about by a notion I had of a metaphor for opium smoking, and once I'd decided that, I had two choices of where to set that part of the novel, and that was either in the Golden Triangle, which is where I eventually went, or else the Golden Crescent, which of course is Afghanistan and Pakistan—and I didn't really fancy that much. So I ended up going to live with the ethnic hill tribes of northern Thailand on the Burma border—Myanmar it's called now, not Burma. These are very interesting people. They're not Thai themselves. They're Tibetan in origin. They migrated to Thailand about two hundred years ago, and brought the opium cultivation skills with them. They're animistic in their religion. They believe in spirits, multiple spirits living around them. I wanted to go and find out how that worked for people, as far as I could, or see the location in which this was happening. So I spent some time living in a village, and I discovered things that I couldn't have found out if I hadn't gone there. There were these structures in the middle of the village, wooden structures, which are actually gates for the encouragement of the free passage of the spirits into and out of the village. Taboo to touch. And they were surrounded by phallic carvings and vulvas and birds and animals. There were also fertility swings that the young girls used to swing on, to encourage the spirits to help them be fertile. These kind of things you can't find out unless you go there.

Q: How did you get the people to accept you and to let you live among them as more than a strange Western tourist?

Joyce: The thing is that they were remarkably nonplussed by the fact that I was there. My guides had to pay them so that I could have one the huts, and we would buy a few chickens off them to slaughter. They'd come up with a dish of monkey-and-mango stew for you now and again. They didn't seem fazed at all by the fact that I was there. They didn't speak English, so I was trying to communicate through my guides, who didn't speak their language very well. I tried to find out the significance of the spirit gate and so on. It was communication by gesture and a little bit of broken English. But they just got on with their work and they more or less ignored me. They were friendly. They weren't hostile. They didn't make a great fuss. They just let me be.

Q: Did they understand you were writing a book about them?

Joyce: No, I didn't say anything about that. I just described myself as somebody who was a traveler, who was interested. There was no trouble. Though there was one hairy moment—you see, these areas are controlled by opium bandits. They buy up the land from these subsistence farmers and they rent it back to them, because the subsistence farmers are now allowed to grow opium for their own use. So that's how the opium bandits get around it. This guy walked into the village with a sawn-off shotgun, and he was a bit too interested in why I was there. The guides told me we had to pay him off with a little bit of money. He was just asking questions about what I was doing there. Maybe he thought I was the law. Maybe he thought I was the DEA or something. I don't know. We just paid him off and he left me alone.

Q: This must give you an advantage. I don't imagine most of the writers in our field do this kind of first-hand research. So, where would you go next?

Joyce: I don't really know. I tend to do a domestic novel and then an exotic novel in turn. I'm still wondering about the next one. I've got some fantasies about Japan. They've got some very interesting ghost-story traditions in Japan, and I'd like to explore that. Or maybe China. I am very interested now in Asia, now that I have been to Thailand. I'd kind of like to go to Laos or Vietnam. Laos is pretty much like Thailand, but without all the hideous aspects of tourism that Thailand seems to have attracted. So Laos might be one target, but that's a bit too similar to Thailand. So maybe I'll end up going to Japan or China.

Q: Do you have another book in progress now?

Joyce: I just delivered my new book, called *The Facts of Life*, and it's about the grandmother started off this interview telling you about. I finally decided to do something about this influence on my life. She had a series of visions of visitors who would come to the door, knock on the door, and she would open the door and deal with them, and then she would wake up in her chair. These phantoms always had some message. Of course I heard these stories second-hand from my mother, but these phantoms came over and over and over to my grandmother. She wasn't particularly frightened by them, but she didn't seek them out, and she didn't think it was a good idea to do anything to encourage them. So I ended up writing a novel where I was exploring this, what was going on, and I incorporated it into the story of Coventry after the War—my home town's Coventry—being rebuilt after the Germans had blitzed it flat. So you've got this story, about the city being rebuilt, at the same time you've got this old woman receiving these phantoms. It's a complicated story about all of her seven daughters sharing around the upbringing of this kid, who is the illegitimate son of one of the daughters. His father was an American G.I. who came over to England during the War and died at Utah Beach. It's this kid growing up, in Coventry. As the sisters are trying to shape his personality with their conflicting values, the city is being rebuilt, and grandmother is having her visions. Is that complicated enough?

Q: It's complicated enough. It sounds interesting. Have you ever had any uncanny experience yourself, or do you just hear about these things?

Joyce: I suppose I have had a few uncanny experiences myself. They're not things that can be resolved into a rounded anecdote. They're always a little bit too strange and a little bit too connected with not having enough sleep or taking the wrong kind of substances. You know what I mean. [Laughs.] There I go again, you see, rationalizing them away.

Yeah, I remember one time in my days when I was young and foolish. We had been messing around with a ouija board. I was on vacation with some friends. We were staying in this trailer park. There were communal toilets across the block. You had to walk across the grass to use the lavatories. It was pitch black after we'd been messing about, and we were still giggling about what had happened with this ouija board. A white horse reared up in front of me, just inches in front of me and then vanished again. It shit me, and just recalling the incident shits me and will for the rest of my life. I don't know what it was. It came. It went. It was the strangest thing.

Q: But you didn't go back the following morning and look for hoof-prints?

Joyce: There was no way that it was a real horse in that place. It was something in my mind, or it was a phantom. I don't know if it was external or internal, but it was enough to cause enough investigation in my own mind to make me write all of these novels.

Q: Thanks, Graham.

Recorded at NECon,
July 21, 2002.

BRIAN LUMLEY

Brian Lumley is not just one of the most popular Lovecraftian writers in the business, but a bestseller for his *Necroscope* series. He began under the tutelage of August Derleth, who published his first book, *The Caller of the Black* from Arkham House in 1971. He began writing in his spare time while stationed in Germany in the British army, before becoming a full time writer in 1980. Some of his other titles include *The Horror at Oakdeane, The Transition of Titus Crow, Khai of Ancient Khem, Demogorgon, The Clock of Dreams, Fruiting Bodies and Other Fungi, Beneath the Moors, Psychomech* and its sequels, and more.

Q: To begin with—

Lumley:

> *I just read a story by Schweitzer.*
> *It gave me a terrible fright, sir.*
> *The heroine's fine,*
> *till she goes down a mine,*
> *and a Burrower jumps out and bites her.*

Q: You realize that is an addition to the Cthulhu Mythos, since the heroine is bitten by a Burrower Beneath, which leads us reasonably into the subject of this interview, which is your long relationship to the Mythos. It's been a long while since you first picked up a Lovecraft book, and it changed your life, did it not?

Lumley: It did indeed. When did I pick it up? I think my first Lovecraft came into my possession in Germany, when I was a young guy, maybe 22 or 23 years old. It was *Cry Horror!* A British World Distributors Ltd. paperback, two shillings and sixpence. While I had hit upon Lovecraftian stories before, Mythos stories, namely Robert Bloch's "Notebook Found in a Deserted House" and others of that ilk, one or two *Weird Tales* stories maybe, this was the first time I'd had a real, complete book by Lovecraft. That was it. That was the beginning. All of a sudden

I wanted to write as well. I had tried one or two short stories when I was a much younger guy, maybe fourteen or fifteen year old, but all of a sudden, I had a real incentive. Lovecraft had shown me the way just as he had shown many other people the way.

Q: He'd shown you the way in a period in which there wasn't a lot of horror fiction being done.

Lumley: That's right. In England we had Ronald Chetwynd-Hayes, who, I think, had already begun to put together some books of macabre fiction. August Derleth at Arkham House, of course. He was called the Dean of Macabre Publishers at the time probably because he was one of the few Macabre publishers at the time. And there was…who the hell was it, Darrell, who wrote *The Haunting of Toby Jugg*?

Q: Dennis Wheatley.

Lumley: Wheatley in England was producing macabre books, and some of them were very good for their time. And that was about it. There really wasn't much happening.

Q: But you just wrote anyway without seriously thinking about the markets.

Lumley: I didn't know anything about the markets. I was in Berlin. Since buying *Cry Horror!* I had moved on to Cyprus and picked up *Dark Mind, Dark Heart*, an Arkham House book, full of Lovecraftian bits and pieces, more macabre stories, really enjoyable stuff. I had started to collect Lovecraft and other Arkham House writers. So, from Cyprus I went to Berlin. In my desk duties, as a military policeman, after the last drunk had been locked up and the last would-be refugee had been cut to pieces on the wire or the wall or shot, there was nothing much to do. But you couldn't sleep. It was a very dangerous situation. It was a hot spot. It could be the beginning of World War III. So you had to be awake. So I was reading Arkham House books. Several of these books carried August Derleth's address, which I still remember . . .

Q: You've often rather forcefully expressed the opinion that the Cthulhu Mythos is still an evolving, on-going concern, and consists of more than reading "The Call of Cthulhu" and "The Dunwich Horror" over and over again. Would you care to expound on that?

Lumley: I think you've just done it for me, Darrell. It's the interest in Lovecraft himself which keeps the Mythos swinging. The reason it is still moving along is because people are still finding Lovecraft as an originator. And of course they always will. There are new generations coming up all the time. Now, I say there always will, but that may not be true. When was the last time you read Edgar Allan Poe?

Q: Rather recently, actually, though I admit I've had to review a lot of it because I've been writing introductions for Poe books published by Wildside Press.

Lumley: Well, yeah…but what happens here is that eventually the stories do become dated. We know they're classics, but they do become dated. I couldn't read *Dracula* again now, for the simple reason that I found it musty in large part twenty years ago, so I've got no doubt I'd find it even mustier now. They do. They do date. And Lovecraft will date as well, eventually. So, the new guys will come along writing in the Mythos, doing it and Lovecraft a favor, because if people stumble across their books first, before they stumble across Lovecraft—which has happened with me on many occasions. People have read my stuff first. I get any number of e-mails which say, "Brian, I am so glad I found your books because I wouldn't have found Lovecraft if I hadn't found your books first, if I hadn't read *The Burrowers Beneath*, *The Transition of Titus Crow*, or some of your short stories. Then I went looking for Lovecraft." When I read Lovecraft, I went looking for Robert Bloch and the other writers in the Mythos. So it will go on, but it's going to take a hell of a good writer, now, to write an original, interesting, intriguing Mythos story.

Q: If you're correct that Lovecraft's own stories will date, does that mean that the Mythos itself has some quality which could outlast Lovecraft? Is it possible that the time will come when Lovecraft is so dated that no one reads him, but people read the Mythos in the work of other writers?

Lumley: Yes, it's possible. Let's face it. Cthulhu has become one of the classic monsters. You now think of the Wolf Man and Dracula and the Mummy—and Cthulhu. It's a fact. He is one of the classic monsters.

Q: He's also a plush toy.

Lumley: There again. What was that outfit that was doing the classic monsters plastic kits?

Q: Aurora. That was about thirty years ago.

Lumley: They didn't have plush toys back then, but there you go. These things have all had their offspring.

Q: It has been argued that Lovecraft is more powerful than other horror writers because he is writing a genuine anti-mythology, an authentic response to the discovery of the vast universe of billions of galaxies, in which mankind can only have a trivial role. Therefore this is a lot more vital than, say, the Mummy, who is surely a local affair. Lovecraft looks outward to the cosmos, where the older mythologies are local and static.

Lumley: Human beings will always want to read about human beings. If we carried your idea about Lovecraft looking outward to the cosmos, the time would come when we're writing stories not about human beings at all, but about the outer cosmos, where we are in fact minuscules in the fate of the universe. I don't see that happening. Writing and reading is human interest. We won't read anything that doesn't have people in it. Yes, we may read about cats because we understand cats. They're our little familiars. But I think people will always primarily have an interest in people and how the universe affects them, and not the other way around.

Q: Lovecraft talks about achieving total externality, with no human interest at all. One wonders if he was talking through his hat a little bit. You can't have a story without characters of some sort.

Lumley: He may have wanted to write without characters. If you check the dialogue in his stories, you won't find a hell of a lot of it. So, you could be right there. He certainly didn't want to write about women much, because the only women in his stories…you had the semi-cretin Lavinia Whateley, who did noxious things with Yog-Sothoth. You had the woman in "The Thing on the Doorstep."

Q: Asenath Waite. But she wasn't really a woman, remember. That was her father's spirit animating and controlling the daughter's body.

Lumley: That's correct. Maybe Lovecraft had something about women, which with his childhood, you could understand, I think. I think that Lovecraft might have liked my stories, but I don't think he would have liked me as a person. Hey, my idea of a man-woman relationship is a whole lot different than HPL's.

Q: People don't faint a lot in your stories. . . .

Lumley: No, I don't let them do much fainting! They actually make love, too. They don't hold pinkies and tell each other how much they appreciate each other.

Q: You realize that if Lovecraft had lived to a normal life-expectancy, you could have met him.

Lumley: Yes, indeed. As you know, I was born just nine months after he died. That was a fact that was pointed out to me by Donald Wollheim, when he came across to Germany one time while I was still in the army. This was a fact which I did not know he intended to use. He put it on the back of one of my early books, that I had "inherited the mantle of Lovecraft," because I was born nine months later. But, you know, if Lovecraft knew I was writing Mythos stories he'd turn over in his grave; not because he wouldn't like the stories, but because they come from a different mindset entirely.

Q: Of course he encouraged all of his friends to write in the Mythos.

Lumley: I know he did, but, I'm saying, would I have been one of his friends? [Laughs.]

Q: He probably would have been polite to you. The only person who ever really got him upset was Forrest J. Ackerman.

Lumley: Really?

Q: The Lovecraft letters are full of unkind comments about Forrest J. Ackerman, largely because of Ackerman railing about Clark Ashton Smith being no good. There was a great flap about this in a fanzine in the 1930's. It was a little undignified for Lovecraft, actually.

Lumley: Yes, well flaps in fanzines have been happening since time-immemorial. Lovecraft was having arguments in his early amateur publications, and I suppose it will go on forever. Let's face it. You and I may be the best of friends, but we've had our arguments about the Mythos and writing and science fiction and fantasy and horror in general. It doesn't mean that the world will not continue because there are flaps in amateur magazines.

Q: I don't think we've ever had a heated disagreement. Lovecraft got really upset. He was quite unflappable otherwise. One wonders how things would have been if Lovecraft had lived until 1970. He would have been 80.

Lumley: Would he have seen anything of mine, I wonder? My first stories were published in 1968. It's possible if he had still been lucid. Doubtless he would have picked up little Augie Derleth's Arkham House books. There's no question about that. I suppose he would have been pleased with most of them. He probably would have seen my stories. If he'd seen my first one, it wouldn't have anything to do with the Cthulhu Mythos. "The Cyprus Shell" wasn't a Mythos story. Maybe I would have been overawed by his presence and backed off and never written *The Burrowers Beneath* or "Sister City."

Q: I think there would have been considerably less of a tendency to continue the work of a living writer, even if he let you.

Lumley: But remember that in his lifetime he was encouraging people to contribute to his Mythos, de Castro, Hazel Heald.

Q: Lovecraft actually wrote their stories and put in the Mythos elements himself.

Lumley: I know. Who were the others? C.M. Eddy.

Q: The Mythos writers who really wrote their own work were such people as Donald Wandrei, Robert Bloch, Clark Ashton Smith, Robert E. Howard, and so on. These were the ones who were real writers and could do it themselves.

Lumley: That's right. Then you had Robert Bloch's "The Shambler from the Stars."

Q: Or Frank Belknap Long's "The Horror from the Hills," which is based on one of Lovecraft's dreams.

Lumley: That's right. And Lovecraft obviously enjoyed this, because after Bloch's "The Shambler from the Stars," he obliged by killing off "Robert Blake" in "The Haunter of the Dark." So Bloch came back and did—what was that third one?

Q: "The Shadow from the Steeple."

Lumley: I've written to Frank Belknap Long. I have letters from him. I have written to Carl Jacobi. It wasn't that I wanted to apologize for using his ideas in "The Aquarium." It wasn't that I wanted to apologize for using Frank Belknap Long's Hounds of Tindalos. I was so keenly interested in these things that I wanted their permission to use them. I would not have done them without their permission. If Lovecraft had been alive, I would not have done my stories without his permission, and there might be a sixth book of Lovecraft's letters from Arkham House, and there would be certain loud-mouth Mythos authorities who wouldn't be able to decry some of the stuff I've done, because I would have had Lovecraft's permission.

Q: You might have had his cover blurbs too.

Lumley: Yeah. That's right.

Q: I'm sure someone would still say, "Well, Lovecraft is just being polite..."

Lumley: Oh course. Of course. He didn't really mean to say that. He hates Lumley, actually. [Laughs.]

Q: Of course it would be a whole different field. There very likely wouldn't be any Arkham House, because it wouldn't have been necessary to memorialize Lovecraft in the late '30s if he were still alive. If he'd lived longer...my hunch is that he probably would not have written much for *Unknown*, but he would have had original stories in *Famous Fantastic Mysteries*.

Lumley: Yes, that's probably about right.

Q: And then some material in *Fantasy and Science Fiction* in the early '50's.

Lumley: Yes, and he would of course have seen the era in which Margaret Brundage's covers would not have needed ripping off the magazines. [Laughs.] But he would have seen a lot of far worse covers—

Q: The grand old days of *Thrilling Wonder Stories* when men were men and women wore measuring-cups.

Lumley: Yes….[Laughs.]

Q: Of course any writer can't keep on doing the same thing over and over forever, Mythos or not. You've certainly moved on to other things.

Lumley: How that happened was very simple. Thirteen years in the army, I was writing, and I had no contact with fandom and with the publishing business. Everything I was getting published, I had to send myself to publishers. These were unsolicited manuscripts, until Kirby McCauley came along. After August Derleth died, there was no Arkham House to send the stuff to. Well, there was an Arkham House, but there was no August Derleth, and stuff was mounting up. Come 1980, when I was due to leave the army, it dawned on me that there was a bigger world out there. There were more real publishers. I had to find them if I wanted to continue writing, and I could not keep on writing Mythos stories when the main publisher of those stories no longer existed as such.

It wasn't that I was stuck in the Mythos or that I should find my own voice. I always had my own voice. My stories have females in them. My Mythos stories had *s*e*x*…filthy words in some of them. "The Return of the Deep Ones" has sex scenes in it. Not explicit sex, but one knew that I wasn't writing from an entirely neutral point of view. There were sexual inferences. So I had to find a new market. I had to do something different. Hence *Pyschomech* and eventually *Necroscope,* when I really found my style, found my mode. But my stories always changed. If you look at the *Titus Crow* series, the first story is a horror story, *The Burrowers Beneath.* The second one, *The Transition of Titus Crow,* is a science-fantasy. I was trying all the fields. The third one, *The Clock of Dreams,* is a pure fantasy. *Spawn of the Winds* is again a science-fantasy, and *The Moons of Borea* is a complete fantasy, and likewise *Elysia* is the most fantastic of them all. I was exploring the entire field.

Q: It seems that the book that made all the difference in your career was *Necroscope*. This is the one that made you a real household name.

Lumley: What happened was, I was living in a little house down in Devon. I had a mortgage. I had very little money in the bank. I certainly couldn't afford to fly across the Atlantic. Paul Ganley, who had published some of my books said to me, "Come across. I've got a thousand books for you to sign. I'll get your air-fare, because there's a cheap fare going," which he did. And Randy Everts, who was publishing a small magazine, *Etchings and Odysseys*, said, "I want to talk to you about using a couple of your stories, and I'll pay for your room in Providence." So I could afford to take my wife, and they could afford to take me, so I went to the World Fantasy Convention. I found the Tor Books party. I didn't know what Tor Books was—I knew they existed, but I didn't know what it was. There was a bouncer who stood in the doorway of the party. He said, "Who are you?" I said "I'm Brian Lumley." He said, "I'm Tom Doherty. Come in to my party. What do you do?" I said, "I write," and I had a dog-eared copy of *Necroscope* in my hand. I said, "You might like to look at this Tom." He stood there doing nothing. He said, "Yeah, I'll look at it." So he's drinking his beer and looking at it, and half an hour later when I went out, he's still reading it. He tapped me on the shoulder when I went out and said, "Get in touch with me. Give me a call when you get back home, will you?" I did. Three weeks later Melissa Singer got on the phone and said, not to me, but to my agent, that she would like to buy this one, and *Vamphyri!*, which was also just out and which we shipped over very quickly. My agent said, "There's a third one, *The Source*, which is about a month away from being finished." Melissa said, "We'll buy that one sight unseen as well." So, the next day I didn't have a mortgage and I was rich. I stayed that way every since.

Q: You mentioned once that the first British edition of *Necroscope* had a cover that didn't work. So they had to recall the book, redo the cover, and then you became rich.

Lumley: Absolutely. The British scene is not as big as the American scene. If you sell 100,000 copies in England, you're doing extraordinarily well. So, the jacket they put on the book in England: there was this rotting skull bursting from the ground. The rotten half was bigger than the fleshy part of the skull. It was a lousy jacket. This was one terrible jacket. And *Necroscope*, the title, was in letraset. You couldn't want for a worse jacket. It wasn't going to sell, and it didn't. So my editor said, "There's something wrong here." So they re-jacketed the book and put a George Underwood cover on it. It went and it kept going, and it still is going. So I was very fortunate. I was fortunate, first of all, to bump into

Tom, who has since become a personal friend. *Necroscope*, incidentally, has sold about 360-370,000 copies in the States alone. It is published in fourteen other countries, including China, Russia, Japan, Greece (of all places), Belgium, France, Germany. I was very fortunate. Yes, this was the one.

Q: You went from there to the very popular subject of vampires—although perhaps it was you who helped make vampires popular.

Lumley: Well, it's possible. I know that Romania is running out of wood. And paper. God knows how many forests have been deforested to print vampire books. In fact they will be printing so many vampire books that there is no wood for stakes anymore. That's why these guys are proliferating. You know that . . .? [Laughs.]

Q: If you drive a book through their heart, it's not quite the same thing.

Lumley: That's not the same, no.

Q: You've done unusual things with vampires, too. I don't think too many people have taken them to other worlds.

Lumley: Other dimensions. Parallel worlds.

Q: Your vampires don't merely come from an old castle somewhere. They have a much more elaborate background.

Lumley: That's right, but the gate is in Romania. That explains why that place has so many bloodsuckers. In fact there is only one place on Earth that has got more bloodsuckers than Romania. That's Las Vegas.

Q: That's a different kind.

Lumley: Vampire City. I've got a lot of friends there, actually.

Q: You've now made the vampire your own.

Lumley: Oh, I wouldn't say that.

Q: Other people have them, but there is a distinct Lumley vampire.

Lumley: There is indeed, and they are, I am told, unique in their way. They have a real reason for being. They have a real background. There is an explanation of why they have not taken over the world, not even their own world, although they have tried hard enough. Yeah. I changed—well, I didn't change it. I suppose I did what I did with Lovecraft again. I took an accepted mythology and gave it a Lumley touch. But I have not incurred the wrath of orthodox vampire lovers.

Q: You seem to have incurred the wrath of certain Lovecraft critics.

Lumley: Yes, indeed. "Nobody ever erected a statue to a critic." Jean Sibelius.

Q: There are critics who see Lovecraft as a major philosopher, which leads one to a kind of doctrine of Lovecraftianism, and maybe you've become heretical.

Lumley: Oh, he did have his philosophy, which was very real and very genuine to the man. But we're all individuals, Darrell. If we all thought alike and did alike, it would be one hell of a dull, boring old world, wouldn't it?

Q: Do you think there's any influence of Lovecraft in your later works?

Lumley: I've just finished a 21,000-word story, a Deep Ones story. Fedogan and Bremer had remarkable success with *Shadows over Innsmouth*. It was a good seller. It went into paperback with Del Rey, was picked up by Gollancz in England, done by a Japanese outfit, and still going, doing well. Steve Jones lives by his editing, as most editors do, and it seemed a good idea to do a second book, so Fedogan and Bremer have just signed a contract for a second *Shadows over Innsmouth*. I don't know what the title will be. It's a similarly-themed book. This time they won't all be English writers. There might be American writers in it as well. I've just done a story called "The Taint," which is an Innsmouth story, set in England. I think it's one of my best. So it's a long time I've been writing Mythos stories. When a good theme occurs, I'll do them again.

Q: Are there echoes of Lovecraft in your non-Mythos writing? Is there a "taint" of Lovecraft which goes through the whole body of your work? Is there anything you've picked up from him?

Lumley: That's an open one—

Q: Certainly he would have been a formative influence.

Lumley: Oh, Heavens yes. Of course he was. I won't say he was profound, the way I've heard some writers say he was a profound influence. I think it was more a desire to be able to write like that. But, having developed that desire and having done it, I very quickly learned how not to write like that. Anything I've picked up from him? I don't know. I sometimes have to fight to stop italicizing the last sentence. [Laughs.] Which I've done, which he did on several occasions. I don't know, a sense of...if you can make your reader believe you're more erudite than you really are, you've halfway there. You might be getting there. A love of words, of course. I mean, I never had to scramble to figure out what "eldritch" meant. It was obvious from his writing.

Q: He's kept that word alive. It's one of his gifts to the language. You don't hear it anywhere else.

Lumley: But I'm wondering, "squamous" or "batrachian." Was that Lovecraft who kept those alive, or was that Derleth? [Laughs.]

Q: They're both from Lovecraft, though we tend to use "squamous" only facetiously these days. A lot of these words we use with a knowing sense of irony. I don't think anyone uses "eldritch" with an absolutely straight face anymore.

Lumley: That's right, yes. We no longer see it as a serious thing anymore, do we? [Chuckles.] I can't really say that there is any one Lovecraftian thing that runs through my work. No. I don't think so. I'm not thinking Lovecraft when I'm writing.

Q: You have a very different kind of protagonist. You have a more go-getter protagonist, rather than someone who sits around sifting papers until he sees a pattern eventually.

Lumley: No, no. That's not my people, definitely not.

Q: You have a very different background from Lovecraft. If he had been in the army, things would have been very different, I'm sure.

Lumley: I'm sure. He would have ended up gibbering if he'd been 22 years in the army. He would have wound up in one of those padded cells he's so fond of.

Q: When Lovecraft actually tried to volunteer for military service in 1917, he said it would either cure him or kill him. But his mother got him first.

Lumley: Yes. She knew it would kill him.

Q: It probably would have, if he had gone to the trenches.

Lumley: I'm sure. No, I don't think he was built for army rigors. There's a point that struck me, some time ago, about "The Call of Cthulhu." You've read *Dracula*. Lovecraft had read *Dracula*. Now then, how do you see these sensitive dreamers, the Wilcoxes and de Castros and what-have-you? If you will recall, in *Dracula*, Renfield equates very much to these people. Renfield knew the Master was coming. He spoke to him telepathically across the waters. He said, "I'm coming." Renfield was munching lesser things. When the Master came, he'd be eating much bigger things. Your sensitive dreamers in the waking world have been contacted by the Master, who's coming. People in madhouses go crazy all over the world. You'll remember where Renfield was. I'm sure that got through to Lovecraft.

Q: I think what also got through to Lovecraft on that story was Arthur Machen's "The Great Return."

Lumley: Yeah.

Q: But he found the Holy Grail to be way too prosaic, so he supplied something a lot more interesting.

Lumley: You're probably right.

Q: Also, the story is very similar structurally.

Lumley: Oh, yes. I think he learned a thing or two from Machen, and from Algernon Blackwood. Of course he had a great love-affair with "The Great God Pan," didn't he?

Q: He particularly liked "The White People"—

Lumley: Yeah—

Q: Which you can see coming out in "The Dunwich Horror."

Lumley: His thing against Blackwood, of course, was that he romanticized too much. He had too much of the soppy, soft stuff in his fiction for Lovecraft's taste. But yeah, I think something of *Dracula* might have gotten through to Lovecraft. But I don't think anything of Lovecraft has lingered in me, really. If I stumble across a Lovecraft theme that needs developing, a Mythos idea that hasn't been done yet, I'll do it. The new one I was talking about, this 21,000-worder for the new Innsmouth book. It's a Mythos story, but you won't find great, old books in it. You won't find long reams of references to Mythos locations and characters. But it's nevertheless a very, very real Mythos story, which you'll find out when you see the thing. I could have, I suppose, submitted it to *Weird Tales*. I know you would have accepted that one. But I rather like Fedogan and Bremer books—

Q: Of course. I can understand that—

Lumley: —and it's an original, so this was obviously the place for it to go.

Q: We're still hoping for another "Fruiting Bodies." That's one of the classics we published.

Lumley: And if an idea occurs which can develop into such a story, you can guarantee that it will be written. Of course. I thoroughly enjoyed writing that one. It wrote itself. I had no struggle at all. It just threw itself on the paper. I suppose every writer does it. They have novels or short stories which some force lifts above the rest of their work. It happens to all of us, and that's one of them. The same for *Necroscope*, of course. It has the same type of force underneath. So it rose up above the rest of my stuff. But it dragged the rest of my stuff along with it. Stories and books which had only been published by small presses are now published in hardback by major presses, on the strength of *Necroscope*. And they're doing well.

Q: You've now got a substantial amount of books out there.

Lumley: Indeed I have. It's very pleasant. I need a bigger house now, for my shelves, foreign editions.

Q: I think the best a writer can hope for is to be hit by lightning like that a couple times in his life. Think of Bram Stoker again. He wrote a lot of other books, but if he hadn't written *Dracula*, no one would care about any of them.

Lumley: That's right. Well lightning has struck me on a couple of occasions. *The House of Doors* did very well for Tor. There were a couple hundred thousand sales there. The *Psychomech* trilogy did very well for Tor, and for me. A good many sales there too. But I think *Necroscope*, the series, is running about…I must be pushing three million in America alone. Well, I'm not going to run out of brandy or cigarettes in a while anyway.

Q: Has there been any Hollywood interest?

Lumley: Oh, yeah. It's got to be the strangest place on Earth, Hollywood. When I get the right contract with the right people, and it has the right names on it, and they're willing to pay—you see, this is not me being entirely mercenary. I wouldn't even attempt to suggest that they stick to the story. They're probably going to want to get rid of Harry Keogh, for instance. You know, "*Necroscope*. Great book. But do we really need this guy who has his own mode of conveyance between places? How about these vampires? Do we really need this vampire world? Can we make the hero a woman?" If it ever happens, I'm going to say, "The contract's good. The number of zeroes on the bottom is correct. Don't approach me to have anything to do with the script." If the movie's great, then I'll say, "Well, what did you expect?" And if it's a stinker, I'll say, "Well, it had nothing to do with me."

Q: So you take the money and run.

Lumley: Yeah. But not because I wouldn't want it to be successful. But I'm absolutely certain that I wouldn't have any influence on it anyway. Once you've sold it, once you've signed that contract, that's your soul, brother, gone. Look what they did to "Necros," on *The Hunger* series.

Q: I haven't seen it.

Lumley: They did "Necros," my story, on one of those trilogies.

Q: And what was left of it?

Lumley: You wouldn't recognize it.

Q: The satisfaction of the printed page is that you can control more of what is on it.

Lumley: That's right. It's not a bad idea to accept the money for "Necros." Of course it was very, very good money for a short story. But it wasn't my short story that they did.

Q: I have a theory that what Hollywood often does, to avoid lawsuits, is find the oldest story they can that's vaguely similar to what they wish to make, buy the rights to it, and then ignore it. Then if someone says, "You stole my idea," they can say, "Take it up with Lumley."

Lumley: Yeah, that's right.

Q: Beyond the new Mythos story you've mentioned, what else are you working on these days?

Lumley: There's a science-fiction story I'm working on. It's a novel. It may be the first time that I've had to go back and rewrite. I've set the thing in the Solar System. But there are reasons now why I may not be able to use the Solar System. I may have to go further out, to find or design another star system. So that's at around 120 pages, and it may stay there while I sort it out in my head. It's very Jack-Vanceish, not a pastiche of Vance, but very Vanceish, because I have been in love with his stuff for a long time. Everything that Jack Vance has written, I've read two or three times. If you read his stuff long enough, eventually you'll start to sound like that when you write yourself. Also, of course, I love his style. So, yeah, I would say a cross between Vance and Lumley, with perhaps some horror, a load of horror, but it will be a real science-fiction story.

Meanwhile, I suppose, Darrell, as the ideas occur, I shall try to write some "Fruiting Bodies" style stories over the next couple of years. I'm not sitting down to write any more novels. There is a new *Necroscope* book due out in June, a couple novelets and a short story, and a couple other bits and pieces.

Q: But no more novels for a while?

Lumley: *Necroscope*, no, it's finished. It's done.

Q: You haven't fallen into that temptation that came to Frank Herbert, when they said, "Here's five million dollars. Write another one."

Lumley: If they offered me five million dollars, I would start writing now. Today. I would finish it in two months' time. It would be just as good as the others, because for five million dollars I can make it as good as they want it. But that's not likely to happen, Darrell.

Q: But you can hope. Thanks, Brian.

Recorded at Jersey Devil Con,
April 27, 2003.

PETER STRAUB

Peter Straub is the author of *Julia, If You Could See Me Now, Ghost Story, Shadowland, Floating Dragon, Koko, Mystery, The Throat, The Hellfire Club, Mr. X, Lost Boy Lost Girl, A Dark Matter*, and more. He has collaborated with Stephen King on *The Talisman* and *The Black House*. He has won numerous awards, including six Bram Stokers, three World Fantasy Awards, and the Locus Award.

Q: Your recent novels, such as *The Hellfire Club* and *Mystery*, have no supernatural content. Your work in the past few years has turned away from the fantastic. Why?

Straub: What you are describing is a very conscious move on my part. After I wrote the novel *Floating Dragon* and then collaborated with Steve King on *The Talisman*, it seemed to me that I had burned out on that kind of material. It was exciting for a long time to work on the kind of conventional metaphors of horror. But after *Floating Dragon*, in which I had deliberately shot my bolt and gone over the top, I felt that I had exhausted that material as far as I was concerned, and also exhausted myself when it came to using it.

It took me a long time to figure out what to do after that. I knew that I wanted to work with matters that seemed more important to me, that seemed central to my own life and self. Once I had started writing *Koko*, it was hard going. It took me at least a year to write the first hundred pages. But once I got into the swing, I saw that I was writing much better than I had been previously, and also that something new had entered what I wrote, which was a better sort of consciousness. All I mean is a deeper awareness of the motives of the characters I was working with, the reasons why people do things. People have different motives which influence behavior. Some are conscious; some are not. Part of the improvement that I noticed is what I was doing was that I was much clearer about the conscious motives and the unconscious motives. It all seemed to work quite well. I was very, very pleased with the book when it was finally finished. Since then I have been trying to stay at that level and explore whatever it is that comes to mind.

Q: Is this immediacy or increased depth the result of your writing about something that is not imaginary—that is, human psychology and motivations—as opposed to, say, ghosts, which you and the reader both know to be made-up? So, are you gaining this new strength from simple realism?

Straub: I don't know that I ever really believed in ghosts, and I am not sure that I don't believe in them now. So I want it both ways on that one. What was at stake was the quality of my interest in the material itself. I felt that I had done all I could with it, and so that was a way of saying I couldn't "believe" in ghostly matters, if you put the belief in quotes. It didn't suit my imagination.

Q: Did your older books still mean as much to you, even though you could no longer work in that mode, or did your supernatural novels now seem to be on a lower plane, in retrospect?

Straub: I didn't lose any of the affection I had for my earlier books, and I didn't think they were any lesser accomplishments. At the time I was doing them, I was enraptured by the material of the supernatural, that is, ghosts and various surreal elements of the supernatural category. I remember thinking that stuff was like blues. It was bottomlessly deep. You could swim down into it forever. That is probably true for a lot of people, but for me I just got to the bottom, and it wasn't so good anymore. I suppose the real point was that I saw that if I were to keep on doing that, I would just wind up repeating myself, which has never had much appeal to me.

Q: This would seem to be an occupational hazard for horror writers, and a recently developed one. That is to say, prior to Stephen King, there was no such thing as a professional horror novelist, someone who made his living entirely from writing horror novels. The classic writers of the farther past, like Poe or Le Fanu or Edith Wharton, or, a little more recently, E.F. Benson, were general men and women of letters. They wrote all kinds of things, including some horror. Not even Fritz Leiber or Richard Matheson wrote one horror novel after another. They got to vary their tone. I am amazed at how well Ramsey Campbell has held up under the pressure of genre.

Did you find editorial or marketing forces trying to turn you into this new kind of writer?

Straub: In a way I think we all did become a new sort of writer. Remember that I started out about the same time as Steve. He was a new person when I was a new person. When I was writing my first books like that, I had never heard of him. I only heard of him because he gave a blurb to one of my books. He wasn't a phenomenon at that point. It never occurred to me that there was any trouble at all in writing decent works of fiction which were also horror novels. That seemed like a non-issue. I thought, of course you could do it, as long as you did it the right way. What I liked about King's work was that it was clear that he was doing it in what I thought was the right way. It took Ramsey a longer time, because he was doing mainly short stories. It was well into my acquaintanceship with Ramsey Campbell that he started to do novels, and it took him a time to find his feet there.

Now, no matter what I said before, if people are asked to describe me, they first thing they will say is that I'm a horror writer. Whenever I publish a book, and it's reviewed, nearly the first words out of the reviewer's mouth is "horror writer." Often on the blurb, they say, "the newest work by the master of horror, Peter Straub," or whatever. This word comes in. It is inescapable. That's cool with me. I am comfortable with that, because even if I'm writing a book about a woman who's kidnapped, as in *The Hellfire Club*, there is plenty of actual horror in that. Really what I like about this is that it pushes the definition, way, way out, so it overlaps with mystery and suspense.

Q: This brings up a question I've posed before. What would happen if Stephen King wrote *The Sound of Music*?

Straub: It would be a horror musical.

Q: Well what if you wrote something that was as far removed from your usual horror novel as *Chitty-Chitty-Bang-Bang* was from the James Bond series? You can imagine that must have given Fleming's publisher a turn. What would your publisher do?

Straub: I think we'd probably have to have a long talk. Of course it would depend on the actual strength of the manuscript. Because I am me, and my reflexes will always lead me down certain paths, the book would never be that far afield. It would never be a romance novel. It would never be a historical bodice-ripper. If it were, there would be lots of stuff ripped besides bodices. So you're talking about a case that would probably never come up.

Q: We're in the age of the specialist writer, who is expected to produce just one thing. But look back at, say, E.F. Benson, who was a great ghost-story writer but is better known today for his social comedies.

Straub: Yes, Mapp and Lucia. It would be fun to do something like that. But it never occurred to me to think of myself as a specialty writer.

I see myself as the sole proprietor of ground of certain dimensions, and my job is to tend that ground and see what will grow. It's all the same, because it's all my ground. There might be corn or peas, but they'd be my veggies. So I think that all of them have a distinct commonality. Even if they were as different as corn and peas, they would still be recognizable as mine.

That is indeed part of the point. If you pick up a book by Stephen King, no matter what the content is, you read a page and you know it's him. Either that or it's one of his imitators who happened to have a good day when he wrote that page. That's the real point. You are supposed to discover your voice or your manner and work it as hard and as well as you can.

Q: Of course in *The Talisman* there are parts where each of you is deliberately imitating the other's voice in order to fool the reader.

Straub: That was a nice little joke. I'm sure it worked. I know I threw in allusions to things King liked, and several times I saw Steve put in allusions to Zoot Sims and Dexter Gordon and try to persuade people that I'd written that. There's also the matter of style.

The other day I looked at *The Talisman* because I get a lot of mail about it, and I opened up the book and thought, "That's Steve," and then I remembered that I'd written that. I had deliberately used Steve King's cadences.

Q: Surely in a collaboration a communal voice comes out anyway.

Straub: That's right. In coalesces, so that jokiness evaporated fairly early on, so we settle into what was a fairly consistent common voice.

Q: Would you ever consider doing it again?

Straub: I don't think so. I don't think anybody in his right mind would do it at all. [Laughs.] I don't want to collaborate with anybody again, and I don't think Steve would, but I certainly wouldn't want to collaborate with anybody but him.

Q: So everything is going to have to come out of your head—

Straub: It's supposed to. Those are the ground rules.

Q: It's supposed to. Do you ever feel that you'll use up everything you've got that's based on your own life?

Straub: In the sense that I'll run out of invention and be unable to recombine matters in a way that wouldn't imitate effects in earlier books? I don't know. That has never actually occurred to me. Part of the reason I think that it may be unlikely is that every character imposes a new world, a new set of circumstances. Every character brings with him his own world of complexities. So you have your own built-in freshness every time you begin.

Now. Having said that, I'll have to backtrack a little bit, because I am clearly always interested in certain things, which will go from book to book: complicated families, books inside books—people reading books, sometimes about other books—this is just something that I like. I might get tired of that, and then I'll stop doing it. I think I'd like to move at some point toward simplicity and have a good, straightforward book that begins with A and ends with Z. For me it is a lot more fun to work it the other way around and to put in all these layers and go back in time and uncover things that happened long ago that reverberate in the present. That really seems to be what my instincts do. But at some point I'd like to do a nice, simple chase. That could be fun.

Q: How much research into realistic matters do you do? Do you go to locales and get to know people in the professions of your characters? I know that, for example, if I were to try to write a novel about military officers, I'd be in deep trouble, because I don't know how they think and act and what their lives are like.

Straub: In regard to places, if it's a truly exotic place, then I have to go there or I know I'll get it all wrong. So for *Koko* I took a long trip to Hong Kong, Singapore, Taipei, Bangkok, and so forth. I took careful notes and I took photographs, and, basically, I remembered how it smelled, how it looked. I also had maps of these places. I figured out where the characters were living, where they could meet to talk to one another, and all that. So that was very helpful. More generally, though, I just make it up. It you make up a town, you can't get it wrong, as long as, the first time a character goes to Jones Street and he turns left, he always turns left later on. I also make it fairly easy on myself by fairly often writing about writers. If I were to write about military people, I'd have to find some somehow and hang out and hear the way they talk. But because I have met and known people from a wide variety of professions, I can pretty well draw material from banks of impressions that I have stored. I should probably talk to more policemen. I used to know some cops in Westport, and I got a lot of stuff from them, but that's probably not too accurate anymore. The area where I feel kind of endangered would be if I were to write about people in their twenties, because I probably don't get at all how they think, and I probably don't know how they speak either. It would be lovely to write a story about a young guy starting out with a law firm or an ad agency and going to sports bars—the kind of people I see around New York all the time—but I would have to live in one's hip pocket for a week before I could get it right.

Q: Or else you would have to set it in the past, when you were twenty.

Straub: That's right. Set it back there with jousts and chain-mail.

Q: Inevitably most of the stories that we see about childhood these days are set in the '50's or '60's.

Straub: Certainly mine are. Or late '40's.

Q: Let's talk about the beginning of your career.

Straub: I sold the first novel I wrote, which was called *Marriages*, and it did abysmally. I had been writing a second novel, which was much, much better, but the publishers I had at the time, Coward-McCann and Andre Deutch, rejected it. I thought it was because of the book, but of course it wasn't. It was because they hadn't done anything with the first one. So if I had asked my agents to keep trying to sell that novel, *Under Venus*, they would have eventually found a place to sell it. But I thought it was my fault, and I spent a great deal of time rewriting it, until I was hideously depressed. I spent a lot more time lying in bed thinking about not rewriting it than I actually spent rewriting it.

So the agent that I had at the time suggested that I write something new, and I thought that it might possibly save my life if I wrote something that had some kind of acceptability to it. So I walked around Hampstead Heath when we were in London, and I had an idea that did something for me. It gave me a little chill. I thought that was what I ought to do. It was more of a horror idea, not especially an adventure thing. When I started to write it, it really worked. It was called *Julia*. It came out very nicely. There were no problems. I was satisfied with the writing. I didn't understand all the story when I started, but it all connected up. It connected itself to itself as it went along, so I understood right away that I had found a subject and a field in which I was alone. So I had no problem with trying to work that a little more.

Q: Had you grown up reading this sort of stuff, *Great Tales of Terror and the Supernatural*, Lovecraft, and all the rest?

Straub: *Great Tales of Terror and the Supernatural* was one of my favorite books. When I was about twelve or thirteen, I remember carrying it around. I remember taking it to Boy Scout Camp. I just loved that book. I don't think I read Lovecraft except for what was in that book, and I don't remember which stories. I think there were one or two.

Q: "The Rats in the Walls" and "The Dunwich Horror."

Straub: Then I moved away from all that, and it wasn't until I had finished writing Julia and had probably started writing *If You Could See Me Now* that Tom Tessier started telling me the people I ought to read.

So because of Tessier, I got a lot of Lovecraft, and I got some Richard Matheson stories, Bob Bloch stories, some Lovecraft Circle people, and so began to find out what was actually there, to learn who my grandparents were. It was wonderful. It was a great experience. I had a tremendous time, just wading in.

Q: Horror, like Science Fiction, has some aspects of a club. But it seems that a lot of horror writers like yourself came in from the outside, and didn't discover the club until their first couple of novels gave them credentials.

Straub: Yes, exactly. In a way I'm glad I wasn't in the club. I had to invent a lot of things for myself. My attitudes hadn't been hardened by group opinion, and also I didn't waste a lot of time on fanzines, and other things they do in science fiction.

Q: Fanzines may be a fine idea when you're sixteen years old.

Straub: In my case I would have been better off doing what I did, which was reading yards and yards of fiction.

Q: When did you actually start writing?

Straub: I wrote in grade school. I wrote some stories in high school and then didn't write much fiction in college. In fact, I don't think I wrote any. I wrote a lot of other stuff. I really started writing seriously after I got out of Columbia, after I got my master's and started teaching. Then I began reading lots of poetry and, as if infected, I started to write it. I spent a lot of time doing that. It was only when I was about twenty-six or twenty-seven that I realized that I had always thought of myself as a novelist, and it was time to do something about it, or it would just be a fantasy. Whatever I had to be of use there would be lost. So, without much of a plan I just started to write a novel by hand in a big journal, and when I finished that journal, I just bought another one. There were two or three of those books. I wrote about five hundred words a day. It felt wonderful. I didn't know if it was any good or not. Then I typed it up and mailed it to a publisher, Andre Deutch, and some woman there—Jill Mortimer was her name—wrote to me to say that she quite liked the book and would try to convince the board to accept it. Three months later, they did. It didn't seem difficult then. The difficulty came later.

Q: What were the difficulties? You seem to have been blessed at that point. Many people struggle for years to get a two-thousand-word story into print.

Straub: The struggle happened when the second book, *Under Venus*, was rejected. Then I thought maybe I'm a one-book wonder. I had no confidence that I could repeat what had seemed a success, especially given the fact of a subsequent failure. But when I started writing *Julia*, I knew half-way through that book that if I could stick it out, everything would be fine. So we're talking about a period of somewhere like two or three years, in which my confidence was shattered and I was working blind.

Q: I'm still impressed that the first substantial piece of fiction you attempted was a novel and you sold it. I always tell beginners that if it takes you thirty tries to get it right, that could be a couple years with short fiction, but thirty novels is another matter entirely. Call this a coward's approach. You don't write novels until you are already selling stories, so at least you know you are writing on something approaching a professional level.

Straub: I told myself I would actually give it three tries. If I wrote three whole novels and none of them were accepted, then I would go off and be a fireman or a brain surgeon.

Q: Would you really have given up?

Straub: I don't know. I never had to learn.

Q: Certainly *Ghost Story* was the one that made you a bestseller. It must have changed your life.

Straub: Incredibly. It changed my life enormously, in ways that were almost all positive. I had to leave England, because of taxation, which was a bit of a blow. I had intended to come back to America anyhow, but not that soon. We had to do it fast. Apart from that, in the millions of readjustments that followed, it meant that publishers knew my name. The editors knew my name. It was easy. Suddenly people were asking me for work. That hasn't stopped. I still get all these requests for stories for anthologies. I could live comfortably. I could live at the level of comfort where you no longer have to ask the price of just about anything, which is a great spot.

Q: Do you find your life market-driven, in the sense that there are now thousands of people out there depending on you to make millions for them and they won't let you stop?

Straub: To some extent that's true, but I'm not Stephen King. I try to resist that course, in that I am far more interested in seeing where I will go following my personal voices. I think I would resist if I were given instructions as to what the topic should be.

Q: In essence you've become a brand name.

Straub: Dean Koontz is a brand name. I sort of was Dean Koontz once. If I had kept on writing books like *Ghost Story*, now I would be selling seven hundred thousand hardbacks. But I didn't do that and I didn't move that way. I moved another way. Everything is still being taken care of very nicely. I think it would be nice to be a brand name, but I don't think that's quite what I am.

Q: You are in the sense that, say, *Mystery* was not published as a mystery novel, but as a Peter Straub book.

Straub: That was my goal from the start. I know Steve King felt that way too, because we used to talk about this back in the days of our boyhood. He didn't want and I didn't want to be published as a genre writer. That seemed like instant death. It was like confinement on constriction. I'm not sure how or why but it was easy for us to be published as mainstream novelists with a left-hand tilt. Speaking personally, I think that made it a lot easier for me to find readers.

Q: Getting back to the idea of your writing the equivalent of *Chitty-Chitty-Bang-Bang*, don't you become your own genre, in the sense that everyone has their idea of what a Peter Straub book is?

Straub: That's the point. Right from the start, I thought that I wanted to be my own genre, a genre known and identified by my name. And by now I think I have done enough work so I just about have achieved that. People all have a general notion of what it is, and some will be curious enough to lay out $27.50 or whatever it is that hardbacks cost these days to see what the new product is like.

Q: What are your writing methods like? I ask because I collect them. I've never found two writers who are quite alike. Some people write all sorts of notes on index cards and pin them to walls, while others just plunge in.

Straub: I'm sort of a plunger. I spend about six months literally walking around making notes, and then when I have lots of notes and a firm notion of the characters in the story, then I write a long thing which I call notes but is in effect an outline, in which I describe what happens step by step. I begin by following this outline, a process which is like walking along a nice safe path through the forest. I have every confidence that I know what I'm doing and where I am going. Then the trees crowd in. The path disappears. It is night. The outline was lost long ago. The safe road that I thought I was following doesn't exist anymore, and I have to find my way through the forest unaided. When I started doing that, it was scary, but when I found it worked every time, then I felt I ought to do it that way and it felt good.

Q: Is your approach any different when your story contains fantasy—things that are impossible?

Straub: I don't think so. It is unusual now for me to describe something that I know is impossible. When I do that, there is sort of a pleasant imaginative tingle. I am conscious of having fun. There's a very sweet little buzz that I get from that. But that's more about the interior of my head than what goes on in the writing.

Q: What kind of fan-mail do you get? Do you get strange mail?

Straub: No. The strangest stuff is from prisons, usually. Sometimes that's kind of harmless and pathetic. Other times it is just guys who want help. They want money to fund their appeals. The rest of the mail is just kindly and appreciative. It's always very nice to receive. I answer all of it, unless somebody wants something that is unreasonable. If they want me to basically write their thesis about me, I write back and explain they're on their own.

Q: Do you get the ones where somebody has a great idea and they want you to write it and split the profits fifty-fifty?

Straub: Yeah, I get those, about four a year, and I always right back and say I have too much to do to take on this project.

Q: So you haven't gotten to the point where you're crushed by your celebrityhood.

Straub: No. Mine is very tolerable.

Q: I've heard that Stephen King's mail is screened to make sure there aren't any screenplays, novels, or stories in it, lest somebody say, "My novel has a ghost in it. Your novel has a ghost in it. You stole my idea. I'm suing your for ten million dollars in damages."

Straub: He was sued two or three times on precisely that basis. I think the suits not only didn't go to court; I think the evaporated because the people bringing them were flakes. If I were in his situation, I'd be wary too.

Q: Isn't it just the case that when you become that famous, you attract the attention of extortionists whose real idea is to sue for five million dollars and settle out of court for fifty thousand? It's a living.

Straub: I suppose. You're a target. But I haven't noticed this happening to me, so I guess I'm not famous enough.

Q: What are you working on now?

Straub: I am in the very early stages of a book that I though could be called a doppelgänger novel. When I was beginning the process I've described and making notes, the point at which I got excited was when I realized that it was a classic doppelgänger situation. That instantly for me put a kind of magic in the heart of the story and it suggested all sorts of possibilities that I hadn't seen before. I don't want to say too much about it.

Q: It's a supernatural story?

Straub: I suppose it is. There is a hugely irrational element at work. It may be made up. It may be a lie. It may be an invention by the version of me who is in the book. The manuscript is passed from hand to hand until it comes to me, and I'm the person who presents it to the public. So I may have loused up the story and added it. But if you take it as literal truth, yes, there's a strong supernatural element.

Q: So you're not quite done with the fantastic yet.

Straub: Obviously not, because I got so happy when I thought of it. All I can say is thank God it isn't vampires or werewolves.

Q: There's a wonderful quote from David Schow that vampires have become the Star Trek of horror.

Straub: Exactly.

Q: Thank you, Peter.

ABOUT THE INTERVIEWER:

Darrell Schweitzer is the author of the novels *The White Isle*, *The Shattered Goddess*, and *The Mask of the Sorcerer*, plus about 300 published stories, most of which are collected in various volumes available from Wildside Press, the most recent of which is *The Emperor of the Ancient Word*. He is a critic, essayist, reviewer, anthologist, a former editor of *Weird Tales* magazine. He is a four-time World Fantasy Award nominee and one-time winner. He has been interviewing writers since 1973. His first book, *SF Voices* (1976) was a book of interviews.

CPSIA information can be obtained
at www.ICGtesting.com
Printed in the USA
LVOW12s0132080716
495263LV00001B/3/P